M000252258

GNOMON

LUCHIA DERTIEN

DSP PUBLICATIONS

Published by
DSP PUBLICATIONS

5032 Capital Circle SW, Suite 2, PMB# 279, Tallahassee, FL 32305-7886 USA
http://www.dsppublications.com/

Gnomon
© 2015 Luchia Dertien.

Cover Art
© 2015 Olivia Coy.
Cover content is for illustrative purposes only and any person depicted on the cover is a model.

ISBN: 978-1-63476-108-6
Digital ISBN: 978-1-63476-109-3
Library of Congress Control Number: 2015930654
First Edition September 2015

Printed in the United States of America
∞
This paper meets the requirements of
ANSI/NISO Z39.48-1992 (Permanence of Paper).

Dedicated to every single person who believed in
these stupid terrorist boys.

AUTHOR'S NOTE

GNOMON: NO-mon, from Greek, literally "one that knows or examines." On a standard sundial, a gnomon is the upright knifelike piece that casts a shadow based on the position of the sun to tell the time of day.

CHAPTER 1

Somewhere in Russia—Moscow; {Paris}

DELAURIER'S WIKIPEDIA article does him no justice. Then again, few things do. Renaire's pretty sure that's why he kills people.

Justice and freedom and equality and all those idealistic dreams of the young didn't fade away in Emile Delaurier like they do for most people when nobody believes or even listens. His dreams twisted instead. Bitterness made him sharp, tempered his spirit of burning iron into cold, violent steel.

They call him a terrorist—the modern extremist, a threat to all governments his esoteric criteria judge unworthy—but Renaire sees him for what he is. He's a man with a cause that means more to him than life itself and weaponry he knows how to use very, very well.

Heaven bless whoever first put a gun in that man's hands.

It's three in the morning in a medium-sized city in Russia that Renaire can't even remember the name of. It's partially because he's somewhere between drunk and hungover, which averages out to mostly sober. He knows Russia pissed Delaurier off recently, so it wasn't exactly a surprise when he and Delaurier hopped onto a train headed straight into the heart of the massive country and then rented a car to go even farther. But Russia's a sprawling monster, so Some Russian City is about as good as he can do right now.

Renaire sucks in, dragging another breath of smoke from his half-ashes cigarette, and watches the other man. The cold of an early Russian spring leaves Delaurier breathing out almost as much of an unwelcome cloud in the air as Renaire. Delaurier is packing up, knives and guns and wire and pliers sliding into the secret pockets of his red coat. He's looking more fanatical than usual and isn't bothering with gloves. They must be killing for The Cause today.

"We're just killing them?" Renaire asks and finally taps his cigarette. Ashes scatter into the frigid air. "Or is this one of your 'send a message' plans?" Those are fun. Sometimes. Depends on the message.

"This one's mine," Delaurier says, and *fuck that*, but he lets the man talk nonsense anyway. "Just watch my back."

Renaire smirks. Delaurier reddens slightly, bless him, and scowls. He is the most violent, adorable thing in the world, and if he's actually blushing, not to mention giving Renaire that obvious of an opening, he's probably as sleep deprived as Renaire.

"You know what I mean," Delaurier says and slams the weapons case (also known as "the suitcase we put the guns in," but Delaurier does love his dramatics) shut. He puts it back into the rental car, so they're not going to be running out and lying low. If it's a message killing, it'll be a quiet one until the authorities find out. Delaurier will probably call them in a couple of hours and deliver a quick righteous-fury, justice-and-equality speech. He screws the silencer onto his preferred pistol with the ease that comes from long years of practice. "There probably aren't any guards."

"Probably?" Renaire echoes, more surprised than objecting. Usually Delaurier has everything from a building's blueprints to guards' middle names already memorized. Renaire takes another drag of his cigarette, trying to figure out what the hell is going on here. "Is this you throwing a tantrum by murdering people?"

Delaurier obviously wants to snap at him but restrains himself, tucking his pistol into his most accessible coat pocket. "They have to be dead before dawn," he says instead.

So it's a rush job, then. If Delaurier didn't call Glasson for some emergency research, it's somehow personal. If Delaurier wants Renaire to stay out of it, it's even *more* personal. Renaire isn't exactly his favorite person, but Delaurier trusts him to keep his mouth shut about anything he's told to.

Renaire takes one final drag of his cigarette, exhales, and drops what remains of it into the snow. "I'll cover you," he says and pulls his own black leather gloves on.

The building is the same huge concrete block as every other late Soviet-era apartment complex in the country, and nobody impedes their entrance. Delaurier walks in easily, and the elevator dings open for them the moment they hit the up button. Floor 5 is a lot nicer than the simplistic entryway, with pristine carpeting that Renaire thinks will probably look beautiful in its own way when there's blood on it. Killing on carpet is always better than hardwood. They're less likely to slip on it.

Delaurier actually has to check the list of occupants and rooms on the wall, which is definitely a first. He reads the Cyrillic script like a pro since it only takes a moment, and then they're down a hallway and another hallway and finally stop in front of a door that looks like every other one. He hesitates, but finally looks back at Renaire and mouths, *Pick the lock.*

Renaire shrugs and decides to try and do it the easy way first by actually turning the handle. Sometimes people are stupid enough to leave their doors unlocked, but not this time. He pulls out a bump key and one of his longer-handled knives and shoves the key into the lock, twists, and jabs the hilt hard into the key. It's fast and louder than he'd like—a *clonk* over late-night silence and the muted huff of the heating system, but Delaurier just pushes him lightly to the side so he can go through first. Renaire gave up on going first long ago, so he just steps out of the way and makes sure he has a good enough view to see the interior.

The door swings open quietly, and there's nothing in the room beyond the expected—couch, television, kitchen, framed articles and faded landscapes hanging on the walls. They walk in easily, and Renaire wonders what the hell kind of person they're taking out, with no guards or any kind of security at all. While Delaurier looks at the three doors off the room, trying to figure out which one leads to where he wants to go, Renaire closes the front door, just enough that it rests on the doorframe so they've got a quick exit but a passerby might not notice they've broken in to kill people.

Delaurier finally opens a door. It's a closet. Renaire doesn't even bother hiding the snicker. The other man takes a moment to flip him off before moving to another door, which leads into a bedroom, and Delaurier steps in with his usual confidence.

Then he shuts the door behind him.

Renaire rolls his eyes and turns the handle to follow Delaurier in, but it doesn't open. Really, he thought they got over this during their first few months working together. Renaire grits his teeth, glaring at the door because of course Delaurier knows he's only got the one bump key on him tonight, and fine, *fine*, if Delaurier wants to do it this way, that's the way it's going to be. Renaire slumps into one of the kitchen chairs and wishes he had brought his flask along.

When Delaurier finally comes back out, he has a laptop and file folder in hand and that look he gets before running into a firefight, eyes wide and feverish and jaw set, like death itself couldn't stop Delaurier from taking action. It's not a good sign.

"We're done here," he states and walks out the door. Renaire follows, not even glancing at the bedroom. It's just as easy getting out of the building as it was getting in, and they're back to the rental car in under a minute.

Delaurier presses shaking fingers on the driver's side door, hand shuddering against the metal for a long moment. Renaire carefully rests a hand on his shoulder. The fact Delaurier doesn't shrug him off or bite out something cruel toward him is another bad sign.

Delaurier doesn't like killing people. He's good at it, and he likes that it actually gets things to change, likes the results, but he doesn't like death. He never hesitates, never flinches, and runs into things like this with eyes open and iron-hard determination. It's what he believes in, it's what needs to be done, but he doesn't like it. He doesn't regret it, but he never likes it.

Which is one of the reasons why Renaire is always with him, since he genuinely does not give a fuck. He tries to sometimes. It doesn't stick.

"I'll drive," Renaire says, since this isn't a time for trying to get even a hint of reaction from Delaurier. He explodes sometimes, and they don't need that right now.

"Are you sober?" Delaurier asks, not the slightest bit of disgust or anger in the words. It means this is an *exceptionally* bad case.

"Close enough," Renaire says, and doesn't bother asking again, just fishing the keys out of Delaurier's pockets with his free hand. "Passenger seat."

In a stunning role reversal, Delaurier actually obeys. Renaire gets in and starts the car, and only a few moments later realizes Delaurier is starting to look normal again. He's clutching the file folder and laptop as if he wants to try and break them with his bare hands. "I'll tell you where to go," he says, not looking at him. That works fine for Renaire. It always will.

THE NEWS hits the world a little before six in the morning, Russia-wise. A reporter, murdered in her bed last night. Security footage and DNA already tells them it was Delaurier, and the STB supporters are already muttering among themselves, confused by their fearless leader killing someone so neutral.

The press is going crazy, screaming for the blood of someone who dared to kill one of their own, and Renaire really wishes Delaurier would actually talk to him. He won't even *argue*. What the fuck is he supposed to do on this train if Delaurier won't argue with him? He obviously can't sleep, since Delaurier is sleeping. Unconscious is probably a better word for how he slumped into his seat and passed out, but Renaire's taking what he can get at this point.

He calls Glasson, who knows all. He's the information demigod of STB, their justice-obsessed organization. Renaire doesn't know what it stands for, so he likes to believe the T stands for Terrorist. The triumvirate of Delaurier, Glasson, and Carope started the group as something light and optimistic, but as time went on and their ineffectiveness bit at them, STB became the excited group of dedicated idealists seen today.

In a lot of ways, they're a family, always supportive and accepting of each other, even Renaire. In a lot of other ways, they're terrifying, because STB is starting to make a difference in the worst kind of way.

Glasson is the living hub of all the little threads of influence the rest of STB puts in place, most on his command. He's the patient, friendly spider sitting in the center of their criminal web, the true facilitator of Delaurier's mad vision for the future. Where Delaurier charges forward, Glasson maps the terrain to make sure he doesn't fall on his face and break his neck.

"Even I can't put up with him like this," Renaire says. It's a lie, but it's still nice to say.

"Your sacrifice is appreciated," Glasson says, and there's a rustling in the background. "Do you know why he did it?"

Renaire sighs, slumping deeper into his seat. "I only have guesses. It was fast and dirty, he didn't even know the floor plan. Locked me out and left with a file folder and laptop."

It's easy to have a conversation that uses minimal specifics by now. He had trouble with that early on, and still has issues with it when he's talking to someone for reasons that aren't job related, but this call is more important than most he makes. Renaire doesn't usually worry about things. There aren't enough things he cares about for it to be a problem.

"Did you get a look at what's on them?"

"Right now? *He* is on them. Apparently they make great seat cushions," Renaire says, glaring at the sleeping blond. He looks like a cherub that grew up lean and severe and furious about that being a fallen-adult-cherub thing. Delaurier wants heaven back, and he wants it for the whole fucking world, ready to storm the pearly gates with pitchforks and torches.

There's no amused exhalation or frustrated noise when Glasson hears what little information Renaire can give him. Glasson is silent before he finally speaks. "I don't like this."

Renaire hesitates but says, "Whatever's going on, it's personal. He wasn't doing well when we left." He glances at the pallor of Delaurier's skin. "He still isn't."

"Keep him alive and bring him home. We'll be in touch," Glasson says and hangs up.

That was already the plan, but it's still nice to know there's not going to be a firing squad waiting for them when they make it back to Paris. Unless it's reporters. He knows why Delaurier never wears a mask or anything that could be confused for a disguise when it comes to The Cause, but it drives Renaire insane trying to deal with any authorities that are unlucky enough to find them. The rest of them can run around easily without any fuss, but Delaurier wants to be a *symbol*.

It's just one more thing that makes him so fucking ridiculous that Renaire considers punching Delaurier. He has that feeling a lot, these days. At least Renaire has the sense to keep his head down. Well, usually—pretty much everyone knows someone travels with Delaurier. Who he is and why he's content to be Delaurier's killer shadow, not so much.

Delaurier wakes up four hours later, snapping upright and grabbing onto his armrests so tight that the plastic squeaks and bone's visible beneath his knuckles. He takes a shuddering breath, blinks a few times, and exhales while staring straight at Renaire. He looks awkward. It's unsettling. "Get some sleep," Delaurier says.

Renaire is unimpressed. "That's it?"

Delaurier frowns. "What do you mean?"

"No thank you? No asking where we're headed? No explanation?" Renaire asks. "An explanation would be really good right now. If I get to pick something, it's that."

"You don't get an explanation because you don't need one," Delaurier states.

Renaire isn't letting this go. "You're the one who says I can't reason my way out of a paper bag, so why wouldn't I need you to explain things for me?"

"You just proved you can reason," Delaurier points out irritably. "Right there. You beat your own argument by making it."

"Which only an idiot would do, proving—again—that I'm a reasonless fool who needs an explanation," Renaire says. "So stop trying to deflect and tell me *what the fuck is going on.*"

"There was a threat. I removed it."

Renaire feels like tearing his hair out, watching the stubborn set of the other man's jaw, the unyielding stare right back into Renaire's eyes. He shook after killing a reporter, but there's not a thread of regret in Delaurier. They've killed screaming politicians and begging CEOs and maybe five times as many people in collateral damage, not to mention what the rest of the organization has done. This may have shaken him, but Renaire has plenty of nightmares about seeing soul-deep regret on Delaurier's face, and this is a thousand shades away from that.

"Is that all I'm going to get?" Renaire asks, because he is a creature of eternal (pathetic, useless) hope when it comes to Delaurier.

"Go to sleep," Delaurier says. "I'll need you alert when we get to Moscow."

Renaire doesn't ask what's in Moscow. Their working relationship comes down to Delaurier deciding everything and Renaire choosing whether or not to go along with whatever it is. Renaire can remember saying *no* probably twice. Maybe three times. It's not like Renaire has anything else to do.

He leans back and closes his eyes, and he's gone.

MOSCOW IS gray and biting and doesn't care about the two young men who get off the train and leave the station through one of the close-to-forgotten stairways, one of those places only the janitors remember. It's almost worrying how easy it is for them to get around. Despite being on every wanted list in the world for the past two years, and quite a few for the three years before that, Delaurier has been arrested exactly one time.

Renaire doesn't know what everyone higher in organizations thinks will happen when they tell their angry, underpaid employees to catch the man who travels the world killing terrible bosses. It's actually pretty common for them to go through security receiving nothing but a slip of paper with a guard's employer's name and address on it. Problems only come when management is around.

Delaurier leads them deep into the city outskirts to one more concrete monstrosity. Paris may have spoiled Renaire, but the artist in him shudders at the rigid lines and blunt impact architecture the soviet era inflicted on the country. Other parts of Moscow are beautiful. This street is far from them.

He doesn't know too much Russian, but he can recognize the word for hotel above the door. There's no doorman, no valet, nothing but a sign and an arrow. Renaire hangs onto Delaurier's bag (*their* bag, actually—they share one nondescript duffel bag, and the other is The Suitcase We Put the Guns In) while he speaks to the concierge, and wonders how alert he really has to be. Russia has the good alcohol. It's one of the few things he likes about the country. Good alcohol, impenetrable art, and a fantastically bizarre sense of humor. It's not his preferred place to lose himself, but it's probably in the top ten. If Delaurier dies here, it'll get the job done well enough.

They get a room—one room, not that it means anything—and Renaire has barely tossed the bags onto the floor with the standard complaints before Delaurier is gone again, out of the room and down the hall to the bathroom. Delaurier comes back showered and changed into some of his more diplomatic clothing, collared shirt and already half-undone black tie along with the ever-present red coat. Renaire follows his example, not bothering with looking nice because he can't be picky anymore, hasn't done laundry in a hell of a long time.

That was somewhere in Finland, he thinks. The world's an indifferent blur even when he's sober.

"We have somewhere to be," Delaurier says and leaves.

Renaire follows, because he always does.

THE SUN was setting when their train arrived, and it's already night by the time they get to the suspiciously club-looking door Delaurier stops in front of. There aren't many people, since it's barely nine in the evening, but it's still kind of hilarious to see Delaurier here—the bouncer lets them in without a single glance at anything beyond Delaurier's face, and the man knows it. Delaurier could be wearing rat-chewed pajamas and get inside a club, even at peak hours.

"I know you're not one for nightlife, but getting into a club at nine is starting early," Renaire says. He'd usually be happily on his way to drunk by now, but he decides to treat this like a learning experience for STB's fearless leader. It's worth every single scowl. "They don't even have the good music out yet. You shouldn't lower your standards like this. If you're going to broaden your horizons, do it right, you know?"

Renaire lights another cigarette as they move up from the first and most populated floor to the upper deck. Three separate bars wait within the club, which is promising, but he doesn't stop at one of them, not with Delaurier walking forward with body language that screams confrontation.

"If you want to waste time here, fine," Delaurier says. "I have more important things to do."

"You always do," Renaire says. "It's just one more reason you should stop and do some shots, since the important things have led you here." He grins around his cigarette. "What are the chances? It must be destiny telling you to loosen up."

"I hate you so much," Delaurier mutters, half sighing in aggravation.

"It's you hate me *often* more than *so much*," Renaire says, because it's an important point to make. "You tolerate me half the time, at least."

"And the other half of the time, I fantasize about beating you to death with a wine bottle," Delaurier says.

Renaire smiles. "Do I moan when you bludgeon me?"

Delaurier doesn't even try to respond to that one.

They weave through the people trying to reserve tables for later in the night, and Delaurier leads them to a door placed between two lit curtains. The colored lights are drifting from green to blue and will likely be shading their way to purple any second now. There's another bouncer guarding the entrance. Yet again, the bouncer takes one look at Delaurier and lets him through, although it's for different reasons. He tries to stop Renaire, though, standing in his way with a firm stare and crossed arms. It's cute. And stupid.

Before he can do anything, Delaurier snaps a hand around the intimidating-looking man and grabs a fist full of shirt, dragging Renaire into the room with him before the bouncer even knows what's happening. Renaire loses his cigarette in the process, which is a tragedy. No drink, no cigarette, no *nothing* in a half-empty nightclub.

The room is open to see the dance floor below, the same color-changing backlit curtains bedecking the walls, like they're trapped in a magical snow cavern. It's generally ridiculous, just like the man sitting behind a table with two more bodyguards flanking him. He's dressed in a metallic shirt and bright teal pants, with sharp-spiked hair.

"The year 2002 called. It wants its fashion back," Renaire says and slides into one of the chairs closest to the entrance. Delaurier twitches just enough that Renaire knows he would've laughed or groaned at that. *Mission accomplished*, he thinks, because the idiot is glaring at him instead of watching Delaurier. Renaire makes sure to give the man his best smartass grin in case the insult (not exactly his best work) wasn't enough to keep his attention, and lights another cigarette.

"Who the fuck let this asshole in?" the man snaps, pointing violently at Renaire, so it must have been good enough.

"I did," Delaurier says, completely unrepentant with just enough disdain that the man will probably be more professional from now on. Disdain from Delaurier is a dangerous thing. It makes you want to impress him. "You seemed anxious to meet. Here I am."

"Right, right," the man says, gaze still flicking between Delaurier and Renaire. "I don't want anyone overhearing. I send my men away, and you send yours, and we can talk."

"He's not my man," Delaurier says. "He *is* mine, though, and he always keeps a secret, even if he can't keep his mouth shut. You can trust him as much as you trust me."

"Fine," the man bites out and leans forward, closer to Delaurier. He's smart enough to know there's no point in pressing Delaurier on the subject. It's a point toward him not being a complete moron. "It was a messy business, killing that reporter." He waves a hand through the air. "But that's not why I wanted to speak with you. I've heard news that an Interpol task force is being put together, just for you and the rest of STB. I could give you more information, if you did me a favor."

"Or I could shoot you right now and find it out myself," Delaurier says. The man's face falls. It falls even further when he says, "And I already knew that."

Renaire didn't.

Delaurier lets out a deeply unimpressed breath and says, "If you want an exchange for services, there's always the option of paying me."

The man looks stunned.

"This is what happens when you're an international beacon of righteous fury and justice for the oppressed masses," Renaire says. "Everyone forgets you kill people for a living."

"My competitor is moving in on some territory that's been ours for a long time," the man says. He's much younger than your average head of a Russian mafia group, but then again, Delaurier is only twenty-seven. Age has nothing to do with what someone does in life. "I'd much rather be dealing with his successor."

"This is a business rivalry killing?" Delaurier asks.

When the man cautiously nods, Delaurier names a price. They battle back and forth on it, and this is Delaurier's least favorite part, dealing with the practical aspects of being a terrorist-assassin. It doesn't keep him from being good at it, though. In the end, it comes down to them making a lot of money for killing a lot of people.

"If the money isn't in our account by the time we've completed the job, we come for you next," Delaurier says simply.

Nobody expects anything different from a professional murderer.

"Fine. Now take your shadow and get out of my lounge," the man says when they have a name and an address and a signed but vaguely worded agreement.

"Gladly," Delaurier says and once again grabs a fist full of Renaire's clothing—the shoulder of his well-loved jacket—and pulls him out of the room.

The club is packed now, the later hour making it a pulsing grind of humanity that Delaurier glances down at with a sense of resignation so deep that Renaire wonders once more about how he actually sees the world, and what he thinks is important. What he thinks about humanity at its core, with all the ideals and dreams stripped away to leave drunken flesh sliding against the nearest welcoming warm body.

Sometimes (*right now*) Delaurier's disdain for true humanity, for the real, primal instincts that drive the average person far more deeply than principles and noble causes ever will, makes Renaire so angry he can't even think. It's like watching a god be disappointed with his creations, and what the fuck is he fighting for if he refuses to accept what people are naturally, anyway? He fights for their freedom while disapproving of what they'd do with it.

It's not like he needs me now, Renaire thinks, and slips around Delaurier, heading to the bar without another word. It's crowded, but he has a lifetime of experience at fighting his way through the senseless herd of humanity. Mobs in France, mobs in El Salvador, mobs in Russia, they all work the same. The only difference is the tone of senseless babble that comes from one voice on top of a hundred others.

He ends up standing next to an attractive brunette woman, her darker-haired friend squished next to her. They've managed to hold down a small section of the bar, the brunette leaning hard against the gauche glittery surface. The club isn't going for class, just exciting lights and sparkles. Renaire can respect that.

"Look at the new guy next to me," the brunette says to her friend in Portuguese. "Do you think I speak enough Russian to convince him to come back to the hotel?"

"Buy me a drink and find out," Renaire replies with a grin, also in Portuguese.

It's a promising start to the night.

He's barely two shots in (shots are a wonderful ice breaker, anything that's a competition to see who can get drunk faster is always good in his book) when Delaurier finally makes his way over, shoved left and right and looking even more irritated than usual when he manages to plant his feet and stand firm against the tide of shifting bodies. "You were sober for two days straight," Delaurier states.

"Why do you think I'm drinking this fast?" Renaire says, smiling in a vicious way that's just a raised eyebrow away from mockery.

"Can we get him in on this too?" one of the women asks with a laugh, pleasantly lost in the way monolingual tourists develop as time goes on.

"He's married," Renaire replies.

"I don't see a ring," the other says.

"That's because he's married to *liberty*," Renaire tells the women in Portuguese.

Delaurier looks from Renaire to the Portuguese women. "What are they saying?"

He rolls his eyes at Delaurier. "Do you really want the answer to that?"

He looks at the way the Portuguese women are pretty much propositioning him with body language, and sighs. Delaurier knows what he looks like. "We're leaving."

"*You're* leaving, maybe," Renaire says. "I've made some lovely new friends, and we're going to get better acquainted."

"Could you find your way back even if you were sober?" Delaurier asks.

He raises his eyebrows. "I wasn't exactly planning to go back," Renaire says dryly.

Delaurier is not an idiot. In fact, he's one of the most intelligent people Renaire has ever met. But somehow that beautiful brain of his has no idea how to deal with sex, or any relationships that don't revolve around a greater goal or years and years of familiarity. Or the other person being Renaire, and even then Delaurier doesn't seem to know quite what to do with him. The man can inspire a packed theater, incite a park full of people to rise up and fight, can talk fire and action into (almost) anyone's soul, can debate with knife-sharp arguments and crystal clear logic, can deliver orders like the most experienced of generals, but flirting just…. It doesn't work with Delaurier.

It would be hilarious if Renaire didn't want to weep from it so often. He can readily recognize innuendo from Renaire, at least. It's taken two years for him to get to that point, but hey. It's progress. Renaire will take what he can get.

"You're going to waste time with…," Delaurier says, and ends up waving a hand in the air like it can encompass women, sex, alcohol, and things that aren't The Cause in one grand swoop of his wrist. "We have things to do, plans—"

"How does our relationship work, Emile?" Renaire asks, leaning back against the bar so he can look the other man in the eye. "Do I *plan*? Do I do anything other than follow you into the fray?"

Delaurier doesn't speak, and the club's bass beat is loud enough that the floor feels like it's shaking beneath them. Renaire sighs, shakes his head, and turns back for his next hit of alcohol.

"Just come back with me," Delaurier says.

"No." Renaire doesn't even bother looking at him.

Delaurier makes a frustrated noise. "We don't know anything about them, they could be—"

Renaire turns and outright laughs at him for that one. "Yes, because Portuguese tourists are such a dangerous bunch," he says. "And what 'we' is this? It's not like you'd be climbing into bed with them."

Delaurier obviously doesn't understand this. Most of his friends who are in relationships are in long-term, *committed* relationships, and Renaire is the only person he's known to regularly do the one-night stand thing, as far as Renaire can remember. Delaurier knows Carope does it sometimes, but he's never actually had to acknowledge it like when Renaire doesn't come home some nights. He realizes that even after two years of dealing with Delaurier's shit, this is also the first time they've even been in the same building while Renaire does it, not to mention first time he's *seen* it.

He sighs and turns to the women, saying, "Excuse me for a moment, I need to explain something to my friend." They nod and wave him off with all the friendliness one could ever ask for while Renaire grabs two fingers of Delaurier's coat sleeve (he never touches him, never even brushes skin, not unless he thinks it's absolutely necessary). He pulls him toward the nearest quiet bit of wall he can find. Delaurier does a commendable job of ignoring the couples using the wall for other reasons. "I'll put this bluntly. I'm trying to get laid. Leave me alone."

"I'm not an idiot," Delaurier says, outright glaring at him now. "You have *no idea* how dangerous it is to be out in the open like this right now, and that's not even starting on being alone or being that vulnerable with *strangers*—"

"I hate you so fucking much," Renaire snaps. "Do you know how many times a day I want to punch that lovely face of yours? I don't have any idea about how *dangerous* this is because *you don't tell me anything*! And then you just expect me to know it anyway, and you want me to just follow along, follow *orders* without even questioning it—"

"All you ever do is follow me!" Delaurier shouts at him, and fuck, now is not the time for him to explode, not when there's a Russian mafia crime lord somewhere on the second floor and Renaire is too angry to deal with this. He's having trouble even caring about the danger because Delaurier is in his face, the world is red, his ears are ringing from the music and everything is focused on Delaurier, furious and close. "You're accusing me of taking you for granted, but I'm not. I just know what you do! You do what I tell you! And for some reason you're *not doing it now* and the only difference I can see is *them* and—"

"Don't you *dare* act surprised that I'm like this," Renaire bites out.

"—I'm trying to *protect you* and you just keep trying to ruin yourself like the idiot you are, and you don't even have the common sense nature gave lemmings, and you're risking yourself for *them* while I'm standing right here asking you to choose the smart thing for once!"

"Which is what, *you*?" Renaire says, halfway to sneering.

Delaurier looks like Renaire just slapped him, eyes wide and stunned and staring at him. Strangest of all, he doesn't look hurt. Delaurier can be ice-cold, but the reaction and the eyes don't match up. Maybe it's just one more example of the magical disconnect between Delaurier's brain and body. He waits and watches the man get his thoughts in order because he wants to hear what Delaurier says next. He wants to be able to slap him back down if he says the wrong thing.

"That *is* what I'm asking," Delaurier says, rigid and awkward and stunned. If he was staring down the barrel of a gun, the tone would make sense. Not so much here.

Renaire still can't think clearly, he can't deal with this. He's still furious and seriously tempted to keep shouting, to grab Delaurier by the shoulders and shake him even if it would do no good whatsoever, and he's *still* too sober. "If I leave with you, you will give me explanations," Renaire says. "You will let me drink, with no snide remarks or disappointed *you could be so much more* commentary. And you will keep your fucking Cause to yourself for the rest of the evening, because I'm already sick of arguing with you."

Delaurier still looks unsettled, and it must be particularly disconcerting since it takes no time at all for him to agree. Hell, he even goes up to the bar and gets a bottle of something for Renaire to take back to the hotel. If this is an apology, it's the best one he's ever received, but Delaurier doesn't apologize. He'll acknowledge he's made a mistake, and he'll compensate for damage, but he never, ever apologizes. He's a creature so full of impossible conviction that regret doesn't even exist.

They get a taxi back to the hotel, and the ride is dead silent.

Their room has two twin beds, and Renaire sits on his child-sized beige duvet with his bottle and watches infomercials flicker in the dark of the room, with Delaurier still looking shaken on the adjacent bed but concentrating on the reporter's laptop. They absently disagree about the advertisements, about the weather, about *your mom* and beyond because they're never too old to reach that level, Delaurier is too proud to let anything sit, and Renaire is too drunk to just stop fighting back (not that he even does that sober).

It's all habit. Just what they do naturally in each other's presence. Delaurier keeps glancing over at Renaire, and he desperately wants to call him on it, but they've had plenty of screaming at each other for the night. Quiet halfhearted arguing is already draining.

Renaire falls asleep with about a fifth of the bottle left for the morning. Or his flask. Probably both.

Delaurier watches him the whole way down.

HE DREAMS of when they met. Not when they first saw each other (or at least when Renaire first saw him) but when they met. When they spoke.

Dreams are flashes of light and memories jumbled together, nonsensical information dumps of a desperate brain trying to recover from the day. Renaire drinks because of them, sometimes. He doesn't like dreaming, but above all else, he hates remembering. He can't stop remembering, not unless he's drunk or high or completely absorbed in something else—painting, fucking, killing. But he doesn't have those options in his sleep.

So he remembers.

He'd been worse then—a feat that impresses even Renaire now. He wasn't quite to junkie levels of addiction, not yet willing to do absolutely anything for a hit of whatever his escape of the day was, but he'd been getting there. He just hadn't hit bottom quite yet.

Renaire couldn't even remember the name of the man he'd been sleeping with. He does know he was nice enough, a good way to pass the time, and always more than happy to provide Renaire with whatever kind of recreation he wanted. The man had been fucking obsessed with him, him and his art, would sit himself in front of a window and give Renaire some sort of come-hither look that Renaire hadn't been the slightest bit impressed with, and say *draw me, R, paint me, R,* begging to be immortalized.

He'd been a nice enough guy, and he went to work at odd hours, and Renaire was grateful for that, glad to go for stumbling drunken walks at all hours of the day or night. And, two days earlier, he went to the park and saw Delaurier. But that wasn't what his mind focused on. It was a small awareness, a distracting intrigue and a strange queasy feeling that'd stuck to him ever since he'd seen the bastard, but Delaurier didn't rule him. Not yet.

That hadn't stopped him from painting the man, though.

Renaire remembers that, remembers that the easel in the corner of the unhealthy mussed bedroom already had an attempt at Delaurier on it. He also remembers learning how stunningly accurate it managed to be a few minutes later, when his shock of a muse was shoved through the door by one of the big burly men that were probably intimidating and followed What's-His-Name around sometimes. He'd been bloody, nose bleeding freely, blood in his teeth, blood sticking golden hair to his skin.

The burly man had obviously not realized Renaire was in the room, or hadn't cared he was in the room. It was barely noon, sunlight trickling far enough in that it still managed to make Delaurier fucking glow.

Or it was the drugs.

It was probably the drugs.

Either way, Delaurier was watching the burly man like a lion about to rip the throat out of a gazelle.

"Who the fuck do you think you are?" the burly man had shouted at Delaurier, still oblivious to Renaire, and he'd pulled out a knife. That *definitely* glinted. Renaire had already been quietly pulling out useful brushes and knives and even a tube of paint (cadmium yellow; it had somehow seemed appropriate), and waiting. Swaying, but waiting. "You think some snot-nosed little shit—"

Renaire laughed. It was one burst of a *Ha*! at the idea of someone calling *that* a snot-nosed little shit that did it, and the burly man hadn't thought it was funny. He'd glared, sneered, done all the appropriate posturing. "If it isn't the painted whore."

"Paint*ing* whore," Renaire corrected.

"He doesn't have anything to do with this," Delaurier had said.

At the time, Renaire had rolled his eyes, thinking Delaurier was some kind of idealistic moron. Now he knows he's not a moron, but he is about twenty times more of an idealist than anyone sane could ever be. The bodyguard had seemed just about as impressed, with Delaurier struggling to get out of the handcuffs and flailing to try and find some semblance of control while flopping about on top of the unkempt bed like a waterless fish.

Renaire had sighed. "Listen, I just—" He'd swayed, pointing toward Delaurier while he took drunken steps toward the man. "I just want to paint him. Why are you tossing him around?"

"He tried to kill our employer," the man said, still trying to make Renaire feel bad or disgusted or whatever. Still going with the whore thing. It didn't work, since Renaire gave even less of a shit back then. "The fucker's a terrorist."

He'd blinked, looking back at Delaurier. "Seriously?"

Delaurier had fucking *shrugged*, unrepentant, a perfect nonverbal *yeah, so?* if ever there was one.

It's nice to be able to pinpoint the exact moment you sold your soul to someone.

People don't believe how easy it is to kill someone. Renaire never forgot, probably never will. He *wants* to, but he also knows he's pretty good at it. Art and murder, the two things he's decent at. The burly man hadn't even noticed when Renaire pulled the knife out of his relaxed, unsuspicious hand and barely gasped when Renaire almost casually sliced his throat open. It was a lot easier than what he'd been planning to do with the paintbrushes.

Renaire had been drunk enough to pat the newly dead corpse on the head before letting it fall, saying, "Nothing personal."

The man's body hit the hardwood floor. The room was silent. And spinning, just a bit.

"Who are you trying to kill, again?" Renaire asked, wiping the knife's blade on the edge of his shirt.

Delaurier had rearranged himself to an almost respectable pose by then, legs under him and probably capable of getting up off the bed if he did some very determined rocking. "You didn't have to do that," he'd said, watching Renaire intently.

"Actually, I did," Renaire said. "Again—who are you killing?"

"Jean-Auguste Loudin," Delaurier had replied cautiously, because Renaire had probably looked like a drunken crazy man. Which was mostly accurate.

"Who?" Renaire had asked and then frowned. "Is that What's-His-Name?"

Speak of the devil, What's-His-Name had burst through the door right then looking frantic and panicky with wide eyes and a gun (a revolver, of all things) in hand. He had looked at the newly dead man and then at Renaire and then at Delaurier, and somehow that made him run over to Renaire, looking so very worried. "Are you alright, R? Did they hurt you?"

"I'm fine," Renaire reassured him, and for some reason What's-His-Name (Jean-Auguste, probably) had actually been relieved. "Do you have the handcuff keys?"

What's-His-Name had frozen like Renaire just pulled a gun on him. "What?"

"No, see, this was all a misunderstanding," Renaire said and sat himself down in the *paint me*, *draw me*, *love me* chair, dropping everything but the knife so he could light a cigarette. "We'll talk it out like civilized people. No more random killing."

He could already see Delaurier about to object, but Renaire had shot him a look sharp enough that he'd shut his mouth. Renaire's pretty sure that he'd been in shock.

Apparently, What's-His-Name had trusted Renaire completely, since he'd actually helped Delaurier into a reasonable sitting position and unlocked his handcuffs. And they'd actually fucking *talked*.

Jean-Auguste Loudin was a brutal exploitative businessman who was blah-blah equality, blah-blah crimes and justice. Renaire had zoned out pretty fast on that. He'd been far more interested in watching their faces, watching Jean-Auguste turn from What's-His-Name into the harsh man Delaurier had claimed him to be.

Apparently Delaurier wasn't just a crazy person intent on murdering people. He was an *idealist* intent on murdering people. Renaire wasn't sure if that was better or worse.

Renaire had gotten bored pretty fast, watching them shout and threaten and snarl at each other, like debating would ever change either of them. He still hadn't known Delaurier's name then, so he'd looked at Delaurier's sunlit hair and proud blazing eyes, half convinced he was a divine impossibility. He crushed the remains of his cigarette against the windowsill and called out, "Come on, Apollo, get the job done and let's go."

Jean-Auguste had been shocked enough to look at Renaire instead of Delaurier, and spent his final moments looking stunned and betrayed and hurt even before Delaurier had wrestled the revolver (Jesus, it was a *silver-plated* revolver, how much of an asshole was What's-His-Name?) and shot him twice in the chest. It was fast, and Jean-Auguste had fallen to the floor with his eyes wide open and staring straight at Renaire.

Delaurier had followed his victim's lead after that, but in a very different way. He'd watched Renaire like a hawk watching a cobra, trying to figure out if it'd attack, and which one of them would come out on top if he did. "How drunk are you?" Delaurier had asked as if that could explain away everything he'd just done.

"Drunk enough to kill, high enough to do it well, sober enough to never regret it," Renaire had answered, and pointed straight at Delaurier. "I'm going to paint you."

Again, Delaurier looked at Renaire like the crazy person he was. Delaurier had hesitated, though. He'd looked around at the bright airy bedroom and the blood and corpses on the floor and Renaire's little art corner by the window. Delaurier had wanted to ask something, but instead he nodded and said, "You saved my life. It's the least I can do, but not here or now."

"I'll follow you," Renaire said.

Delaurier had nodded again, looking around the room and finally paying attention to the details, probably judging Renaire by the clothes tossed across the floor and the empty bottles and bags arranged neatly on the nightstand. "Do you need to take anything? We have to leave quickly—"

"One thing," Renaire agreed, and Delaurier had looked strangely relieved. Renaire had almost expected him to be gone when he came back from the other room. He *had* expected the frown on his face when Renaire walked out with nothing but a wine bottle. Renaire also tossed a damp cloth to Delaurier so he could wipe the blood off his face. "I'm taking the good stuff. For services rendered."

Delaurier had hesitated, but he'd asked. Sort of. "Are you really a…." He paused as if he couldn't actually get the word out, more from trying to find a polite way to phrase it than actual embarrassment.

Renaire had taken pity on him and said, "No, I'm not a whore. This is just me appropriating compensation for creative infringement and emotional damages."

And then Delaurier had stared at him for a long, long time, but finally held out his hand. Renaire shook it like a sane and reasonable human being who wasn't really dangerously thrilled to touch him for the first time. "I'm Emile," he said, the simple words one long unstoppable breath.

"Emile," Renaire had repeated, delicately tasting the two syllables in the process, and smiled. He liked them.

He still does.

"Delaurier, I mean," Delaurier had said, emphatic, eyes wide, still staring into Renaire's.

"Is that so, Emile," Renaire said, and couldn't stop smiling.

"Emile *Delaurier*," Delaurier repeated. "I go by Delaurier."

"Then I'm Renaire," he'd said, not even a little bit tempted to share his own first name, and tried to decide whether or not a handshake that had lost the actual shaking movement counted as hand-holding, because it was lasting a lot longer than was appropriate.

Renaire's hand had dry paint splattered across it and felt like it was vibrating against Delaurier's warm, slightly sweaty palm. Renaire could feel the strange shift in Delaurier's fingertips, the tiniest sweep of his index finger against the edge of Renaire's palm, an infinitesimal move that still somehow felt like a caress.

But Delaurier had eventually looked away from Renaire's face, down to look at their hands, and jerked away as if Renaire had burned him or was contagious or something repulsive. It had hurt. Even then, it had hurt.

After that, after that single moment, it was always *don't touch him*, always two feet away from him, miles between them as Delaurier's preferred definition of personal space. Renaire would think he was watching him, sometimes, but Renaire knows he's reached a level nearing insanity after two years of *don't touch, don't look, don't even fucking breathe*. He couldn't escape even if he wanted to.

It's that single moment that haunts him. That single, burning moment. Eyes locked into infinity, hand in hand, the world insignificant beyond them.

He wakes up in the night cold and alone, and Delaurier is barely three feet away.

SUNLIGHT WAKES him up the second time, searing into his eyes before he tosses a blanket over his head. *Why the fuck is Moscow sunny today?*

"There's water on the nightstand for you," Delaurier says from the other side of the room.

"You opened the window, didn't you," Renaire accuses.

"Yes, I did," Delaurier says, completely unrepentant. Renaire wishes he had something to throw at him other than the pillow. He refuses to give it up, even for petty vengeance. "Do you want your explanation or not?"

Normally Renaire would keep being difficult just for the sake of being difficult, but *that* makes him peek out from the sheets toward Delaurier. He's sitting on his own bed with what looks suspiciously like a PowerPoint presentation waiting on the laptop next to him. Renaire gets subjected to those for any jobs that require more than sneaking in and killing people, so he's not really surprised.

Delaurier is also obviously trying very hard to not laugh at the ridiculous position Renaire's put himself in, head peeking out of the blankets he's cocooned around the rest of his body. He even has a glass of water waiting for Renaire on the shared nightstand.

This is going to be very bad news.

He disentangles himself from the fabric, still fully dressed in the same clothing he wore yesterday, and most likely the day before that as well (excluding shoes and socks, thank God), and gulps down half of the provided water. He finally crawls his way out of the bed, stands to stretch, and sits himself into the single small chair, drinking more of the water. "Okay, go."

And up goes the PowerPoint. It's a picture of a smiling, professional-looking woman, black and white and slightly fuzzy, like it's been ripped from a newspaper. Which it probably was. "Irena Ivanova, age thirty-seven, one of the foremost investigative journalists in Russia, and the world."

Next slide—headlines. Too many headlines for Renaire to even really read them, particularly with how fast Delaurier runs through them. "She helped expose significant crime and corruption in the Russian government, as well as helped raise awareness throughout the world about the extraordinary amount of human trafficking taking place in Eastern Europe."

There's an awful lot of admiration in Delaurier's voice. Whatever this lady did to make Delaurier run unprepared into Russia to kill her as fast as humanly possible must have been horrific.

Next slide—Ivanova at a restaurant somewhere, talking to someone. The only important thing about the slide is that it tells Renaire very, very clearly that someone was having her watched. "She is—*was*—regrettably pacifistic, believing that violence never solves anything. And it did work, to a point. Sometimes action would be taken on things she exposed. Overall, it made her a threat to the rotten cores of political parties, but not enough of a threat to try and take out."

Delaurier actually hesitates before moving to the next slide, which is strange since it's blank. It must be a placeholder slide, since Delaurier hands him a file folder that looks suspiciously like the one Delaurier had taken from Ivanova's bedroom.

The first page is notes in Russian, Cyrillic, once again defeating Renaire, so he flips to the next page. Delaurier's picture is paper-clipped to the next six pages. It's one of the semipropaganda pictures, where it's candid but Delaurier is just so unnaturally photogenic that STB can still toss it onto fliers and it looks inspirational. The first few pages beneath his picture are in Russian, but the last two are readable.

And terrifying.

Renaire didn't even know half of what's on the first page about Delaurier.

"She was very good at her job," Delaurier says quietly. There's almost a touch of regret to it.

"I don't understand," Renaire says, because it's always better to say that than try to figure it out himself. "You've never made a secret about—"

Delaurier reaches over and turns the page, moving from one paper-clipped bunch of papers to the next. Glasson's calm thin face is looking up at him. Another candid. Either someone's been spying on them, or someone's camera was stolen, or something else went wrong. Glasson has four pages, and Renaire does him the courtesy of not reading them. Carope is after that, with another four pages.

And then it's Renaire.

He has even more pages than Delaurier, because *everything* is inside instead of a consolidated summary. Birth records (and he's surprised at the lack of commentary, considering his first name and birthday), arrest records (mostly drunk and disorderly), hospital records (something he doesn't even want to look at), transcripts (including his halfhearted attempt at law school, with one sterling grading period followed by flunking out), even his fucking military record, including deployment and dishonorable discharge. There are copies of old drawings, one copy of that very first painting of Delaurier (which is worth an obscene amount of money, probably thanks to blood spatter and the admittedly interesting provenance). He learns what his family's been up to since he left. His parents died four years ago in a car wreck. His sister is still alive, married rich like she'd always hoped, and is now named Michelle Mannon.

Ivanova knew more about Renaire's life than Renaire did.

The file folder keeps going through the ranks of STB, all the way down to thirteen-year-old Chason.

"I asked her to not publish it," Delaurier says. "I tried convincing her. I offered her bigger stories. I tried to find a different way, but she wouldn't listen. She said even if she didn't publish it, she'd still send it to Interpol, and she was—"

"Thank you," Renaire says. It's quiet, but he means it.

Delaurier did what Renaire had never, ever thought him capable. He compromised his ethics. He put something ahead of The Cause. Renaire doesn't doubt for a moment that Delaurier feels awful about it, but he also doesn't doubt that Delaurier would make the same choice if it were put before him again.

"I couldn't let her endanger you," Delaurier says. Not *The Cause*, not *STB*. You. He went against his moral code for the sake of his friends. Delaurier leans forward as if he has to make Renaire understand, even if Renaire knows it's himself he's justifying his actions to. "You're mine to take care of. I waited as long as I could, kept trying to reason with her, but I would *never* let someone hurt you like that, not when I could find a way to stop them."

"Thank you, Emile," Renaire says again, and he leans forward to grab onto Delaurier's hands with his own, because Delaurier needs *something*. His hands are shaking, just a bit. Renaire pretends to not notice. "You saved us. We're safe now, because of you."

If Interpol had this information, they'd get arrested, and they'd be sent to prison, and it would be a French prison. That's to be avoided at all cost. The United Nations sent a commission to investigate the French prison system in the 2000s and evaluated it to be one of the worst human rights violations the commission had ever seen. They have one of the highest prisoner suicide rates in the world for a reason.

It's yet another thing Delaurier is fighting against.

He thinks about hugging Delaurier, but doesn't.

"Did you tell Glasson?" Renaire asks. He's still holding Delaurier's hands, and he's not letting go until Delaurier actually notices. Delaurier shakes his head, watching Renaire intently as if he's expecting something. Renaire has no idea what it'd be. He lets go of one hand in order to fetch Delaurier's phone. Since that makes Delaurier look down and realize his other hand is being held, Renaire drops that one too before presenting his prize to Delaurier. "Call Glasson, give him whatever information he needs while I'm gone."

Delaurier frowns. "Where are you going?"

"I am going to go take a shower," Renaire says firmly, grabbing some of the hopefully cleaner clothing out of their bag before turning to look at Delaurier. "It's going to be a very long one."

That actually earns him a quirk of a smile. It's tiny and genuine and directed straight at Renaire before he turns to the phone. "Enjoy."

"Oh, I intend to," Renaire says, and turns to leave.

"Wait," Delaurier says when Renaire already has the doorknob in hand. Renaire turns to look at him. Delaurier looks *nervous*. Renaire takes a moment to look out the window and see that no, the sky is not falling. "I read your file. You should know that."

Renaire remains still and breathes in a reasonable rhythm. "And?"

And oh, he knows it's coming the moment Delaurier's eyes get that idealist shine to them. Renaire mouths the words along with him bitterly, rolling his eyes as Delaurier says, "You could be so much more." It pisses Delaurier off, of course, and he lets out an aggravated huff of air. "I mean it, Renaire. You *could*! Your test scores are superb, and your grades were as good as mine when you actually tried. If you'd only—"

"I'll be in the shower," Renaire says, and is very proud of himself for only slamming the door a little bit behind him.

RENAIRE DOESN'T go back to the room. He buys himself a sketchbook and steals the charcoal and sits in some park or another. It's a nice enough place, and he spends the day sketching the courageous yet battle-hardened pigeons of Moscow. Very few city pigeons are unscarred or have all their toes or are healthy, period. It's barely above freezing, but the locals don't seem to care. It's a sunny day, and Renaire's fingers are stiff from the cold, but really that just averages out to standard dexterity.

The one physical feature Renaire appreciates on his own body is his hands. They're coated in black now, turning his cigarette gray and probably putting streaks on his face, and one final angry pigeon is glaring up at him from the sketchbook when Delaurier somehow finds him. Renaire's pretty sure he installed a tracking device during one of Renaire's (many) drunken stupors.

"You could've just called," Renaire says around the cigarette, not even bothering to look up from his irate stubby bird. It's missing an eye, yet his life model still somehow manages to be glaring at Delaurier with the strength of five disapproving grandmothers.

"I've been told that wasn't an appropriate response to learning everything about your entire life," Delaurier says, wry and the slightest bit self-effacing.

"I didn't really expect you to have an appropriate response," Renaire says simply, taking a moment to tap ash off the tip of his cigarette. He'd hoped, yes, but never expected, not really. "I came to terms with the fact you're a possessive, self-important asshole with a superiority complex a long time ago."

"Somehow, that's reassuring," Delaurier says.

"You can still apologize if you want, though," Renaire offers with one final smudge to the pigeon's rumpled tail feathers. "You won't mean it, but it's still nice to hear."

Delaurier doesn't apologize. He reaches into Renaire's jacket and pulls out a cigarette for himself. Renaire puts the charcoal down to fetch the lighter, since a hand into his jacket is fine but a hand in his pants is *not*.

"Even when I learn literally everything about your life, I still can't make sense of you," Delaurier says. Renaire doesn't dare watch him smoke, so he picks a tourist—a harried brunette with a beret already halfway to falling off her head—and turns to the next page. "I can predict you, but you're still… nonsense. If anything, this makes you even more frustrating."

"You flatterer," Renaire says with something halfway to a laugh. "I bet you say that to all the boys."

"I really don't," Delaurier says, sounding far more serious than Renaire is willing to pay attention to right now. It doesn't last long, though. He stretches, arm hitting Renaire in the shoulder slightly, and Renaire does *not* take the bait—he is not looking while he stretches. Delaurier has apologized by being art eye candy three times, and they were all incredibly awkward, and he is *not doing that right now*. "Are you done sulking?"

"Sulking, yes. Drawing, no," Renaire says.

Delaurier makes an intrigued noise and picks up the finished drawings Renaire has sitting under a rock, just in case the wind picks up. "I like them."

"Of course you do. They're the cruelly oppressed creatures of society," Renaire says. "Look at how the bourgeois humans have hurt them, how they're forced to huddle near sewer vents for warmth in this brutal freezing world. These poor souls need your help, Emile. Look at their plight, their misery. Save the pigeons."

"Why do you do that?" Delaurier asks irritably.

"Why not?" Renaire shoots Delaurier a quick smile before turning back to sketching the tourist. "You could use a little more self-awareness. Pigeon #4 is for you, by the way. You'll like Pigeon #4."

Pigeon #4 is the most offended pigeon Renaire has ever seen. He hadn't even known pigeons could look offended until Pigeon #4 came around. It makes Delaurier laugh.

"Alright, I'm done," Renaire says with one final scribble to her hair and finally turns to look at Delaurier. His talk with Glasson obviously did him some good. It usually does. "Are we doing the job today?"

"Tonight," Delaurier says and takes Renaire's sketchbook away from him so he has two hands to wipe the charcoal off his fingers with a tissue Delaurier provides. "Let's eat, and then I'll show you the plan."

"I don't need to see the plan," Renaire says as he always does.

Likewise, Delaurier says, "You can never be too prepared."

Delaurier stands up and starts walking, flicking his pinched-off cigarette into a nearby trash can.

Renaire follows.

CHAPTER 2

Moscow—Warsaw—Budapest

RUSSIAN MAFIA offices never actually close. In general, illegal businesses do most of their work long after standard operating hours, which means Delaurier and Renaire do their work around the same times.

They're to make a statement, it turns out. Delaurier has plenty of plans and timetables and employee rosters, and pulls out blueprints that Renaire doesn't even pretend to do more than glance at. Delaurier isn't quite an optimist, but he seems to live with the eternal hope that one of these days Renaire will actually give a shit. That day is not today.

"I've never understood why they're always referred to as the Russian mafia," Renaire says while Delaurier tries to tell him about electricity grids or something. He hasn't given the man too bad of a time today since he also bought Renaire ice cream. It's not alcohol, but any and all bribes are appreciated. "I mean, it's not the Japanese mafia, it's the *yakuza*. Drug cartels aren't quite the same thing, but they're close enough, and nobody calls them the Colombian mafia. Or—"

"*Bratva*," Delaurier says. "But it usually refers to a single group. *Vorovskoy mir* also works. But 'bratva' would be like 'family' in the traditional Mafia. There's not really a word for the entire collective, so Russian mafia is as good as we can do, now will you at least *pretend* to pay attention?"

"You bought me ice cream, so that's fair," Renaire says graciously. "Oh, and Wikipedia says we're a crime syndicate."

"We are *not* a crime syndicate," Delaurier says, glaring at the spreadsheets on the table. "We're an extremist group, at the most."

"Oh, we're in there too," Renaire says. "Crime syndicate is a new addition."

"There's no syndication in what we do," Delaurier says. "There's not even any crime—"

Renaire laughs.

"Any crime *beyond this*," Delaurier says. Renaire watches the wheels turn in his head, even if Delaurier doesn't want to discuss it right now. "Fine, there's a little bit of cyber warfare, and we don't pay taxes appropriately, and there's occasionally blackmail or theft or arson, and there's organization and small affiliated groups around the world, but that's it. We're *revolutionaries*, not criminals. We're the vanguard of a—"

"You're going to go and edit the page, aren't you?" Renaire says, finishing off his ice cream.

"Of course I am. It's wrong. Stop stalking our Wikipedia entries," Delaurier says. "You always start getting *ideas*."

"Heaven forbid," Renaire says dryly. "Weren't we going to pretend I'm listening to your plan?"

Delaurier sighs, looking up to frown at Renaire. "When you get *ideas*, things always end up going wrong. The past three times one of us nearly died, it was because you had an *idea*."

Renaire rolls his eyes. "You don't think that's a suspicious correlation there? I voiced an *idea* because we were about to die!"

"Do you really expect me to believe that Tripoli—"

"Tripoli doesn't count," Renaire says.

"Finding you had almost *literally* drank yourself to death doesn't count?" Delaurier snaps. "You had a blood alcohol content of .47 *percent*—"

"You know why Tripoli doesn't count, we are *moving on*," Renaire says.

"Is it that hard to just listen to me? To just follow my orders? You do it well enough when we're *not* in a life-threatening environment," Delaurier says. His hands are clenched into fists now, leaning hard on the table toward Renaire.

"You don't get to control me, Emile," Renaire states.

"Yes, I do," Delaurier says, and stands, heading for the door. "I just try not to. I'm heading out at eleven tonight. You can choose whether or not you're coming along." He takes a moment for a single parting shot. "Although we both know what it'll be."

"And we were having such a nice day," Renaire says, and the door shuts behind Delaurier. He is seriously tempted to throw things at it.

But eleven rolls around and Renaire is standing in their hotel room, ready to go.

Delaurier doesn't even have the courtesy to look smug.

WHEN THEY get there, the office is nothing special, sitting in the outskirts of Moscow (interestingly, the complete geographic opposite of the outskirt area of Moscow their hotel is in). Renaire isn't surprised to see there are still lights on in the building. Crime doesn't sleep, for either side of this encounter. Delaurier has his unremarkable brown coat on this time. No question about what kind of job it is.

"Should be about nine people inside, three guards, at least half will be armed," Delaurier states, not even glancing over at Renaire.

Things are still snappish and tense between them, but Renaire is pretty sure they'll be able to make it through this cleanly enough. They have before. Of course, the other times hadn't included a suddenly emotionally expressive Delaurier who looks about ten seconds from exploding. Renaire is telling himself that professionalism will override Delaurier's natural urge to scream at him, because otherwise he is going to end up trying to convince the idiot to postpone.

"Do you have everything?" Renaire asks.

"Of course I do," Delaurier snaps, and *fuck this*, Renaire doesn't have to take this shit. He can leave whenever he chooses to. But Delaurier shoves his hands deep into his coat pockets and starts striding his way toward the office's back door. As ever, Renaire follows. "You're just backup, understand? You cover me, and that's all."

Renaire can't deal with this, not sober, but he never lets himself bring alcohol when they have a job, so he has to settle for a cigarette. His hands twitch with the urge to strangle Delaurier, just a little bit.

"Don't do anything stupid," Delaurier says. "In fact, don't do anything at all."

"What kind of weaponry do you think they have?" Renaire asks, because that *little bit* of strangling is turning into strangling until he turns purple. Even if they were running into a military base to try and take out a tank battalion, this would still be ridiculous behavior for Delaurier.

"Maybe you should just wait out here," Delaurier says when they reach the door. They do this so often that Renaire is certain Delaurier doesn't even realize he's stepped aside to have Renaire open the door, one way or another. "Or back at the hotel."

"Or in Paris," Renaire suggests, rolling his eyes. "You know, you might as well send me to Antarctica."

When he does the standard twist of the doorknob, it's unlocked. These people are either very confident, or very, very stupid. He can see Delaurier is thinking the same thing, lips pressed tightly against each other, and standard procedure takes over once again. Delaurier lightly pushes him away from the door, Renaire lets himself be pushed, and Delaurier already has a gun drawn and is in the building by the time Renaire has his hand on the doorframe.

It's not chaos inside, because Delaurier is too good for that. It *is* already bloody and loud. Two bodies, obviously the guards, were efficiently put down in the small room off the side of the hallways that was their station. Renaire supposes that's another point in favor of Delaurier's thing about memorizing floorplans and shift changes and grabs one of the corpse's AK-47s. Louder than he'd like, but the shouting and occasional scream tearing its way through the building isn't any worse than the gun would be when it comes to noise control.

Delaurier always tries to be kind of polite about killing noncombatants. It's why he's not using anything bigger than a pistol, and it's also one more ridiculous thing he does that makes Renaire want to grab him by the shoulders and shake him until he sees stars and sunflowers and fucking *unicorns*. There's no actual targeting going on, mostly panicked gunfire from the mafia office workers that's hitting their own people more often than it even gets close to where Delaurier is crouched patiently in one of the closest office cubicles.

Renaire has the AK-47's shoulder strap held loosely in his hand, cigarette in his other when he sits down next to Delaurier. "They're going to call the police if they get near a phone," he says.

"This office belongs to the Russian mafia, they're not going to call the authorities," Delaurier says.

"It's *Russia*," Renaire points out but doesn't have time to discuss any further since Delaurier is moving. He's moving toward people who obviously have no idea what the hell they're doing with those guns (which is surprising—he knows more than a few USSR schools taught how to field-strip an AK) so he slings the gun onto his shoulder and makes sure he has some knives on hand. Civilians are predictably unpredictable when they're facing the wrath of God known as

Delaurier, meaning that Delaurier will probably have to dodge whatever erratic behavior they have, meaning that Renaire would have to predict *two* erratic patterns, and it's just a mess. So. Knives.

He doesn't even need to worry since Delaurier takes the other three down in that conscientious yet brutal way of his.

"Five down," Renaire says helpfully around his cigarette, and there is something seriously wrong with Delaurier because he just *glares*, and when he walks past Renaire, he shoves him. Hard.

"Wait here," Delaurier says, firm and frustrated.

Renaire stumbles and ends up falling into the seat of an office chair, spinning for a good few moments while he tries to recover from the shock. By then Delaurier is gone again, and there's more gunfire.

This isn't how it goes. This isn't how it works between them, not on a job. It's the one place they understand each other, the only time Renaire *knows* Delaurier trusts him.

The lights are flickering now, and he doesn't know if that's because something got shot or someone did something intentionally, but either way it's frustrating.

The office complex is set in a *U* shape around the boss's office, which Renaire remembers is either unoccupied or they're not supposed to fuck with it or something. They came in on the end of the left side, and the gunfire is coming from what sounds like the corner leading into the right side of the office.

When Renaire walks over to see the fuss, there's one more body, and two people who've sequestered themselves behind a makeshift barricade of office furniture and a water cooler. They're shouting in Russian, and it sounds very intimidating while they shoot the good old reliable rifles of Russia at no discernible target.

Delaurier, who is smart, is nowhere to be seen.

Renaire continues to think they should look into grenades one of these days.

There's no way to shoot them out, so the only real method Renaire can see for this is to either convince them to come out, overpower them, or wait them out. At the rate they're going with the random shooting, they'll probably be out of ammunition pretty soon. But then again, this is Russia.

Convince them to come out, then, Renaire thinks, and heads over to the nice coffee table next to a couple of very basic chairs. It's heavy, so Renaire takes a moment to admire how good it looks for something so shoddily made, before shaking one of the table legs out. It still has nails on it. There's also a potted plant that used to be on top of the table, so he grabs that too.

Renaire realizes this is one of those *ideas* Delaurier keeps shouting about. But right now Delaurier can go fuck himself.

He hefts the potted plant for a moment—it's a small one, probably a jade plant—and then looks at the distance between him and the remaining office workers (one of which is probably the remaining guard) and then looks at the surprisingly decent ceiling height. And then he lobs the plant over to them.

It hits right on the top edge of one of their overturned desks, shattering and spraying dirt and plant all over. The men scream, and one of them stands for some reason. Renaire sees Delaurier take him out, even if he has no idea where Delaurier is stationed.

The other man, having realized his cover is actually more of a waiting death trap, takes what he thinks is his chance. He stands and starts shooting erratically toward Delaurier while he runs toward Renaire and drops the gun when he gets past that hallway, grabbing onto his dead friend's gun instead.

He gets off a shot or three when he spots Renaire waiting around the corner, but they're nowhere near him. Renaire just grabs the table leg like a baseball bat, and swings. And then swings again. And again. After that there's not really anything left to do beyond watch the man fall to the floor.

He drops the gore-covered table leg onto the hallway's once beige carpet, right by the last man, and walks to the flickering lights of the main entrance. He wonders if Delaurier's screaming at him is going to be the thing that finally gets them arrested.

When Delaurier storms around the corner with wrathfully long strides, eyes already burning at him, Renaire just raises his chin and stands his ground. Delaurier doesn't even try to step around the blood seeping into the carpet. His boots step right into it, trailing footprints all the way to Renaire.

Renaire's entire body stiffens for a single moment, but it's Delaurier's feet, on carpet. The world turns again.

"I told you to wait," Delaurier says, voice low and dark, body shaking from the adrenaline. He steps closer, close enough that Renaire can feel his breath against his skin. The fistful of fabric Delaurier grabs is tight and furious. "I *told you to wait*, that was completely reckless and senseless and *stupid*, you could have gotten yourself killed—"

"I did what I had to," Renaire snaps back, unrepentant, watching Delaurier's eyes glint in the flickering fluorescent lights of the office. "And it *worked*. What else do you want?"

"I want you to *obey*," Delaurier says, and his grip is impossibly tight, fabric straining beneath white-knuckled fingers as he shoves Renaire with a fist. His back hits the wall with enough force that a nearby picture frame rattles. "You don't make the plans, remember?" There's a bitter twist to the words, and fuck, is this *still* down to his control issues?

Renaire glares at him, hands clenched against the weak plaster of the office wall. His fingernails scour bloody arcs into his palms, and the pain grounds him. The world always blurs when Renaire gets angry, always makes his vision center on one thing, and now he can't see anything but Delaurier and his golden fury.

"I choose whether I obey," he says, and every syllable is difficult to get out. His throat makes them sound rough and raw and damaged. "You don't make my choices."

Delaurier lets out a harsh, angry laugh. "Oh that's right, because yours are always so *sound* and *healthy*."

Renaire doesn't even pretend to make smart decisions anymore, which is why he grabs Delaurier's wrist in an effort to get the son of a bitch to leave him alone. "I'm choosing not to break your perfect fucking nose, aren't I?"

"That's not a choice," Delaurier says and drops the fabric of Renaire's shirt, twisting his wrist to catch the restricting hand and slam it onto the wall above their heads. The frame rattles again. His grip is just as tight on Renaire's skin as it was on his clothing. "That's not a choice, Renaire. Not for you. That's an obsession."

Renaire tries to calm down, but he ends up staring into Delaurier's deadly serious eyes.

They don't talk about that, not really. They have avoided talking about that for two fucking years. They don't talk about it when one of them is close to dying. They don't talk about it when Renaire is drunk enough to let himself try and draw the bastard. They don't talk about it in silent shared beds on starless nights that leave Renaire awake and shaking and curled into a fetal position to keep himself from trying to do anything, or say anything, or *be* anything more than the half partner, half friend, all irritant of STB's fool of a fearless leader.

He wants to say that Delaurier isn't cruel enough to use this, but he really, really is. Renaire takes a deep breath, bows his head, and squeezes his eyes shut.

"Look at me," Delaurier orders harshly. When Renaire doesn't obey, Delaurier's other hand snaps forward to tilt Renaire's head back up, back to eye level. His eyes shoot wide open at the feel of warm, calloused fingers pressed against his jaw. "Just do what I tell you to."

There's a slight sheen of sweat that keeps Delaurier's hair sticking against his skin and looking like cream silk in the flickering lights. His lips are right there, *right in front of him*, but this is Delaurier. This can't be what Renaire wants it to be. This is just Delaurier exploding in a new way. He doesn't dare shut his eyes again, but he does try to concentrate on something that isn't painful to look at while he can feel the other man's erratic, fury-hot breath against his skin.

He wants to swallow down the dryness of his throat, wants to be able to *think*, but instead he ends up staring at Delaurier's mouth. He doesn't lean into the way Delaurier's fingers cup his chin, doesn't lean forward, away from the wall and toward Delaurier. He stays perfectly, rigidly, stone still right where he is.

Delaurier's thumb is tracing his jaw line, his fingers gliding featherlight against Renaire's cheek, and this is every nightmare and fantasy he's ever had combined.

When he manages to take a breath, manages to calm down enough to trust his mouth to open and say actual words instead of babbling all the things he doesn't get to want, he looks Delaurier in the eye. "You don't own me," Renaire says. He wants to shout it, but it comes out close to begging.

"Yes I do," Delaurier says immediately, right on top of Renaire's words. They're fierce and full of conviction, like he believes it just as much as he believes in equality and freedom and every other soul-deep creed he fights and kills for, everything else he worships. "I've owned you since you first saw me, and you *love it*, you wouldn't even know what to do with yourself if I didn't."

"Emile, *please*," Renaire says, he *begs*, because he can't survive this. He will die. Delaurier is cruel and beautiful and is murdering him with words and glances and with every single confident brush of his fingers. "You don't do this. Please."

"I made a choice," Delaurier says as if that explains every single thing about the past few days, and suddenly Renaire can't breathe or think because the hand against his cheek has twisted, and now his thumb is tracing Renaire's lips. "Now it's your turn to make one."

It's the lightest of touches, but he gasps anyway.

There's no choice to make, not really. He can see it in Delaurier's eyes that this is just the final feeble lock on a gate about to burst. There's no choice to make, because he was right. It's not a choice—it's an obsession that has consumed him since one ill-fated afternoon in Paris two years ago. There was sunlight at the right angle through the right trees, Delaurier smiling in the right direction, a breeze tossing Renaire's papers at the right time and teasing Delaurier's halo-struck hair to the perfect degree. A single moment of eye contact.

Fuck, he hates himself so much.

Delaurier's thumb stops moving, resting gently at the middle of his lower lip, like he might be having second thoughts, and Renaire *panics*. His free hand grabs Delaurier's shoulder before he can even think, and Renaire knows he probably looks as desperate as he feels, because how can he not? He wraps his fingers in brown fabric and says, "Kiss me."

Delaurier doesn't hesitate. His hand moves from tormenting Renaire's lips to combing its way into the hair behind his neck, and then pulls him forward. Delaurier drops Renaire's hand from the wall and wraps his arm around his waist, dragging them flush against each other's bodies, and Renaire moans against Delaurier's lips just from that.

When Delaurier smirks, Renaire takes the opportunity to press teeth against his lower lip, and Delaurier shudders. Renaire bites down hard enough to hurt, and Delaurier fucking *whimpers*, fingers digging into Renaire's hair hard enough to yank his head back for a new angle to slide their lips together, and fuck, he is not going to last long at all.

Delaurier pulls his mouth away to attack Renaire's ear, biting his earlobe like it's been tormenting him for years. "I want your shirt off," Delaurier says, rough and urgent. Renaire can feel him against his thigh, the skin on his cheek heating and cooling from the unsteady shaking breaths Delaurier takes against Renaire's face, and it's the most intimate thing he's ever felt. He speaks into Renaire's skin like he wants to taste what the words might bring out of him. "I want your shirt off, and I want your pants off, and I want you naked, and I want it *now*."

"One more good plan," Renaire says—babbles, really, words desperately tripping over themselves almost as much as Renaire's body as he tries to strip out of his shirt while somehow keeping as much contact as possible with Delaurier. "But—bed. Please. *Please* let there be a bed." It's ridiculous, it's a fucking office, but he is going to beg anyway.

"There's a couch," Delaurier says, because he memorizes blueprints. He plans. He is leaning back enough to strip Renaire's shirt off with his own hands, thumbs making a point of sliding up his skin, and Renaire stares because the other man looks like it's physically painful to not be kissing him. He tosses the shirt aside without looking away from Renaire for a single second, and starts moving down the abandoned hall.

Moving down the hall doesn't work so well, since Renaire can't stop touching him, but can't make himself tug at Delaurier's clothing, can't even reach beneath fabric after years of restraint and training. *Don't touch, don't look, don't speak*, his mind screams at him, and all it means is that he has fingers tangled in Delaurier's hair and is trying to swallow every breath and gasp. He tries to kiss Delaurier, so mindless that there's no chance of this stopping.

Delaurier doesn't stop. He walks backward, and Renaire follows until they hit a wall. Delaurier *laughs*, and it's beautiful. Renaire pulls away just enough to speak, but he's still close enough that his nose is brushing against Delaurier's. "Tell me what you want."

"I did," Delaurier says, walking him farther down the hall again. He speaks when he can pull himself away from Renaire's mouth. Now that Renaire is trying to taste every wonder of Delaurier's mouth with his tongue and then sucking in every gasp right along with Delaurier's lower lip, it doesn't happen very often. "Fuck, you're so—" He stops, pulling Renaire's mouth away with a jerk of his hand, baring Renaire's throat and nipping at the exposed flesh. "The only reason you aren't naked yet is it's hard to walk and strip at the same time."

Renaire squeezes his eyes shut, breathing hard while his nerves war between pain and obsessive pleasure at the feel of Delaurier's teeth as they get sharper and sharper—either way, he wants more. He follows the shuffling steps Delaurier leads with. He always follows. Renaire's back hits another wall, but this time he groans, pained at the impact because something just slammed right into his back.

Delaurier pulls away just enough to look at the surface—the door, thank all that is holy. There is probably a couch in there. He would fucking love a couch right now. He wants a horizontal surface so, so badly. Renaire takes the opportunity of Delaurier's shaky fumbling with the doorknob to hesitantly suck on Delaurier's throat.

"Fuck," Delaurier snaps, a hand bashing against the door, and Renaire freezes, jerks away from Delaurier's neck, and looks him in the eye immediately. Delaurier is snarling at the door, but his hand is resting possessively on Renaire's shoulder while he does it. "It's not opening."

Renaire is not the problem. The door is the problem.

"No couch?" Renaire asks frantically. He wants that couch. *He needs that couch*; why the fuck does the world hate him? He will take a fucking loveseat or an extra-large chair without complaint at this point.

Delaurier groans, forehead banging lightly against the metal door, like he can scare it into opening through close quarters loathing. "I am so glad we killed these people," he mutters.

"I hate doors," Renaire says.

"Let me just—" Delaurier says, and separates from Renaire to ram his shoulder into the door as if he can force it open. "This fucking door, I am going to burn this building to the ground and salt the ashes *just for this door*."

Renaire feels like he's going to hyperventilate, but he can't just let this opportunity pass. And if Delaurier says no, he'll obey, because he always does. And fuck, fuck, he wants it so bad. He doesn't bother giving a warning; he just grabs Delaurier's shoulder and turns him back to face each other, and then presses him against the door with a hand. He takes a deep breath, feeling feverish and panicky, and practically trips over his own legs as he falls to his knees, fingers already sliding into the waistband of Delaurier's pants. "Please," Renaire begs. "Please, let me—"

The string of profanity that Delaurier groans out makes even Renaire pause. It's a good thing he stops, because this way he gets to watch Delaurier's quaking fingers undo the button of his pants and unzip the fly, with zero showmanship beyond the slower speed of anyone who looks this close to shaking apart. He's hard, and Renaire doesn't even take the time to see more than that before he grabs onto Delaurier's hips and wraps his lips around Delaurier's cock. It's almost delicate, his tongue flirting with the tip, and Delaurier groans like Renaire is ripping him apart.

"How rough do you want it?" Delaurier asks, hoarse, one hand braced on the doorknob while the other has that same possessive grasp of Renaire's hair. "I know what I want, and I know you'll give me anything I ask." Renaire groans again, and Delaurier gasps at the feel of it, the hand in Renaire's hair tightening so much it feels like the strands will be ripped out if this goes any further. "What do *you* want?"

Renaire doesn't want to move his mouth, doesn't want to release Delaurier when this is still so new and impossible. So instead of answering, he locks eyes with Delaurier and stays still, mouth loose and open and waiting.

"Jesus Christ," Delaurier breathes out, and doesn't wait. He takes a single sharp breath in, slowly thrusts forward, and Renaire moans.

He waits for the bite of nails in his scalp, waits for Delaurier to fuck his mouth so hard and deep that Renaire will be hoarse for a month, but he doesn't. Delaurier's eyes are fixed on his own, occasionally flicking down to watch Renaire's lips swallow him with every agonizingly slow thrust, but he always comes back to Renaire's eyes, like they're magnetic. "Your fucking *mouth*."

He can't just let praise like that stand, not like this. Not when Renaire isn't even struggling to breathe or keep up, not when it's like this. Delaurier lets out a sound that's half hum, half moan, and so fucking satisfied, and this is too easy to deserve that reaction. Renaire presses a hand against his own hard cock, still trapped in his pants, but the moment Delaurier sees it, he tugs *hard* on Renaire's hair and *growls*, "Don't you dare."

Resolve jolts down his spine, and he moves his eyes from Delaurier to concentrate on grabbing the man's wiry hips and dive down as far as he can on Delaurier's cock on his next agonizingly slow thrust. He can't even get close to swallowing him completely, this has never been what Renaire is best at, but he's choking on it, and Delaurier groans like he's been shot when Renaire twists his tongue.

It doesn't last long—he's barely taken two breaths, heart thundered twenty times, before Delaurier's hands are in his hair and dragging him off his cock. Delaurier is still panting almost frantically against the door, but it doesn't keep him from looking like wrath personified. "If I wanted you gagging, you would be," Delaurier says, breathy and harsh.

Renaire has to clear his throat before he speaks, saying, "You won't break me."

"I'm trying not to," Delaurier says, and Renaire can tell they're talking about different things but doesn't have enough logic in him right now to figure it out.

Delaurier doesn't give him time to even try. He wraps a hand lightly around Renaire's throat and guides him onto his feet to stand in front of Delaurier, and the moment they're near eye level, Delaurier leans forward to press their mouths together and then their tongues. Renaire whines when Delaurier separates—first for breath, and then Renaire has to rest his head on Delaurier's shoulder when the other man's hand sneaks beneath his pants, unzipping and dropping them with little finesse and absolutely no patience.

"God, I want to fuck you," Delaurier says into his hair, a hand gripping his hip hard enough to bruise, and Renaire doesn't even mean to bite Delaurier's neck, but his mouth can't do anything else, not with sweat-slick skin beneath his lips while Delaurier strokes him and, fuck, while he talks. Renaire clutches at his waist and tries to think coherently enough to remember what's allowed, what's not, what is even happening anymore. "I've wanted to fuck you for years."

Renaire has no idea what he says at that, only that he feels like he's lost every bone in his body, and he's suddenly babbling into Delaurier's skin and drowning in the feeling of *Delaurier's hand*, saying, "Oh Jesus Christ just fucking touch me, Emile, I will do *anything*—"

"What do you want, Renaire?" Delaurier says, biting his ear. His hands are doing impossible things to Renaire just grazing his skin, tormenting him with gentle brushes of fingertips, only to follow them with a bruising grip, and Renaire moans like he's dying when Delaurier grabs his ass. "I'm not doing anything else until you *tell me*."

"I don't know," Renaire says, frantic, with no idea what he can do. He's barely restraining himself from giving in and thrusting against Delaurier's leg, or leaning back into his hands, can't do anything beyond cling to him. "Fuck, I don't know. I can't even think. I just fucking want you." It's like asking a starving man what he wants to eat at a five-star restaurant. He has two years of fantasies, and they all fail him in his time of need, and fuck, *fuck*, he hates himself so much.

Delaurier makes a pleased humming noise, though, so it must have been enough. His hands slide from Renaire's ass to his hips, just a finger's width away from his thighs, and shoves Renaire against the adjacent wall. "You'll have an answer next time," Delaurier promises, and Renaire can feel every syllable as their lips brush with the movements, and he grinds his cock against Renaire's.

Renaire is going to die. The noise he lets out at the feel of Delaurier's cock against his is completely inhuman, a hoarse rasp of a whine that Delaurier rips apart between their mouths, thrusting again. Delaurier's pants are still hanging onto his hips and the fabric digs into his thighs with every thrust, metal a cold jagged press against his skin in a feverish world. Renaire is going to die, and he doesn't give a fuck, because he'd be dying with Delaurier.

Next time, Delaurier had said, and Renaire shudders just at the thought. Their pace speeds up, and Renaire wraps an arm around Delaurier's waist in an attempt to get them even closer together. Fuck, he wants to feel Delaurier against his skin for the next week. *Next time*, Renaire thinks again, and he can barely manage to breathe at the feel of it all. *Next time.*

"Tell me," Delaurier says, almost a question.

Renaire is fucking grinning, eyes sliding shut as he decides to just screw it and ride the crazy train that is whatever the fuck they're doing right now. "You said *next time*," Renaire says, words a low purr. He really does not give a shit about what he sounds like, but apparently Delaurier really, really does, since he makes a noise more appropriate to getting stabbed than frottage in the hallway of a crime scene.

"There will be so many times," Delaurier moans into his neck, and *Jesus fuck*, his hand is wrapped around Renaire's cock, around *both of them*. Heaven save him from the things this man can do with his fingers—he will never again be able to watch him even fucking *type*. Delaurier is panting against him, and Renaire can't think anymore. "Renaire. Tell me. What do you want?"

Renaire can't think, he *can't*, but Delaurier wants him to so he just begs his mouth to make word noises. It does, and Renaire breathes out, "I want to come in your mouth."

Delaurier drops to his knees.

Delaurier looks up at him with eyes as desperately devoted to Renaire as they are to The Cause.

Delaurier barely has time to wrap his lips around Renaire's cock before he's coming with an agonizing groan, *inside Delaurier's mouth*, and Delaurier fucking *swallows*, swallows like he's starving for it, and sweet motherfucking God if he could come again *he absolutely would*. As it is he fights to stay standing, and it doesn't last long—he slumps to the floor and kisses Delaurier like he's dying, which he still feels like he is, and he can taste himself in Delaurier's mouth. The world is beautiful, and nothing in it could ever be as beautiful as Delaurier.

Blowjobs are not Renaire's specialty. He can be passionate, and he can be *extremely* enthusiastic, but he will always be best with his hands. Renaire wraps a hand around Delaurier's cock and jerks him off ruthlessly, Delaurier fucking *whimpering* into his mouth as Renaire twists his wrist and strokes him hard and fast, other hand curled in Delaurier's sweat-damp hair.

Delaurier's eyes are squeezed shut, but they snap open when Renaire whispers his name. He's staring at Renaire when he comes in Renaire's grip, obviously trying to stay silent, but a choked-off whine still escapes his throat.

Delaurier takes three deep, desperate breaths and grabs Renaire's wrist. His hand is still shaky, but his grip is firm and absolute, and he's pulling Renaire's hand up, away from his body.

Renaire wishes he was surprised. He wishes he didn't know Delaurier was about to declare this a terrible mistake, add it to yet another bizarre action taken in whatever insanity Russia has infected him with. It was nice while it lasted. It was *very* nice. And if things go even worse than he expects, well… he trusts Moscow to do the job well enough.

Renaire watches the slow progression of his hand up toward Delaurier's face, trying to be impassive about the look in Delaurier's eyes, and *oh Jesus fucking Christ and all that is sacred or profane*—he is licking the come off Renaire's fingers. Renaire is probably hyperventilating and Delaurier looks so fucking smug, and he needs to kiss Delaurier *right now*.

Delaurier lets him. Delaurier is making a happy humming noise that Renaire only knows from when he's managed a particularly impressive feat for The Cause. It's a strange, leisurely kiss, like Delaurier is just happy Renaire's there. He's not smiling when they separate, not quite, but he looks… fuck, Renaire doesn't even know. Smug and content and confident.

"Get dressed," Delaurier says simply, standing and grabbing articles of clothing they'd managed to lose. Renaire gets his pants thrown right in his face. "We have a building to burn down."

Well.

Professional face back on, then.

Delaurier doesn't say anything about the fact they just had sex and the fact there were a lot of things said, and Renaire doesn't have the courage to bring it up.

When they get on their westward-bound train at dawn, Delaurier sits right next to him. And, after some uncharacteristic fidgeting, Renaire ends up with his fingers wrapped together with Delaurier's own, both firmly silent as Delaurier carefully holds his hand.

THEY SWITCH trains to head southwest when they hit Warsaw, aiming for Budapest in a night train for no reason beyond it not being a (semi)direct link from Moscow to Paris.

It's very, very strange. They've done this a hundred times before, but Renaire still has no fucking clue what he's supposed to do, and from the impossibly uncertain look Delaurier keeps getting, neither does he.

Delaurier seems to be getting the hang of hand-holding, though. It's the only real physical contact since Russia, and even that keeps Renaire halfway to a panic attack, and *he doesn't know what is going on.* Delaurier's grip is tight and warm even in his sleep, and reclaiming his hand is more difficult than it should be. Although he'll admit that quite a bit of the difficulty is that he really, really doesn't want to let go.

There's no arguing, no needling, no discussion. It is quiet and awkward and terrifying.

He escapes into their car's tight corridor and calls Glasson while Delaurier naps through eastern Poland.

"Is he dying?" Renaire asks, quiet and urgent. "Does he have a terminal disease? Am *I* dying? Oh God, am I *already dead*?"

"You're too frantic to be dead," Glasson says, and there's a strange clunking noise. "Wait. Are you saying what I think you're saying?"

"I'm not a fucking mind reader, how should I know?" Renaire hisses out, already starting to pace. Glasson doesn't deserve this, but he's the official head of operations for STB. If someone's going to get screamed at, it's usually him. "Fuck, I have no idea what's going on. He talked to you. I *know* he talked to you—"

"Did he actually kiss you?" Glasson asks, obviously disbelieving. There's another muffled noise in the background, like a shout quickly stifled. Renaire's guessing Glasson chose to cover the phone instead of another mouth. "I'm asking you very seriously. Did he kiss you?"

Renaire drops his head, forehead thudding against the train car's window. Even with the reflection, he can't tell if he's smiling or grimacing. "You could say that."

More muffled noises, and then rattling, and Renaire realizes, "Oh *fuck you*, I'm on speakerphone!"

"We've been waiting two years for this, excuse us for—" he can hear Carope call out, only to be muted. Renaire's guessing it was done forcibly.

Glasson comes back on the line after a few more moments of movement. By now Renaire's curled on the carpeted floor of the train car, leaning against the outside wall and trying very hard to be soothed by the rocking. "I'm sorry about that," Glasson says, and sounds genuine. "We thought—"

"Just tell me if he's okay," Renaire says, because this isn't helping. At all. He wants this call finished as quickly as possible, and then he wants to find a hole to die in. "Is he brainwashed, or poisoned, or on mind-altering drugs, anything like that?"

There's a long pause, and then the vague, ever-present muffled noise of speakerphone is gone. It's just Glasson now. "I won't say he's in his right mind, but he's himself, and you know he never does anything unless he means it," Glasson says simply. "Is a kiss really that surprising, after two years?"

Renaire doesn't correct him, doesn't even consider going into more detail. He wants to ask *why now*, but that's obvious—Delaurier has been very, very strange ever since they sprinted to Russia and killed Ivanova. He desperately wants to ask *why me*, but he's terrified to hear what the answer would be. So, instead, Renaire says, "It's pretty fucking surprising after *two years*, yeah."

"Have you considered talking to *him* instead of me?" Glasson asks. "I'm not exactly fully informed. I don't even know where you are."

"I'm on the floor," Renaire says because he's very helpful. He grimaces. "I'm *sober*, and on the floor."

Glasson is mostly a good person, so he makes a sympathetic noise. But he's only *mostly* a good person, so it's more of a "sucks to be you" kind of noise than anything else. "You're the only person I know who can ever make him change his mind," he says.

Renaire thumps his head against the wall again. "So what, you think he loves me for my arguments?" he asks, the words acidic and disdainful.

"Basically, yes," Glasson says. "Also, you should know I heard some of what's in your Ivanova file. I didn't share it with anyone else, but—"

Renaire hangs up before he can hear the rest. It takes him a moment to sift through the self-loathing to find his mildly helpful masochistic streak, which is really the only thing that helps him stand back up and turn toward the compartment Delaurier managed to talk their way into.

He really wishes he was surprised to see Delaurier waiting in the open doorway for him. He is rumpled and pale, but even with slowly developing circles under the eyes he has trained on Renaire, he is perfectly alert and awake. They just stare at each other for a long while, train rocking beneath them.

"I didn't do this right," Delaurier finally says quietly.

Renaire sighs, shoulders slumped as he averts his eyes. He'd rather not do this at all. "I'm too tired for this," he says, which is mostly honest.

"Too bad," Delaurier says, and it's a familiar move when Delaurier grabs him by the shirt and drags him through the door. He releases Renaire much more quickly than usual, though. Renaire tries to tell himself it's because he needs two hands to shut the compartment door.

He's folded the beds out. It's a sign of nothing beyond it being past midnight in a sleeper car. Renaire stays standing in the tiny amount of space left between the bunk and the other wall, braced against the tiny table built in to the side. When the door is closed, Delaurier looks from Renaire to the layout of the small compartment and then tucks the upper bunk back into the wall with the efficiency that comes from years of experience.

"What happens now?" Renaire asks, because he really has no idea. He isn't the one who plans. He's just the one who follows, and even that he barely manages.

He knows the look of Delaurier preparing to make a speech, has seen it over and over again from impromptu street corners, and huge months-long planned secret rallies, and righteous angry phone calls at least once a month. "Now I try to be reasonable about you," Delaurier says. The hurt from that statement must be painfully obvious on his face, since Delaurier jerks to his feet and says, "Not like *that*, I meant that—fuck, I can't even *think* around you anymore. I don't even know what I need to explain, it's not like I've ever dealt with something like this before."

Renaire covers his eyes with both hands, rubbing at them hard enough to see spots, and wonders how well the train's wheels would get the job done. "It's fine. You're not exactly yourself right now. We can pretend it never happened."

"Where are you getting this from?" Delaurier outright *shouts* at him, offended and furious. "What do you think is going on here? If you don't want me, just say it!"

He seriously considers just sitting back and letting Delaurier shout at him, but it's not in his nature. He glares and says, "After *two years*, you decide this is what you want, and you don't think I'm going to be a little suspicious?" He waves a hand toward their gear and the world outside the train car, everything that exists beyond this ludicrous conversation. "You think I'm going to just mindlessly accept how strange you've been acting recently and how you suddenly decided that you want to fuck me now and not wonder if the two *just might be related?*"

"Of course they are," Delaurier snaps. He's lost some of the anger, though, and almost all of the defensive rigidity of his spine. "I told you, I made a choice."

Renaire laughs bitterly, leaning hard against the wall, arms crossed. "And it was what, fuck me now or wait for someone else when we get—"

Delaurier has a hand over his mouth so fast it leaves Renaire speaking into his palm. He looks stunned. "Oh God, you actually believe that, don't you?"

He can't speak, so he settles for glaring the best *don't you dare patronize me* glare he can manage when trapped against a wall with Delaurier's hand over his mouth.

Delaurier takes a deep breath. "Right. I can understand not believing anything said in the heat of the moment"—and Renaire can't help the bitter laugh that Delaurier's hand muffles—"so I'll try to explain this to you, very, very clearly. Are you listening?"

Renaire wants to bite his palm. He nods instead.

"I've been—" he begins and then stops, that same tactical speech-planning expression taking over for a while before shifting into something frustrated, and then terrifyingly intent on Renaire. "I've been attracted to you since we met. There has never been a time when I didn't want to fuck you, and there will probably never be a time I don't want to. I am very fond of you, even if I want to bash your head into things sometimes. But I thought this would change me, and make me less focused on bringing the change the world desperately needs." He pauses. "You scare me. But I killed a good woman to protect you, and I don't regret it. I want you, and I realized I don't care any less about the cause for admitting it. Nod if you understand what I'm saying."

Renaire stares at him, and is pretty sure he can't feel his arms anymore, but he manages to nod.

"I like to think I'm a good person, but I know I'm not perfect, mostly because you make a point of rubbing it in my face," Delaurier says. "I know I treat you like shit sometimes, and I'm a possessive asshole who likes controlling you more than is healthy, and that we argue constantly. But I'm—" He lets out a long breath. "—I don't just *care*, Renaire. I am very, *very* fond of you. And I would like it if we tried being together."

Renaire keeps on staring.

"Just to make sure we're on the same page, snap your fingers if you can actually process this," Delaurier says. He actually sounds nervous.

He tries to reply, but there's a hand in the way, so all that comes out is muffled syllables.

Delaurier removes his hand, frowning. "What did you say?"

"I can't move my fingers," Renaire says.

"That's unfortunate," Delaurier says, eyes wide. Renaire is reminded of horses running through fire. "I really like your fingers." He takes a deep breath. "Would you like to try and sleep with me in the very small train bed? I'm exhausted, but I want to touch you, so I'd really like it if we did that."

"We're not going to fit," Renaire says. "There's no way we'd fit."

"I still want to try," Delaurier says. "If you're willing. It might be difficult, but we can try at least, can't we?"

Renaire might be close to hyperventilating. He really doesn't want to be sober. "I'll cramp you or I'll fall or we'll end up—"

Delaurier interrupts him with a hand pressed against his cheek. "Renaire. Yes or no. Do you want to try?"

"I don't like multilayer conversations," Renaire says a little bit frantically.

"Deal with it, you're good at them, we're tired and multitasking," Delaurier says. "Yes or no."

"Fine, yes, I want to try," Renaire says, and shit, he can't remember where he put his flask.

He doesn't have time to look for it, or even to glance over at their gear, because Delaurier leans in to press their lips together, soft and cautious. It lasts only a moment, a heartbeat or four, before he pulls back. Delaurier is smiling. It's dawn personified.

"I really don't think we're both going to fit, though," Renaire says.

Delaurier gives him a stern look, and starts pulling Renaire's shirt off in a somehow affectionate, yet businesslike way. Renaire is helpless to do anything but let him, and toe off his own shoes.

"Not in the double-layer conversation way," Renaire says, although he still thinks that too. "In the train bed way."

"Humor me," Delaurier says, and gets Renaire down to his boxers.

Renaire has no idea how this remains nonerotic. It might be because Renaire hasn't slept in over twenty-four hours. It's probably also because this feels like just about every other night they've been half-dead on their feet, from Delaurier being the one to undress him and sit him on the bed, to the way Delaurier stumbles over someone's shoes after he's undressed and turned off the lights.

It is very, very awkward trying to be in the same tiny bed. Renaire first pushes himself against the wall, on his side, but that doesn't seem to work with Delaurier's plans. Then he ends up sprawled almost completely on top of Delaurier, who tries very hard to keep the *oof* whuff of air in but fails. He's too stubborn to admit that trying to use Renaire as a blanket is about the same as having ten iron blankets draped on top of him, so Renaire sighs and says, "It's not like we can't try to do this when we're not on a train."

"This will work," Delaurier declares.

Renaire rolls his eyes. "These beds are small for *one* person—"

"I said it will work, and it will," he says and does some more shifting so that they're on their sides, facing each other. Delaurier is now squished against the wall, and Renaire is pretty sure if the train encounters any bumpy patches he'll fall right out of the bunk, but Delaurier obviously thinks he's succeeded since he's looking painfully smug. He also has Renaire pressed against his chest, arms wrapped around him, and Renaire's face is pretty much planted in the crook of his neck. "I told you we could do it."

"Yes, I'm very proud of you," Renaire says, and really, he doesn't mind the position. His nose is buried in Delaurier's hair, his cheek is resting against the curve of his neck, he can feel Delaurier's steady living pulse, and it's marvelous.

Delaurier has a hand in Renaire's hair. That is also nice. "We're safe. Go to sleep," he says. He sounds satisfied and a little bit something else that Renaire doesn't dare try to analyze.

Renaire obeys.

CHAPTER 3

{Tripoli}; Budapest—Munich—Paris

HE REMEMBERS Tripoli.

Well, not Tripoli. Tripoli is there, or what he can remember of it at least, but it's Leptis Magna. They'd visited the astonishingly well-preserved Roman ruins before some job or another, Renaire neither remembers nor cares. But they'd had time, and Delaurier (still Emile to him in all ways then—the oblivious idiot inside the striding steel ideal) was more than happy to follow him two hours from the city in a car Renaire may or may not have stolen for the day.

It'd been a miserable day, weatherwise, a dark gray sky with a wild wind ripping the clouds into dangerous shapes and occasional bursts of rain. Renaire had brought a sketchbook and pencils anyway, because it could always clear up, and if all else failed, he could sketch clouds and ruins. Emile had brought a thermos of coffee and not even frowned at the weather. He'd looked around, proclaimed it good since there wouldn't be anyone else there, and been almost as excited as Renaire to see the site.

Renaire would perch on small damp ledges with no concern for his clothing while careful with his paper, and draw while Emile examined every facet of the ruins, calling out Roman factoids and history that seemed the slightest bit relevant at any given moment. The only arguments were debates, and the only insults were directed toward the long dead. It lasted that way for hours, with no rush to their exploration, just the eagerness of sharing new things with new friends.

It'd been probably five months since they met, then, still at the point when Renaire's excuse had always been *of course I can't leave, I still need to paint you.* He knows Delaurier could see right through it because there are many things someone can mistake Delaurier for, but an idiot will never be one of them. Still, it was an excuse—his *one* excuse.

He doesn't remember where exactly they were in Leptis Magna, can't remember the features or building or what direction they were facing. He just remembers Emile, turning back to smile at him against the backdrop of once sacred battered columns and savage clouds that suddenly broke, and there was light around them, and Emile was incandescent. Light itself was in love with Emile in that moment, and Renaire was helpless to do anything but follow its lead.

Renaire's dumbfounded fingers had dropped his sketchbook as he gaped at Emile, who had frowned, obviously growing worried. When he'd shifted, meaning to move toward Renaire, Renaire had *screamed*, "Stop!"

Emile froze instantly.

"I need to paint you," Renaire had said, words falling on top of each other as inelegantly as the shaking fingers trying to pick his sketchbook back up. "I just…. Just stay there—fuck, I don't have paint. I guess I can sketch and paint it later, just *stay right there*."

Emile's easy smile was gone, but Renaire remembered it vividly. He sketched frantically, feeling close to tears for no reason he could explain. The profile and background and light were done fast enough, the image so eternally cemented in his mind that it took no thought at all to transfer it to paper. And after that it was Emile's face. First that *smile*, and then the shock and concern when Renaire had shouted, and the moment of undecipherable horror, and then endless resignation. Exhaustion. Watching Renaire sketch, impassive, as if he was politely humoring a complete stranger.

Love is a quiet ache, more often than not, like a splinter in your soul. At that moment, Renaire had understood that it wasn't a splinter. It was the tip of a massive iron spike, and that single day, that single image, had been the strike that finally impaled him, brutal and inescapable.

He could've gotten out before that, maybe. But after Leptis Magna, he was nailed down forever, heart fixed so completely he would be ripped apart if he ever tried to twist away.

Renaire was grateful when it started to rain.

The drive back to Tripoli was silent, with Emile not even looking at him as Renaire kept on sketching. He sketched until his hands hurt, and Renaire made it to their hotel room in a daze. Now he knows that Delaurier had steered him into the building and through their door, but logistics hadn't existed for him at that moment.

It's a blur from there—he remembers wandering a market and looking for the perfect paint. The perfect brushes. The perfect canvas and easel, and every single item he might need, and then a spare or five in case something went wrong. Emile was gone, then, disappeared off into Tripoli to do *something*, but Renaire had seen nothing but a painting in his mind.

He doesn't know how long he painted, only that he had, and it had been an unhealthy length of time, not that it mattered. Renaire didn't sleep. He didn't eat. He painted exactly five portraits of Emile; three of them based off Leptis Magna and the other two more the result of a feverish madman than any specific image.

When he stopped, there was a lukewarm bottle of water on a nearby table. He'd chugged it, and then fallen into the nearest bed and slept like the dead.

When he woke up, Emile's things were gone. All that was left in the room were paintings and art supplies and a small bag with Renaire's meager belongings inside of it.

Renaire had taken a minute or two to look around frantically for *any* sign of Emile, anything at all, and found nothing. He'd ended up vomiting in the bathroom and then stared at the paintings with a knife in his hand, trying to decide whether or not to rip them apart. In the end, Renaire had stabbed the knife into the wall, deep and cruel.

And then Renaire took a shower. He watched the dizzy whirl of paint slide off him and mix into nothing but a gray puddle staining the skin of his feet and said, *fuck it.*

Tripoli wasn't the best place for it, wasn't where he'd prefer at all, but Renaire could manage. It would take some work, take some serious dedication, but it would get the job done.

Alcohol is illegal in Libya, but Renaire was a man possessed. He found his way into a market, and then a market from that market, and finally found what he was looking for. The man selling it had grinned at Renaire and said, "What would you like to buy?" Renaire had taken one look at the bookcase full of alcohol, tossed his entire wallet to the man with an elegant flick of his discolored hands, and said, "*Everything.*"

He'd gone back to the hotel room because it only seemed polite. Renaire had lined up all five of the fucking paintings against one wall, sat himself against the opposite, and started drinking until he couldn't see straight. And then he'd kept drinking. Drank until the pillowcase of contraband was full of empty bottles, and he couldn't feel his hands and then his arms and then couldn't feel his entire body, couldn't think, couldn't do anything but lie on the floor in a worthless heap surrounded by shards of glass and broken things and stare at the fucking paintings, fucking worthless masterpieces that Renaire had destroyed everything good in his life just to create, wanting to burn them down right along with the whole fucking world before he downed one last bottle (that was always the way, *one more, one more, and then it'll be over*) and begged nothing in particular that he'd never wake up.

He did, though. He woke to a hospital and a furious Emile that nurses had to physically remove from the room when he grabbed Renaire by the shirt and shook him viciously, scared and shouting demands of *"Don't you ever do that again you son of a bitch, don't you ever fucking make me come home to see you like that ever again,"* at him.

Tripoli's not a pleasant memory, except for the parts where it is. Renaire doesn't like Tripoli, doesn't like thinking about the whys and hows of it. He's actually made an effort with the drinking, since Tripoli. Not much of one, but enough of an effort that Delaurier is less twitchy and Renaire's hands shake less when he needs to be sober for jobs—which is good, when he needs to pull a trigger.

Emile (but Delaurier, now—any and all hopes of being closer had vanished) stayed until Renaire was released from the hospital, when he'd held out their bag. *Their* bag, the first time he'd admitted their belongings were intermingled to the point that neither of them actually having untouchable belongings; they swapped shirts, they shared mismatched socks, did their laundry in one exhausted load, and said, "We're going to Copenhagen, if you're ready."

Tripoli was many things. Renaire understands absolutely none of them.

RENAIRE JERKS awake to the sound of his phone bursting to life with the very memorable chorus from The Turtles' 1967 hit song "Happy Together" and he flails himself all the way to the floor.

"Mnarmfrr," Delaurier says from where he's face-planted into the pillow. It might be something like Renaire's name. Or cursing. The two usually sound the same from Delaurier.

"Sorry, sorry," Renaire whispers and manages to grab his phone. His sleep-addled mind notes that it's pretty fucking weird his phone is singing out Delaurier's custom semi-ironic ringtone when the other man's phone is charging right next to Renaire's. He probably sounds half-dead when he answers with a rasping, "What the fuck, *hello?*"

"It's nice to meet you too, Renaire," a woman—young but mature, friendly and sweet—says. She sounds amused. "Are you able to have a private conversation?"

He scrubs a hand through his even wilder-than-usual dark hair, still trying to really get his bearings. "I'm not buying anything," he says. "I'm an artist. I have no money to buy things even if I wanted to."

"It's more what we can do for you, actually," the woman says, and she's on the edge of laughter. It's the pleasant kind of laughter, the sharing-a-joke kind of laughter that he can't help but smile back at. She could make a killing as a phone sex operator. "Listen, I'm about ninety percent sure you're with or near Delaurier, is there any chance you could get away for a moment?"

That definitely wakes him up, and he moves forward to put a hand over Delaurier's mouth, giving him a stern look that (hopefully) conveys the fact there's something serious happening. It works, since Delaurier's morning dazed grumpiness is immediately replaced by his alert planning face. "What makes you think that?"

"The fact you're Renaire and he's Emile Delaurier," the woman says, dry and strangely affectionate. "Can you get away?"

"He's asleep, is that good enough?" Renaire asks.

"For the start of our conversation, sure," she says. "But you'll probably want to find somewhere else to speak in a few minutes."

"We'll see about that, but whatever, what do you want?" Renaire says and grabs one of his sketchbooks. *Lady wants private convo*, he writes and then adds a music note with an arrow to signify his ringtone that is labeled with *yours when called*. Delaurier gives him a quick nod of understanding.

"I'm part of a task force that's been created to respond to STB's threat," the woman says, and *fuck*. Renaire freezes, and Delaurier tenses just from his reaction. Renaire can see why she thinks he wants to talk without Delaurier around because, yeah, he actually really does want to do that now.

He clears his throat. "I'm kind of not wearing pants right now, can you hold while I get dressed, and we can talk after I'm somewhere else?"

And now Delaurier is *very* alert.

"Of course. I'll call back in five minutes," the woman says cheerily and hangs up.

Renaire drops the phone and immediately starts to freak out and tries to decide what the fuck to do. On one hand, Delaurier should know about this. On the other, maybe Delaurier *shouldn't* know about this. Renaire has kept secrets from Delaurier for his own good before, and this might be one of those times, but he doesn't *know* yet.

Ironically, Renaire realizes that if they hadn't ended up sleeping in the same ridiculously tiny bed, Delaurier wouldn't be awake to give him the intent, questioning look that is keeping Renaire from immediately putting on clothes and heading somewhere else to wait for her call. If this... *thing* between them hadn't happened, Renaire wouldn't even be making a choice.

"What's going on?" Delaurier asks, looking ready to march into battle.

Renaire looks at him for a long moment and then grabs clothing and starts tossing it on. "I really have no idea, and I will tell you when I actually know," Renaire says, and looks at the time on his phone. It's barely after six; these people have definitely done their homework. Renaire can be awake or asleep at any given moment, up or down (usually down) as needed or desired, but Delaurier is just about incapable of functioning before eight unless there's an emergency.

"Why are you leaving, then?" Delaurier asks.

Renaire shakes his head, stepping into his shoes without bothering about socks. "It's private. I'll tell you if I think you need to know, I promise," he says.

He can tell Delaurier is itching to snap at him and demand answers and try to order Renaire to stay. Renaire would stay if he turned it into an order, but Delaurier doesn't. He sighs, and nods. "I'll wait here," he says firmly, and dear God, the look in Delaurier's eyes is *trust*.

Delaurier trusts him. Delaurier trusts him, and Renaire has no idea what to do with that.

Renaire swallows the sudden dryness in his throat and raises a hand, only to stop, leaving it floating in the air between them. He hesitates, and Delaurier gives him an unimpressed *what the hell are you doing* look. Renaire feels like he's going to vibrate to death. "If this isn't okay, just stop me, I'll stop, I swear, so—" He cuts himself off by taking a deep breath, and feels like he's going to have a heart attack while he cautiously, slowly, lightly rests his hand against Delaurier's cheek.

Delaurier smiles at him. It's a small, pleased quirk of the lips, the sort of thing that happens at the little pleasures in life. There's no flinch, no glaring at him or confused frown toward his hand, no stern disapproving look. He gets a smile.

"Can I kiss you?" Renaire asks, prepared to back away at the slightest signal.

"Absolutely," Delaurier says immediately, muscles tense like he has to restrain himself. He's watching Renaire's lips intently.

Renaire wants to close his eyes, but he's scared that he might miss and end up kissing Delaurier's nose or something equally ridiculous. It's now or never, he's set this up and Delaurier is *waiting for him*, still and almost eager of all things, and it's now or never, and it has to be now because never isn't an option Renaire can survive anymore.

He leans down slowly, watching Delaurier's eyes slide shut when Renaire presses his lips lightly to Delaurier's own. It's a tiny thing, chaste and soft and brief, but Renaire's heart feels like it's going to explode. It's only a moment, and he has to pull away to stare at Delaurier's pleased, not the slightest bit horrified face.

"That was okay?" Renaire asks.

"That was okay," Delaurier agrees, dry amusement in the words, and wraps a hand around the back of Renaire's neck. He drags him in for a firm, breathless kiss that moves from a simple press of lips into Delaurier teasing Renaire's mouth open and doing his best to make Renaire feel *very* welcome.

It's easy to get lost in it, the careful press and movement of their lips growing more daring and desperate by the moment. His hand slides back to grab a handful of Delaurier's sun-struck hair, eyes closed tight as they kiss, and Renaire feels like he's drowning.

And then his phone starts singing that 1967 sensation "Happy Together" and he jerks away and has to ignore the smug, satisfied look on Delaurier's face before he explodes. Renaire grabs the sketchpad and a pencil and stumbles his way out of the compartment and into the corridor, answering the phone with a, "Yes, hello, I'm still finding somewhere to talk. I couldn't find one of my shoes."

"That's fine," the woman says, unhurried and flawlessly pleasant. "We all have those kinds of mornings. How did you sleep?"

Renaire lets out a slightly hysterical laugh. "I really have no idea what's going on here," he says, which is completely, purely 100 percent true. He leaves the train car and moves into the next, which has a miniscule and mostly empty café serving overpriced breakfast food. Renaire sits down at one of the small tables.

"I'm sorry. I know this is probably confusing. It's a strange situation for us too," the woman sympathizes. "But our research has shown us a lot of things about STB, and one of the most important observations is that you don't believe in the cause, do you?"

"I do not," Renaire agrees easily. "But that doesn't mean I'm not affiliated."

"Oh, you're very affiliated," the woman says, humor lacing every word. "But that's not what I mean. You're involved with the group not because of its goals, but because of the group itself, the participants—"

"You *can* just say his name," Renaire says dryly.

The woman's voice has a cautious, concerned frown in it now. "I didn't want to bring it up right away. Some people aren't eager to talk about that sort of thing."

"Which sort of thing are you talking about?" Renaire asks, absently sketching some of the passing scenery. "Are you talking about the gay thing, or the murderous assassin terrorist thing, or the 'he's never going to love me back' thing?" When the woman doesn't reply, he sighs. "I know exactly what useless fucked-up choices I'm making."

It's easy to fall back into what had been the status quo for two years. Mostly because he still has trouble believing it's not the same as it ever was. He'll wake up on a train into Russia, or a rental car outside an ugly building in the middle of nowhere, or sprawled on the floor of his tiny apartment with a hangover, and he won't be the least bit surprised.

"Some of us think you have Stockholm syndrome," the woman says, and Renaire laughs so hard it hurts. "I know. I don't believe that either—some people just don't understand what love can do to someone's mind. Which brings me to my point. Things are about to get very bad for STB, and you have the chance to make those things much less dangerous for your friends."

Renaire closes his eyes, breathing steadily. "If you arrest Emile," he says very clearly, and then has to stop and clear his throat. "If you arrest Delaurier and sentence him and send him to prison for a very long time, and he finally realizes he can't get out, he'll martyr himself."

The woman is very quiet.

"So no, I don't think I'm going to do a single fucking thing to help you," he says, and he's surprised at how amicable his tone is.

"You can keep him out of prison," the woman says softly. "Right now you have the chance to end this entire mess."

Renaire frowns at the passing landscape. "Are you sure you called the right number?"

"We'd like to set up a face-to-face meeting with you. We have information we'd like to share," the woman says.

"I'm stupid, but I'm not that stupid," Renaire says.

"You're exceptionally smart, actually. And that's why you're going to meet with me," the woman says. "Can you be in Paris two days from now?"

"I could be in Bhutan two days from now," Renaire says, and really wishes he had brought his flask. Why does he go places without it? Delaurier needs to stop being so distracting. "Where?"

"The Arènes de Lutèce, at sunrise. I'll be sure to wear a funny hat," the woman says.

He sighs. "You're very determined to meet me sober, aren't you?" he says. Even Renaire has a limit to what time he's willing to start drinking. Well, these days he does. Even if it's about noon. The woman laughs, still friendly and affectionate. "Fine, I'll be there. But I at least get a name."

"That's fair. I'm asking quite a lot of you, after all," the woman says. "My name is Celine Normandeau. Please call me Celine."

"It's nice to meet you, Celine," Renaire says honestly. "You seem like a lovely person. I hope I don't end up having to kill you."

"Likewise," Celine says. "I look forward to meeting you in person two days from now."

She hangs up, and Renaire groans, scrubbing a hand over his face. He writes down some of the basic facts—name's Celine, specified task force, has a lot of research on STB, thinks Renaire will betray them for *love* because he's already proven himself to be an alcoholic moron—

but he makes a point of not writing the meeting place, or the time of the meeting. Or the funny hat.

When he gets back to their compartment, Delaurier has switched the bed back into the bench seats and is dressed and half-asleep. He also takes one look at Renaire and silently holds out his flask.

Just when I think I can't be any more in love with you, Renaire thinks, and takes it as he falls onto the seat. He hands over the notes on his sketch pad and takes a long drink of whatever the fuck is inside his flask today. It burns nicely. "I need to get back to Paris," he says, feeling more than a little numb.

He'd been hoping for some time in Budapest, for a chance to just breathe, maybe figure this thing with Delaurier out somewhere that isn't on a train. And possibly with a bed. He's still not sure if he gets to even think that, but fuck, he has absolutely been thinking that.

"I don't like this," Delaurier says.

"You never like anything you didn't personally plan," Renaire says, and grabs a nearby sweater to toss over his face, leaning his head back against the gently rocking wall.

Delaurier is holding his hand again. "We can fly there if we need to."

There is exactly one thing Delaurier is afraid of, and it's airplanes. He'll do intercontinental travel, long flights that he has to tranquilize himself to manage, and Renaire ends up staying awake the entire fucking time making sure he doesn't overdose or freak out or even wake up, but that's all. They go by train (almost always train), or boat, or car, and one time they actually ended up traveling on horseback, which Renaire never wants to do ever, ever again, but Delaurier does not fly. Not unless the only alternative is a two-week sea voyage.

"We don't need to fly," Renaire says. He doesn't want to say this, doesn't want to say this *at all*, but he says. "And we're under surveillance."

"That's not new," Delaurier says. His thumb is sweeping gentle arcs across the top of Renaire's hand like he can't even restrain himself, and fuck, this is going to be so painful.

Renaire carefully pulls his hand away, using it to grab the sweater on his head and toss it back toward their bag so he can drink from his flask again. Renaire doesn't want to be sober. Mostly he wants to lunge toward Delaurier and kiss him breathless and jerk him off like there's no tomorrow, but instead he drinks. Again.

"But this *thing* we're doing is new. They called me because—"

"I know," Delaurier says simply, and takes Renaire's hand back like there wasn't any intention behind the separation beyond the whole taking the sweater off his face thing. When he *really* looks at Delaurier, it's pretty obvious the other man does not give a shit if there was any other intention. He wants to hold Renaire's hand and destroy anything that tries to make him stop. He makes an aggravated noise. "I don't know how people are supposed to do this, and we can't do it the normal way. I started this wrong, but I promise I'm going to figure it out."

Renaire frowns at him. "What?"

"You have no idea what I want to do to you," Delaurier says, squeezing Renaire's hand hard enough to hurt. "But for now, this is all I'm going to take. This is enough." He takes a deep breath. "I don't want you to take this from me."

"I don't want to," Renaire says. He seriously considers taking another drink. "I really, really don't want to, but what if people start to—uh."

Renaire is stopped midsentence by Delaurier swinging himself around to straddle Renaire, trap him between his thighs, and look him straight in the eye, unblinking and intense in that fiery heart-searing way only Delaurier is capable of. He's still holding Renaire's hand, tight and certain, but his other hand is braced against the wall right next to Renaire's head, keeping him still just as surely as his legs are.

"This is another communication issue, I think," Delaurier says while Renaire stares at him, shocked into silence. "Do you like holding hands?"

"I like holding hands," Renaire says. He's trying to not stare at Delaurier's mouth, and he is failing. It isn't helping that every time he manages to look up into Delaurier's eyes, the other man looks like he's having the same exact problem. "But they'd be suspicious." He has to stop and take a breath and swallow because Delaurier is so, so close to him, he can feel the heat of his skin even with fabric between them, and he's caged between Delaurier's spread thighs. He ends up laughing a little bit hysterically. "Is now really the time to have this conversation?"

"It is if you think it is," Delaurier says. He leans closer, which Renaire hadn't thought was possible but it really, really is—his chest is a deep breath away from Renaire's, their mouths a whisper's width apart. "What do you want?"

Next time, Delaurier had said in Russia.

"What do *you* want? I'll—" Renaire begins, but Delaurier cuts him off with another vicious squeeze of his hand.

Delaurier tips forward to press their foreheads together and moves his hand from the wall into Renaire's hair. The movement of his fingers is somewhere between stroking and tugging at his curls. "Stop making this complicated," he says quietly, even if it sounds like an order. "You're officially allowed to want me. We're at the 'how' part now."

He wants to reply with something witty and sharp. Instead, he lifts their joined hands from the seat to make it feel less like clinging to each other in the face of gravity and more like their hands pressing against each other for the simple fact that they can. Their palms rest together like they're ready to waltz, fingers tangled in the hopes of never losing the other in the ensuing whirl.

Renaire doesn't know how Delaurier understands the gesture, or if he just guesses, or can predict Renaire so well that it wasn't even necessary. He closes what little distance there is between them to press their mouths together, soft and sweet and comforting. Their lips move slowly as if they have all the time in the world. Renaire savors it, memorizes it, feels like he can somehow taste colors in the kiss.

It goes on forever and for only a heartbeat, and then Delaurier pulls away to trail kisses from the corner of his mouth to his cheekbones and his jaw line, and finally Renaire shudders at the feel of Delaurier's teeth dragging against his earlobe.

"I'm sensing you like my ears," Renaire says, voice high and breathless, feeling more than a little bit hysterical. It feels strange to break the silence of everything beyond the ever-present train and the sound of their lips and tongues against each other. His spare hand is still pressed against the seat, uncertain of what to do—he wants to do absolutely everything, but is afraid to try anything.

Delaurier makes a noise halfway between a laugh and a hum. "It's your hands I like most," he whispers directly into his ear, nipping between syllables. Delaurier's fingers skim through Renaire's hair, smooth and teasing. "The dreams I've had about your hands."

Renaire is starting to understand this, he thinks. It's hard to think when he has a lap full of Delaurier who is hell-bent on abusing his earlobe, but the pattern is showing itself. And also he's had just enough to drink that he's more than a shaking bundle of worthless anxiety. He lifts his hand and cups the side of Delaurier's face.

Delaurier is always two steps ahead of him, always and forever, so it doesn't take anything more than that for Delaurier to release Renaire's earlobe and fucking *lunge* for his hand, pulling his own away from Renaire's hair to grab Renaire's wrist and keep him right where Delaurier wants him. It starts with nothing but a delicate nip against his palm, but that doesn't last long—his mouth dives onto Renaire's thumb, and Jesus, the things his tongue does. It's one finger, one single finger, and Renaire is turning into a wordless shuddering mess all over again.

"This is definitely suggestive," Renaire breathes out, and Delaurier laughs, pulling away to go back to kissing Renaire. It's not sweet anymore, although it *is* still a promise. A very different kind of promise, full of Delaurier's clever tongue tormenting him to death. Renaire can feel Delaurier's hard cock pressing against his stomach, and he wants to—fuck, he has to break away and ask, "Can I—"

"Yes," Delaurier answers instantly before ruthlessly reclaiming Renaire's mouth with a gentle bite to his lower lip, and Renaire tries to calm down and *fails completely.*

He groans, a noise of pleasure and anxiety and frustration that Delaurier swallows down, and calls back to Delaurier's voice saying, *Next time.* He leans deeper into the kiss, desperate, and gets a pleased hum for it, and Renaire moves their joined hands carefully, thinking *next time, next time, next time* as he slides their hands between their bodies and presses them against Delaurier's cock, still trapped in his jeans.

Delaurier moans at the pressure, and he releases Renaire's wrist to quickly unbutton his pants and unzip his fly. He moves to Renaire's pants the moment his own are undone, but that's not what Renaire wants, not right now, so he grinds up, jeans harsh against Delaurier's bare skin, and Delaurier freezes with an intake of breath, hand stuttering to a halt. Renaire twists their joined hands—deft and smooth, dexterity has always been his sole redeeming quality—until his hand is wrapped around the top of Delaurier's hand, and that hand is wrapped around Delaurier's cock.

Delaurier's other hand slams into the wall of their compartment so hard that there is no way their neighbors are asleep now. "Oh," he breathes out, shaking slightly, and Renaire can see from the daze in his eyes that this, he is *definitely* allowed. Delaurier's stunned open mouth slides into something like a satisfied smirk before he returns to kissing Renaire hard enough that Renaire's head hits the wall.

Fuck, he really hopes nobody comes to investigate.

Renaire guides their hands slowly up and down his cock, careful and loose, toying more with his grip on Delaurier's hand than his erection. He slots their fingers together and moves Delaurier's hand gently, paying attention to the sounds Delaurier makes into his mouth. He twists his wrist, tightens his grip, teases Delaurier until he has to pull his mouth away to take a panting breath, eyes fiery and lust-fierce as he tries to regain control.

"I knew this was a good idea," Delaurier manages to say, more as syllable-shaped breaths than true words, and drops his forehead onto Renaire's shoulder. His back is bowed in a way that makes Renaire desperately need to close his eyes and think cold thoughts, and even that doesn't help much. He speeds up their strokes, and Delaurier starts *talking*, words like machine gun fire in Renaire's already abused ear. "Fuck, the things I am going to do to you when I get you in my bed, Renaire, we'll need to burn the fucking sheets."

Renaire thrusts up, almost against his will, and Delaurier grinds against him eagerly. Renaire speeds their hands up until Delaurier is making choked noises against his neck between his curses and promises that are sucking the breath from Renaire's lungs. "I'm going to tear you apart and make you come so fucking hard you forget your own name, but I'll know it, and I'll keep it safe while you're screaming nonsense into my fucking mattress," he says and bites down so hard on Renaire's earlobe that it hurts, grinding against him, panting like he's asphyxiating. "Say you're mine, tell me—"

"Fucking hell, Emile. You own me and you know it," Renaire says in a single, desperate gasp. "I'm yours, I'm completely yours."

"You're going to purr for me again, Renaire," Delaurier says against his neck, which makes zero sense, but Renaire is pretty sure he would be babbling out some very dangerous shit right now if he wasn't pretty much speaking on command at this point. "And you're *mine*."

He's using his orders voice, his preaching voice, his conviction voice, and fuck, he's not even done anything beyond rut against Delaurier; he should *not* be coming before Delaurier, but he absolutely fucking is. Delaurier grinds down and fucking *claims him*, and Renaire moans as he comes in his pants like a fucking teenager. Delaurier is only moments behind him, gasping and spilling into their joined hands and panting against Renaire.

They just breathe together for a few moments before Delaurier kisses Renaire again, sated and happy. He's doing that humming thing again. Renaire loves it.

"We disembark in about twenty minutes," Delaurier says, sliding off Renaire's lap, and Jesus, he hadn't even realized they were still holding hands until Delaurier pulls him forward and to the tiny sink in their compartment. He cleans them up as efficiently as he can, but Renaire's pants are nowhere near being capable of cleaned in twenty minutes with a small sink on a train, so he has to settle for a change of clothes.

Remarkably, their train arrives at the station perfectly on time.

They don't have time to do much in Budapest beyond find the nearest Laundromat and eat something that is a mix between an early lunch and a late breakfast (Delaurier says it's brunch, but Renaire refuses to call it brunch; he is not a brunch person—there are specific types of people who have brunch, and he is not that type) while they watch their clothing swirl around in the machines.

Someone in the Laundromat recognizes Delaurier, and then that someone calls his friends instead of the authorities (which is what always happens when someone recognizes Delaurier), and Delaurier gives one of his impromptu small group speeches. Renaire used to think he practiced them, or at least wrote them, or maybe just had bullet points. Now he knows these are really the things Delaurier thinks and believes, and he's pretty much speaking his mind while he seduces poor young Hungarians into believing (and fighting) for The Cause.

Renaire sketches their awestruck faces in front of the ancient rumbling dryers, with Delaurier's silhouette in front of them, and leaves it for the new recruits while he heads to a liquor store and refills his flask. Delaurier is so happy to have done some preaching that he doesn't even look disappointed.

Delaurier looks very, very happy. It's possibly the happiest he's ever seen the man outside of Paris. He has a near-permanent small smile on his lips and looks around Budapest in a way that reminds Renaire of himself, but not. Where Renaire watches for the sharp edges and shadows of architecture, Delaurier looks for the ancient, sturdy stonework, the strength of an arch and the achievement of a spire. Either way, they both watch the city.

They hold hands sometimes. Renaire is pretty sure both of them are fine with it.

THEIR TRAIN arrives in Munich long after dark, and they only have ten minutes from when their train arrives to when the train to Paris departs, and it's a mess overall, but they manage to get on in time, and they have another sleeper car because Delaurier is Delaurier.

Renaire has never understood how sitting on a train can be so exhausting.

They don't even bother messing with anything. Delaurier pulls down one bed, and Renaire stows their bags so that if anything jostles the train, it'll only be the two idiots sharing a one-person bed who go tumbling to the floor.

It seems they're going with the spooning route tonight. Delaurier curls around him, and makes that humming noise again. Renaire admits to himself that he doesn't actually mind the whole "sharing an absolutely tiny bed" thing.

Renaire is dead asleep until eight in the morning, when he snaps awake, momentarily terrified that he's waking up from much more than one night's rest. Emile's arm is thrown across his chest. It keeps him from moving, or panicking, or rolling off the far too small bunk.

He breathes. He stays curled in bed with Emile, because he can.

CHAPTER 4

Paris: *Gare de l'Est—Chéron*

THEY ARRIVE midmorning, Delaurier blurry-eyed but mostly alert. By now they're practically professionals at getting in and out of Gare de l'Est undetected, or at least unimpeded. It doesn't stop Renaire from always sending a polite hello and wave toward the single functional security camera on their route in and out of the train station, though.

Paris greets them like a bad-tempered old aunt trying very hard to not be pleased to see them. It's cloudy, but there's a sliver of sun every now and then that makes parts of Paris shine, even if the metalwork is tarnished. The pigeons of Paris are just as hardened as those of Moscow, but they're also more French, so Renaire tells himself they carry it better.

Delaurier (and by extension STB and Renaire) has never had any problems in Paris. Ever. Some people have tried chasing him, and one time someone was foolish enough to arrest him, but it's an open secret that Paris is in love with Delaurier. The man could probably do public executions and the people of Paris would show up to cheer him on. Then again, maybe not, since one of the reasons Paris loves Delaurier is that he brings mountains of scandal and excitement but no actual discord to their doorstep. Not really.

The irony that the world started paying attention to Delaurier only after he gave up on making it listen will never be lost to Renaire. Sometimes, Renaire wonders if they'd love Delaurier as much if he wasn't a beautiful white boy who is as close to aristocracy as France can comfortably approve of without muttering about guillotines.

And because Delaurier loves Paris right back, and (supposedly) people in love never keep secrets from each other, Renaire ends up with his hand trapped in Delaurier's all the way from the station to the Chéron. The renovation of Paris in 1860 (or sometime around there) changed the city's architecture forever, but ever since Renaire met him, Delaurier has loved the Chéron above all others, so he lives and works and sleeps in it and plans and eats and talks in the street-level café that bears the same name as the building.

Even Renaire's emotional masochism has limits, so he has a very small apartment four blocks north of the Chéron. It is very, very small, and apparently Renaire is not allowed to go there yet because Delaurier is half guiding, half pulling him inside the café and up the stairs to the room that has more or less become STB's coffee-and-alcohol-drinking headquarters. Or just headquarters. Either way, it's where they plan things. They have the very secure option of Delaurier's apartment if something needs to be completely secret, but again, Paris loves Delaurier and STB, and the Café Chéron loves them even more.

There is nowhere more loyal and devoted to STB than their Café Chéron and its regulars, and STB returns the affection. Garrant once punched a man for suggesting the café think about turning into a Starbucks, so he's their second favorite after Delaurier and hasn't paid for a drink in at least a year. Renaire is the night bartender's favorite, which is plenty for him.

Right now the problem is that the Café Chéron is loyal and devoted to STB. This devotion means that the regulars (honestly, they're all regulars) love them, but have a nasty habit of treating STB as their favorite daily drama.

Every single one of them is going to know.

The minute they even get in sight of the place, Renaire can hear whispers and commentary from the outside tables. By the time they actually get through the heavy front doors and into the building, they're clapping. It only gets louder as they cross the checkerboard floor, and by the time they're past the tables and moving up the stairs, there are people fucking *whistling* at them, and Renaire is torn between wanting to stop and kiss Delaurier for ten hours and find a hole to hide and die inside of.

Mostly the "wanting to die in a hole" part of him is winning.

Either way he is infinitely grateful when Delaurier drops his hand to hold the stair banister while also carrying the hard rolling suitcase with the weapons in it up the stairs. They keep everything else in a duffel bag, so it's already slung around Renaire's shoulder. He lights a cigarette with shaking hands (he needs a drink) and tries to not be terrified of seeing their friends' faces. He hopes they won't all be there. Statistically, it's not common that all of STB would be there. He really, really hopes they won't all be there.

Every single one of them is.

Glasson, as ever, stands at the core of things, smiling over the main members of STB while they do absolutely nothing productive. Lile, their medic (not technically a doctor; he left school after getting sick of the politics you don't expect to find in medicine but are deeply entrenched there—he's *very* dedicated to healthcare), sits near him, laughing over something with his partner Bossard, who is sick of *actual* politics thanks to his father being a member of the National Assembly and growing up with a firsthand look at the sort of corrupt backroom shit Delaurier is dedicated to destroying.

Jules, Garrant, and Sarazin are closer to the stairs, their expressions already absolutely thrilled to see Renaire and Delaurier. They are by far the strangest, yet most perfect combination of abilities and personality to ever exist. Together, they can achieve the impossible in almost any task.

Jules is the poet and propaganda wizard, a genderless being of such imagination, courage, and whimsy that it is very much to everyone's benefit that Sarazin is with them. Sarazin is the voice of experience and realistic aspirations, an orphan who lived through plenty of horrible shit, which makes Sarazin the only person who absolutely knew what she was getting into when joining STB. And then there's Garrant, rounding out the trio, being the boisterous, volatile, genial burst of action and initiative that keeps Jules and Sarazin in motion and getting their work done instead of sitting around debating the definition of reality or something.

And last, but nowhere near least, is Carope, crouched next to Glasson, looking ecstatic in a way that speaks of horrible things. She is a blessing and a curse of emotional intelligence, capable of picking up on anything and everything bothering you, which means she picks up on anything and everything bothering you. Worse, she'll usually try to help with it.

It's not even noon yet, and it is completely unfair that Renaire has to explain this to all of them at the same time.

At least there are no catcalls or whistling, although those are still echoing their way up from the ground floor. And if Renaire doesn't look at them, he can ignore the grins and waggling eyebrows. Renaire just walks in, tosses the duffel bag into the corner, and sits down hard at his usual not-quite-separate table in the corner.

His table isn't quite separate because his friends refuse to let him be separate.

Renaire's always felt like a very weird blend of finally at home with the best friends he could ever ask for, and also like an asshole that they tolerate because Delaurier does and they all follow his lead. He's been accepted, but fuck knows why, since he's a really shitty friend.

For example: Renaire blissfully discovers that (almost) all of STB goes by last name, feels perfectly at home going by his own, and continues to refer to Delaurier as *Emile* because, when he started, it pisses Delaurier off to the perfect mild-twitching-reaction level. He then finds out everyone goes by last name because Glasson is transgender. When he and Delaurier were kids, teachers refused to stop calling Glasson by his parent-given first name, and going by their last names was a very easy work-around. When they met Carope, she dropped her first name and immediately joined in, and it's become the standard method of address for STB.

So, now Renaire feels like an asshole, because he was already in the habit of calling Delaurier Emile when he found out that his name choice was actually a really meaningful sign of brotherly love and solidarity with his childhood best friend.

Even with that information, Renaire can't stop doing it. Just for the twitch. And when Delaurier grew out of the twitch, just *accepted* that Renaire's an asshole, it was already so ingrained that Renaire couldn't stop calling him Emile even if he wanted to.

Renaire's one of the gang, but definitely acknowledged as the *complete asshole* of the gang. Either way, he fucking loves every single one of them. Even in this awkward situation of sitting on the outside edge of their five café-sized tables and awaiting the unavoidable relationship interrogation, Renaire ends up smiling. Just a little bit.

Naturally, it's Carope who starts. She pulls her chair up to his table, grinning. "So," she says, "let's talk."

"About what?" Renaire asks.

Carope leans in close, dark eyes eager. "About what you and—"

Delaurier saves him, already up and preaching the good word in front of the window like usual. The projector is already on and aimed toward the white wall they keep bare of decoration solely for Delaurier's dedication to visual aids. Renaire assumes the somber Ivanova PowerPoint they're getting is the same one Renaire received, so he only partially pays attention to the actual presentation. Instead he chooses to watch their faces and body language as the entirety of STB slowly understands what Delaurier gave up for them. They're seeing Delaurier all over again, rediscovering that same sense of awe.

Above all else, until eternity, Delaurier will love his Cause and the ideals of equality and freedom and justice and liberty more than anything else on this Earth. But his friends are a very close second.

Delaurier doesn't hand out Ivanova's file, though. Not this time. Instead, he has more slides, these about how many pages she had on each of them and likely information leaks, and Renaire ignores the mutters when his dangerously large collection of pages comes around. Chason is missing from the meeting, which isn't uncommon since he's thirteen years old and you couldn't tie him down with carbon fiber netting, but Mathieu *is* there, which is definitely out of the norm. He must've slipped in during the presentation, and he's sitting next to Carope, looking worried and nervous.

Mathieu is the only one without a file, because he's not officially one of them. He's a harmless sweetheart who has never killed in the name of The Cause (although you could argue Renaire hasn't either), and a beloved friend who delicately leaves the room when darker conversations start up. As far as Interpol is concerned, he's just Carope's roommate. As far as *Mathieu* is concerned, that's all Mathieu is.

Carope definitely wishes Mathieu was more than that; she's been Renaire's sole competition for the Most Pathetic Lovestruck Idiot award ever since she picked poor Mathieu up from a bench in a Metro station a few months ago. Renaire wins by a landslide, though, even without length of misery included in the competition. Carope handles it well and somehow manages to be the most sincere and truest of true friends to Mathieu instead of staring at him like a creep and following him around Europe killing people.

Renaire does not miss the way Mathieu still looks a little disappointed about not having a file.

"I wasn't fast enough, so she managed to get some information to Interpol," Delaurier says, and this part's new, mostly. "How much information remains to be seen. We have a lead, though, and we're working on it."

He knows Delaurier is looking at him. Renaire just keeps his eyes on the not terribly informative picture of the Interpol emblem and keeps on smoking, because now he feels like he's going to be sick for so many, many reasons. Otherwise he's going to go for his flask, and his hands are shaking, but Renaire is going to make it to noon, or die trying.

"Do we get to know what the lead is?" Lile asks.

"I don't have enough information to say anything other than it exists, and it's being pursued," Delaurier says, blunt but not unkind. "When I do, I'll share it. Any other questions?"

"I want to hear about you and Renaire," Carope says, eager and loud and *right next to Renaire's ear*. Light laughter and good-natured teasing erupts around the room.

Renaire groans and lets his head fall to the table.

"Don't we have more important things to worry about?" Delaurier asks, and God help them all, it's an actual question. He genuinely has no idea what kind of priority this is supposed to be.

"Yes, you do," Renaire calls out, just in case nobody gives him an actual answer.

"But this is still important! Come on, just answer some questions," Carope says, because she is not going to let this go. "Glasson got a very interesting phone call—"

"Which was actually private," Glasson interrupts, and Renaire can imagine the sharp look accompanying it. Glasson is a good person, which is why he sighs and gives Renaire an apologetic look. "I hadn't realized when I first answered, and I'm sorry about that."

Renaire waves a hand through the air, hoping it'll get the *you're forgiven, you didn't really know* across well enough.

"Okay, he's right, that was bad, I do feel bad about that," Carope admits. "But I still want to know what 'you could say that' means. Did you kiss or not?"

"We did," Delaurier says, and the room *erupts*, and Renaire absolutely wants to die. Carope slaps Renaire's back hard enough that he wheezes. "I don't know how much I should say."

"Then you should stop right there," Glasson says quickly. He's barely audible over the rest of their friends.

"This isn't just about me, Renaire, you could at least get your head off the table," Delaurier snaps.

The good-natured chatter dies dangerously fast.

"Oh no," Carope says quietly.

Renaire barely notices. He sighs and doesn't lift his head. He shifts so he's looking at Delaurier, judging he's at about a seven on the one-to-ten explosion scale. "I could," he agrees, and Delaurier spins himself up to a nine.

"You've both been on trains almost nonstop for the past three days, you're both irritable because of it, and you both know it. Take a deep breath, and focus on the new information for now," Glasson says, nice and logical and soothing.

Normally it would work. Renaire has seen it work a thousand times because Delaurier is more of a constant, endless explosion that keeps itself tightly contained than something calm that blows up every now and then. But Delaurier had been happy, and Renaire knows himself. He knows he's being difficult just because he's a selfish, worthless asshole, and that means he knows Glasson doesn't have a chance of defusing this.

"No, we're going to do this *right now*," Delaurier says, bracing himself on the table to give Renaire a steady scowl. "Did you not want this to be public knowledge?"

"That's fine, I don't care," Renaire says, and Carope kicks him in the shin. He lifts his head from the table and looks at absolutely nothing when he pulls his flask out. He can't avoid seeing his watch—it's why he put it there, after all. It's barely eleven, but hey, this week seems to be one for making bad choices.

He expects the usual shout, expects Delaurier's customary *put that down, Renaire*. He's used to that and just as used to ignoring it, or looking straight at Delaurier as he disobeys.

There's no shout. There are careful hands on his own, and Delaurier is standing in front of him, looking worried. "What did I do?" Delaurier asks, painfully sincere.

Oh no, that's just unfair, Renaire thinks for no reason he can explain, incapable of doing anything but meeting Delaurier's eyes and staying silent.

Delaurier sighs, and Renaire expects him to let go and get back to the meeting. He does let go, but it's to grab Renaire's jacket and pull him up—a move so ingrained in Renaire that he doesn't even hesitate to be pulled along. It's an automatic reaction, Pavlov's fist full of fabric by now. When he's on his feet, Delaurier's hand drops to take Renaire's. Again.

"We'll be upstairs," Delaurier tells the room, not an inch of innuendo in the tone. Because it's Delaurier, they probably don't imagine there could be.

Renaire frowns. "But—"

"We need to put the bags in the apartment anyway," Delaurier says, dropping Renaire's hand to put the duffel bag in its place before grabbing the suitcase for himself. Their unofficially private room is connected to one of the building's staircases, through two small creaky hallways that were probably a back way in for servants long ago. Delaurier leads the way up to the fourth floor, silent the whole way. He doesn't even breathe toward Renaire until he's locked the door behind them and set their bags to the left of the door.

Delaurier has an unnaturally clean apartment. It's also unnaturally *secure*, when he pushes the right buttons. As it is, the place has the tall airy windows of an old Paris apartment and a red accent to everything, but only ever an accent; it's in everything, swallowing the décor, but there's still room for other colors, other fabrics. His furniture is sharp and light.

Delaurier sits them down on the brown-red couch, hands joined again. "I really have no idea what I'm doing," Delaurier says. "You have to tell me when I'm getting it wrong."

Renaire groans, slouching into the cushions. He realizes he kind of missed the hand-holding, which is weird. "And you think I know?"

"You know when I'm fucking up," Delaurier says. "I thought I explained this, but apparently not. So. I'm hoping this will be a long-term relationship."

Renaire turns to frown at him. "Really?"

Delaurier looks about two seconds away from strangling him. "*Yes*. What did you *think* I was doing?"

"I don't know!" Renaire says, dangerously close to whining. "Fuck, I still don't know what the hell you're suddenly doing with someone like me—"

Delaurier drops Renaire's hand so he can cover Renaire's mouth with it, giving him a fierce glare. "We need to get our communication straightened out again, don't we?"

Renaire is starting to wonder what the hell Delaurier thinks communication issues really are, since he currently has a hand clamped over Renaire's ability to do any kind of actual communicating.

"I knew you wouldn't believe me about *some things*, but this is just ridiculous," Delaurier says. "We will start very, very small. Do you at least understand that I'm attracted to you?"

Renaire rolls his eyes and bites Delaurier's palm.

"Oh," Delaurier says and moves his hand awkwardly. He just keeps giving Renaire an expectant look. "Well?"

"I can accept that as a fact that I don't understand," Renaire offers. Sort of like how impossibly deep the ocean is—it's difficult to wrap his mind around, but he can believe it.

"That will do for now," Delaurier says, looking completely exhausted for a moment before the resolve face comes back. "Do you at least believe I care? That I like you, as a person? That you're my friend?"

Renaire smiles at that because he can't *not* smile at Delaurier calling him his friend. "I had my suspicions about that one," he admits.

Delaurier doesn't look satisfied with the answer, but he does look less strained when he nods. "So, given those two facts, wouldn't it make sense that I'd want to be in a relationship with you?"

"But it's not that simple!" Renaire says.

Delaurier groans and falls back against the arm of the couch, with his hands covering his face for a moment. "It *is* that simple, I swear to God, Renaire," Delaurier says.

"No, it's not," Renaire says, shaking his head so hard the world spins a little bit. "You're Emile Delaurier, king of the justice-obsessed extremists, and I'm *me*, the worthless—"

"Stop, Renaire. Just *stop*," Delaurier says and stands up, jaw clenched. "Fine. Here is what we're going to do. You are going to grab the weapons case, and we are going upstairs."

Renaire frowns but obeys and grabs the suitcase with the guns in it. "To the armory?"

"It's not an armory," Delaurier says. "It's just a room I keep weapons in, among other things."

There are so many things Renaire could say to that.

Instead he just follows Delaurier up his own personal, ridiculous staircase, to the *second floor* of his apartment. Renaire's apartment is smaller than some cars he's been in. There is a definite reason he doesn't mind how often they're away from home. Then again, he usually ends up collapsing onto Delaurier's couch when they're in Paris anyway, and it made Renaire's definition of *home* a little fucked-up.

The *room with weapons in it* is just that. They're all neatly arranged in drawers and cases and racks behind nice wooden cupboard doors, with some other valuables stored inside as well, so Renaire admits that the term armory isn't entirely appropriate. He slides the suitcase with the guns in it onto the table in the middle of the room, per usual, but Delaurier moves it off the table and to the side of the room. "We're going to need this," he says.

Renaire doesn't mess with the armory. He doesn't choose weapons, only uses them when it's necessary and maintains his own small useful collection of knives. Their relationship always has and probably always will be based on the simple fact that Delaurier leads, and Renaire follows.

Delaurier knows where everything is, of course, and he opens one of the long drawers. Renaire can't see what's inside, but he can hear plenty of clacking as if he's rustling through wooden boxes.

He makes an irritated noise and pulls out Henri Matisse's *Spanish Woman with a Tambourine*.

While Renaire is busy gasping, Delaurier just fucking *tosses* it onto the table, tosses it like it's a painting someone's five-year-old daughter made, and Renaire can't breathe, can do nothing but shout in absolute soul-deep horror as it clunks onto the table with a light *thok* noise. Renaire sprints over to gather it in his arms and pull it away from anywhere Delaurier could even try to touch as he screams out, "What the fuck do you think you're doing?!"

Delaurier looks up to stare at him, obviously confused, and then spots the painting Renaire is holding very, very carefully in his arms. He looks *relieved*, for a moment. And then he clears his throat, shifting his weight slightly. "Oh, that. That's for you. It was going to be a present," he says with a tone that's only five degrees away from awkward, like that's the sole thing that matters at all about the nightmare fuel that just happened. "Happy birthday?"

"Holy fuck, you were keeping this in the *armory*? Are you *insane*? Oh God, do I have to rescue more masterpieces?" Renaire says, and fuck his usual policy of noninterference, he is going to rip these cabinets open one by one. "Jesus, Emile, you don't even like art!"

"I don't *not* like art. I just don't have time to care about art for art's sake," Delaurier says as Renaire opens cabinet after cabinet— guns, guns, knives, drawers and drawers of ammunition. "There's nothing on that side of the room, Renaire!"

"I am going to have nightmares for *years* about this," Renaire says and then realizes in a moment of horror that he's going to have to put the Matisse down to open some of the drawers. There is no safe place here for him to put the Matisse down. He doesn't even *want* to put the Matisse down; he wants to hold it forever, but he has bare hands, and they're eternally shaking from the eight hours of sobriety he demands of himself. This is a catastrophe, an absolute catastrophe.

"Renaire!" Delaurier snaps. "I'm not going to throw another painting, I promise, I didn't realize—"

"Oh God, how could you not realize," Renaire says.

He can hear Delaurier fighting the urge to strangle him. "You do it all the time!"

"Yes, because they're *mine*, not—"

"Do you have any idea how much your work sells for?" Delaurier demands.

Which is a very weird statement, since Renaire doesn't actually sell his paintings, not really. He abandons paintings when they leave a city. He does sell paintings to tourists when he doesn't have room left in his apartment, and could probably make fifty dollars off one if someone was feeling nice, but that's all. He's still kind of baffled at the number of zeros that were on the blood-spattered Delaurier painting, but people pay money for horror stories on top of a pretty blond man.

He very carefully sets the Matisse on the table and turns to see Delaurier holding one of the accursed Tripoli paintings. It's one of the feverish ones that Renaire doesn't even remember painting, an impressionistic blur of Delaurier, made of reds and blacks and gold, gold, gold. Delaurier's other hand has what looks a great deal like a printed-out spreadsheet. When Renaire just keeps staring, Delaurier carefully sets Renaire's painting on the table. Fuck, he throws a Matisse but sets Renaire's down like it's a Fabergé egg, *what is* wrong *with this man*?

"I leave my art when we move," Renaire says when he can finally find words again.

Delaurier nods and pulls *another* out. It's not another Tripoli, thank God. It's from Bucharest, and it's one of his ridiculous ones that started as one thing and ended as another. Originally, it was Renaire enjoying the city's blend of traditional and cutting-edge architecture, but then he'd seen a kid literally cry over spilt milk and stuck the wailing five year old in the foreground. Sometimes Renaire takes art very seriously, but usually, he doesn't. At all.

"I kept this one for myself. I think it's funny," Delaurier says and moves forward to hand Renaire the spreadsheet. "I noticed after our first month that you left your paintings even when you obviously didn't want to. I had the hotel ship them home, but you never asked about them, and I knew you didn't have the room for them all, so I kept them here. And somehow someone's friend of a friend saw one and wanted to buy it, and it expanded from there."

When he finally realizes Renaire is still staring, he puts down the stupid painting (very carefully, again) and starts pointing things out on the spreadsheet.

The titles all start with where he painted them. Renaire immediately skims for it, but there's no sign of Tripoli, thank God. The format is *Location—number—quick description*, and their poetic-souled Jules was in on this because Delaurier could never, ever think of some of these titles. Jules was in on it, and also probably drunk. Renaire doesn't even know what the fuck an amatorculist is. There's a few amatorculists on the list, and he has no idea how one paints an amatorculist, let alone one that could be winsome. Considering the whole title is *Thessaloniki—1—winsome amatorculist*, and he painted a grand total of two paintings in Thessaloniki, with one of them being a seascape, he is guessing it's a painting of his one-night stand. It sold for $10,000.

"You're fucking with me," Renaire says, grabbing the pages and looking at the single column so very full of numbers, with the lowest being at the bottom pages (earliest sales) and those have a *second* column next to them for the following sale. Some of the others do too, and he just.... Renaire takes a deep breath and shakes his head and doesn't *dare* look at the total. "This is a joke, I know it is."

"You're worth over two million dollars," Delaurier says and gently takes the spreadsheet from Renaire's loose fingers and puts it on the table. "I tried to buy that very first one, but it's in a museum and— anyway. We can go see it if you want. I'll show you the figures for your drawings later."

Renaire carefully sits on the floor because otherwise he's going to fall down.

"This is impossible," he says and starts to laugh. It's not a nice sound. It's gasping and hard and desperate. He was starting to believe one good thing could happen, that this thing with Emile could be real, but *two*? That doesn't happen, not in the real world. Not to him.

Delaurier ignores the statement and follows him down to the floor a moment later, surprisingly patient. After he realizes Renaire isn't going to try and speak through the choked noises he keeps making, he reaches out to hold Renaire's head in his hands and looks into Renaire's eyes so fiercely that he has no choice but to focus on Delaurier and his words.

"I have financial and cultural proof you're not worthless," he says.

And fuck, *fuck*, Renaire hates himself for it the moment he feels it coming on, but Delaurier reaches forward and is holding him, and Renaire's heart and lungs twist, and he starts crying. It's ugly how he cries, it's so ugly and loud even when he tries to muffle the sobs into Emile's shoulder, loud enough that he can't even understand what Emile is saying to him, not really, because even if he's culturally significant and netted two million dollars, he could never hope to be worth those words.

It takes him a long time to get himself together, mostly because every time he thinks he'll be okay, Emile ends up doing *something*, and fuck, sometimes just looking at him hurts, but he finally stops sobbing like a three year old. It's stupid; it's so stupid he's crying over people liking his paintings.

When Renaire can finally breathe again, not to mention *think*, he's practically curled in Emile's lap in the middle of the room.

"The Matisse is in direct sunlight," Renaire finally manages to say, voice hoarse and awkward, and tries to get control of himself. He refuses to be this pathetic.

Delaurier sighs. "Fine. I'll put it back. You get in the shower."

The confusion about that particular order vanishes pretty fast after Renaire remembers he hasn't actually taken a shower in about three days. If he'd been stuck with an armful of dirty sobbing man, he'd do the same thing. Delaurier is not soft or gentle, but he is often kind and *always* cares, often to a dangerously passionate level, so this makes sense.

He gets to his feet on his own, even though Delaurier stands over him and is ready to help at a moment's notice, like Renaire was shot instead of having a ridiculous art-based breakdown. It's easy enough to get back downstairs and into the bathroom, since he usually spends more time here than in his own apartment. He stops by the duffel bag since it still has Budapest-washed clothing, and he wants to feel something closer to human.

He's been in the shower for about five minutes, just standing there and feeling zero guilt about basking in Delaurier's divine water pressure, when he finally notices the man is sitting on the bathroom counter. Renaire is surprised at the fact he *isn't* surprised. Delaurier is half watching him, more an intent awareness of how he's doing than actually watching him shower. It helps that the shower is a frosted glass cube in a fairly small room—Delaurier couldn't miss noticing him even if he wanted to.

Renaire just concentrates on washing his hair because he has no idea what's really going on here. He never does. "Are you waiting for your turn?" he asks.

"I brought you clothes, but you already have some," Delaurier says, looking down at his bare feet instead of at Renaire. "Now I'm just waiting for you."

Renaire thinks he might be starting to figure this out, or at least noticing the trend. Delaurier isn't willing to outright ask him for anything remotely sexual, but he has no problem with putting himself somewhere very, very obvious (such as straddling him, or pinning him against a wall—Delaurier is *not* a subtle man) and waiting for an invitation. Renaire can't decide if it's hilarious and adorable or so aggravating he wants to rip his hair out.

He sighs and swings the shower door open, giving Delaurier an expectant look.

Delaurier just looks back at him.

After a few moments of waiting for the other to move, Renaire finally says, "Are you coming in or not?"

"Do you want me to?" Delaurier asks, and Renaire will not strangle him. He will not.

Renaire rolls his eyes and says, "Emile Delaurier, the honor of your presence is requested in the shower. You are cordially invited to have shower sex with me, black tie strongly discouraged—"

Delaurier's mouth cuts him off, and Renaire is more than happy with that, kissing back eagerly as Delaurier backs him into the water, still fully clothed and obviously not giving a shit. Renaire fights to keep up, can only gasp when Delaurier's fingers press against his back so firmly that he feels like he's leaving gouges in the muscle. Renaire's shoulders hit the wall, and Delaurier's clothing is soaked and sticking to him and oh yes, this was an *excellent* idea.

He gets his hands beneath the hem of Delaurier's clinging shirt and doesn't even hesitate trying to pull it off. Delaurier is not helping him, at all, because Delaurier seems determined to drive him insane with his mouth, which has moved to nip and suck at the water dripping down Renaire's neck. Renaire has Delaurier's shirt sticking to his skin just below his ribcage, and he can see Delaurier's entire body beneath the shirt, but he can't get at it because of the stupid fucking fabric.

"This is coming off *now*," Renaire says, tugging viciously at the shirt, and that at least gets Delaurier's attention. He pulls away for the required two seconds to strip off his shirt. It clings at his arms and chest the whole way up because there is absolutely nothing in the world that wouldn't want to be touching Delaurier's bare skin, including Renaire's mouth, which he has latched onto Delaurier's beautiful collarbone while his hands curl their way into the other man's waistband.

Delaurier makes a noise somewhere between a laugh and a groan, and his hands join Renaire's in the fight to strip Delaurier as fast as humanly possible. The pants don't want to come off either, and Delaurier curses breathlessly with frustration, which is a perfect opportunity for Renaire to take advantage of.

He presses Delaurier gently against the frosted glass of the shower, just far enough from the showerhead that the only water left on him is trailing down from his hair. Renaire kisses his way down Delaurier's chest, stopping for a moment to tease a nipple (and Delaurier's fingers press themselves pale against the glass as he breathes in sharply) before moving down to his gloriously defined abdomen, and then his hipbones, sliding to his knees and pulling the water-soaked pants from Delaurier's body.

Renaire can't wait to ask permission because if he doesn't at least lick Delaurier's cock right then and there he is probably going to have a heart attack. He makes it light, and simple, and a little bit teasing when he presses his tongue to the tip and watches Delaurier, desperately hoping this is all right. Delaurier's head hits the glass, and Delaurier whines before he can cut himself off. Delaurier is *definitely* okay with this, so Renaire licks a long, firm press of his tongue to the bottom of Delaurier's cock.

Delaurier's hand immediately lashes out and grabs Renaire's hair, although it's not painful. It reminds him of sailors clutching railings in the middle of a storm. "I'm going to come on your face," Delaurier says, voice shaking slightly, and Renaire can't do anything but moan around his cock, lips and tongue doing their damnedest to drive Delaurier to the edge. He doesn't say another word, just clutches at Renaire's hair and fights to keep his hips still, beyond the small desperate thrusts he can't contain as Renaire sucks him off.

It doesn't last long enough, not nearly long enough for Renaire to memorize the taste and weight of Delaurier inside his mouth, on his tongue. Delaurier pulls his mouth aside with a deep, primal moan, staring straight into Renaire's eyes as the water pours down onto his back, into his hair, across his skin.

"You are so beautiful," Delaurier breathes out, and fuck, Renaire can see his legs are shaking. Renaire just watches him back; watches Delaurier take himself in hand and jerk himself off frantically, the beating downpour of the shower pressing into Renaire's skin and the steam of the heat making Delaurier's skin look luminescent. "Christ, *Renaire*," he chokes out, and comes with a gasp on Renaire's chin and lips and cheek. It feels heavy in comparison to the ever-present rivulets of water, and Renaire wishes he hadn't closed his eyes in that moment, wishes it down to his soul.

Delaurier drops down to the floor of the shower right along with Renaire, a hand pressing against the now covered side of his face. He stares at Renaire, somewhere trapped between shock and hunger. He wraps an arm around Renaire's shoulders, pulling their bodies together, and Renaire's hard cock is pressed tight against Delaurier's thigh. He has to take a deep breath at the feeling—he doesn't know what Delaurier wants now, doesn't know if he's allowed to rut against Delaurier like some sort of desperate animal or touch himself or *what*.

It's slow, how Delaurier kisses him then. Slow, with a lot of tongue tormenting Renaire's lips, and it takes Renaire a moment to realize he's lapping up what little proof of orgasm the shower has left on Renaire. He shudders, and thrusts against Delaurier, whether or not he's allowed.

"Next time we do that, we aren't going to be in the shower," Delaurier promises. Fuck, he's smiling. He's smiling against Renaire's lips, one hand still teasing his wet hair while the other slides its way around Renaire's skin, and Renaire can do nothing but pant and kiss him and wonder what happens next. Delaurier can read his fucking mind and is always two steps ahead, if not more. Renaire should really be more surprised when he makes that glorious pleased humming noise and leans in to Renaire's ear to say, "Do you want to fuck me?"

"Oh holy fuck," Renaire breathes out, grabbing onto Delaurier's shoulders as if he'll float away if he does anything else. He shakes his head, hair spraying water all over, and he does not give a fuck, because they're in the shower and this has to be a no right now, this *has to be a no*, "No no no, I want that so fucking bad but not here, not now, I want—"

"Shhh," Delaurier says, soothing and *affectionate* and ruthlessly killing Renaire with the sweetness of his breath against Renaire's cheek and kisses him again. "Another time, then. What do you want?"

"Stop asking that, I never know what I want," Renaire says, and it's true, it's so true, Delaurier robs all reason from his mind the moment their skin touches. "I just *want you*."

"You have me," Delaurier says, bending to return his attention to catching the water on Renaire's neck and tormenting him in the process. His hand reaches down to loosely circle Renaire's cock, and Renaire doesn't give a fuck about being careful, not now. He thrusts into Emile's grip, hard, and moans so loud the whole fucking building can probably hear him. "You have me, I swear, I just want to know how—"

"Cover me," Renaire gasps out, and he doesn't even know what that means, doesn't know how to *say it*, only that he wants to be covered in Delaurier, enveloped and consumed completely.

But Delaurier knows, because he always knows. He's so clever, and he doesn't even hesitate before standing and pulling Renaire up with him and slamming Renaire's back into the wall of the shower, harder than the last time. He groans, and Emile is pressed tight against him, so tightly their skin is sliding and sticking against each other as Emile cups his hand firmly against Renaire's cock, and he rocks into it senselessly.

"Look at the glass, Renaire," Emile says, hand so tight against him it almost hurts, and Renaire pants against his shoulder, laying almost accidental openmouthed kisses against his collarbone. "Look at the glass, Renaire, look at the reflection."

Renaire shakes his head, because he can't even keep his eyes open, whining high in his throat. That's not an acceptable answer, though, it doesn't give Emile what he wants, so the hand that had been wrapped in Renaire's hair yanks his head up, and he has no choice but to obey.

The glass is frosted, making their reflection look smoky and distant, but he still is struck breathless. Emile's legs, Emile's back, Emile's *everything* is obscuring Renaire, until all he can see is his own face, tight and helpless as Emile presses and strokes his cock. Emile's hand is wrapped in his hair.

Renaire didn't even know his face could look like that. Or that he could make the breathless keening noise that escapes his lips at the sight.

"I've got you," Emile says. "And you have me, and I have you, and I'll keep holding you, I swear."

"You want me," Renaire realizes, and fuck, he is so close. Emile presses his mouth against Renaire's cheek as he hums out an affirmative and then kisses him, and Renaire watches it happen in their reflection. He ends up closing his eyes, reveling in the feel of Emile's ruthless affection and knowing Emile has him and *likes it*, and he purrs out, "You *want me*."

He doesn't know what happens next, only that suddenly the hand against his cock is touching him so good it's *painful*, and Emile is whispering into his ear with a smug, dark, satiated voice, quietly crooning out, "Oh fuck yes, *there's* my boy," and Renaire's fingers scramble against the glass as he comes, and he will swear to God that his eyes roll into the back of his head as the world whites out for a moment.

The world has twisted, somehow. The world has twisted, and they haven't even touched the soap.

They're on the floor of the shower again, Emile holding him with his face pressed into Renaire's wet hair. He's speaking, but it's so quiet that Renaire has no chance of hearing it, not when it's muffled by the sound of the shower, and Renaire's lungs and heart are doing their best to make the world still seem strangely distant.

"The water's going to get cold," Renaire finally manages to say. Emile lets out a huff of an amused breath into his hair, but he does actually shower, at ease with the fact Renaire is still sitting on the floor watching him. Emile doesn't show off—he's efficient, just like any other time they've been in close quarters for something like this.

When he's done, he turns the water off and frowns at Renaire. "Are you alright?" he asks, more confused than concerned.

Renaire realizes he's just been sitting in the same position and watching silently all this time. "I'm still trying to get over the disbelief stage," Renaire admits. He wants to believe, but if it's a lie, if he's *wrong*, he wouldn't survive the pain.

Delaurier doesn't look happy, but he accepts it and nods, opening the shower door and pulling the waiting towel off the bathroom counter. "Stand up, Renaire," he says, and Renaire does, grateful that his legs aren't shaking. Delaurier wraps the towel around him, and it's warm and soft as Delaurier dries him in that same caring and attentive but oddly not-sexy way.

He's starting to think that Delaurier only has an off or on setting with anything sexual, or even sensual. Either he's some sort of ravenous new lover Delaurier, or he's the same untouchable comrade Delaurier that Renaire has dealt with for the past two years.

When Delaurier seems to be satisfied with his work, he dries himself off with far less attention to detail and pulls Renaire out of the shower by the hand. Renaire lets him lead with little objection, but when Delaurier starts moving toward the clothing like he's going to *dress him*, Renaire shakes his head and says, "I do *not* need you to dress me."

"He speaks," Delaurier says with a small smile and moves out of Renaire's personal space. It takes him a moment to realize that Delaurier isn't leaving him, he's just picking up his completely ruined clothing from inside the shower and dumping them in the sink, probably so they don't drip all over the floor. He then wraps up in one of the other towels while Renaire dresses himself like the adult he is. "I'm going to get dressed, and then I'll be right back."

The play-by-play is more than a little strange, but he doesn't ask about it. When Delaurier doesn't leave, Renaire frowns and says, "Okay…?"

Delaurier still doesn't move. He keeps watching Renaire, for a long time. Renaire is fully dressed, and Delaurier is in nothing but a towel, and somehow Renaire feels like he's the naked one.

"I'm still doing something wrong, aren't I?" Delaurier says.

"No you aren't," Renaire says. If there's a problem, it's Renaire. "I'm going downstairs for lunch."

Delaurier gives him a stern look. "And you *will* tell me if I'm fucking this up."

"I'll do my best," Renaire says, because it's as much of a promise as he can ever give. It seems to satisfy Delaurier since he nods, but he still hesitates.

Renaire is in the process of rolling his eyes and telling him to *just go, already* when Delaurier moves forward and kisses him. It's chaste, a soft press of lips to lips, and it stays that way for a long, sweet moment. Delaurier pulls away with a cautious smile before finally leaving the room.

This was a very busy morning, Renaire thinks a little numbly.

He takes a deep breath, tries to feel like some sort of adult, and for some reason when he reaches the stairwell, he doesn't stop descending until he's at street level. His feet have him headed toward his own apartment, which works fine for him, even if he has no idea *why*. Renaire doesn't want to be a complete asshole, though, so he sends a quick text saying he has to check up on it.

His apartment is about the size of a pickup truck. It has a bathroom and kitchen squeezed in beneath a mezzanine someone else installed, which Renaire tossed a mattress onto. The only thing he likes about his apartment is the light. What isn't covered in bottles and discarded clothing is coated in spatters of paint and pastel and places he's dragged charcoal and pencil accidentally—it's pretty much unavoidable in this small a space.

Normally, Renaire goes out and tries to sell paintings to tourists when he runs out of space. He really has no fucking clue what to do about that now that he's supposedly a famous artist.

He doesn't have the mental capacity for that right now, though. Renaire is tired, down to the bone, so he doesn't even glance around his tiny apartment. The windows (beautiful, bright things that face south and can swing open or be shut tight or be completely blacked out or lightly shuttered) are open all the way, with the early spring sunlight of noon shining in, but that doesn't keep Renaire from mounting the tight spiral staircase up to the mattress and passing out within moments of hitting the sheets.

RENAIRE HAS these sorts of dreams often, and this one more than any of the others. It's not a nightmare, but it's not a happy dream. And yet, it isn't unhappy.

There are no words, no voices, even though he somehow *knows* what's said. He doesn't see where they are, or who they are. He only feels and knows.

Everything he loves is about to die. His mind summons up Delaurier now, as it has ever since he first saw the other man. Before that, there wasn't anything beyond a sun-bright figure. But now Renaire stands and wordlessly screams *I'm going too, I'm coming too, don't leave me, let me die with you* as he walks past whatever threat there is to Emile.

There's warmth, and a joining, and a sense of acceptance and contentment, and then a bite of pain that Renaire doesn't mind at all. The dream cuts off sharp but peaceful, and he always wakes up feeling better than when he fell asleep.

Sometimes Renaire thinks he should worry about the fact that the most peaceful and soothing recurring dream he's ever had is the one where he gets killed.

His worst dreams are of surviving. They're of fire and burning fields, of the way blood is sucked into warm, thirsty dirt and coagulates into a rigid half-mud adobe-color stain while boots and tire tracks trail the remains of the dead carelessly across unpaved roads through the beautiful greens and emeralds of screaming terrified birds and tropic heat and pain. So much pain. He walked until he couldn't hear people or smell burning or find his way back, and in his dreams he never escapes it.

Renaire started *really* drinking because of memories, tried to drown himself until he couldn't remember when he closed his eyes. He drinks and doesn't ever mention his past and refuses to set foot anywhere near Cote d'Ivoire no matter what Delaurier might want— one of the two or three times he's ever said no.

His dream of dying is soothing. It's desperate and sweet and vague, full of acceptance and peace. His dreams of living are sharp and vivid and painful and so, so real.

He'd choose death any day.

CHAPTER 5

Paris: Chéron—Gallery—{Vienna}—*Arènes de Lutèce*

RENAIRE HAS a dawn meeting with Celine, the dangerously well-informed Interpol agent.

When he flails his way out of the mattress and its ancient mint-green sheets to grab his phone, singing out that wonderful Turtles song again, it's not Celine, or Interpol, or Delaurier slowly dying alone in a pool of his own blood, or any other nightmare. It's Delaurier, who is not dying, saying, "I am inviting you to dinner."

The sun is setting already, not that he expected anything different. His apartment is cold and bathed in dim golden light, and Renaire really needs to have a place that doesn't require coordination to get in or out of his bed. It was always a good excuse for passing out on someone's couch. Either way it's awkward to make his way down. Or up. There's a reason he only stuck a mattress up there.

"I'll be there," Renaire says, sitting down on the bottom steps of his tight staircase and scrubbing a hand over his eyes. "I just needed to get some sleep."

"That's understandable," Delaurier says, rigid and awkward. Renaire is torn between affection and exasperation. "You'll be back soon?"

"I'll be there," he repeats.

"Good," Delaurier says, still awkward but not *quite* as awkward, thank God, and hangs up, and Renaire has a meeting with an Interpol agent in less than twelve hours.

He isn't stupid. She may have sounded friendly and honest, but that doesn't mean she actually is. People are rarely what they want you to believe. He'd bring someone for backup, but they have information on every member of STB. A lot of information. A lot of very good and therefore very *bad* information.

But not on Mathieu, Renaire remembers.

He isn't exactly Mathieu's friend. They're good acquaintances, and they've gone drinking together, and definitely don't hate each other. Mathieu is a weird combination of naïveté and earnestness that somehow then got stuck in a blender with being painfully stubborn and rebellious just for the sake of being a part of something bigger than one person.

When Carope brought him back to the Chéron like a stray puppy, Renaire had thought he was just another runaway that Carope would rehabilitate and send on their way. But Mathieu got caught up in the fever, in the *excitement*, in the idealist part of STB that still remains of the original little activist club the triumvirate started. He empathized with the cause, and he stuck around, and Carope fell fast and hard.

Mathieu is a pure soul. Carope is used to trying to polish the poor fucked-up and tarnished members of STB. Renaire can see how that might appeal to someone like her.

So, Renaire likes Mathieu, in a cursory kind of way. It's probably going to be an awkward conversation, and he doesn't know if Mathieu could even keep his mouth shut for twelve hours. When he gets excited, he starts talking. A lot. But it's either Mathieu or nothing, so he'll deal with it.

The call is quickly answered, Mathieu's cheery greeting making Renaire wonder if he should technically bump Mathieu up to official friend status. "Renaire! What's going on?"

"I'm meeting someone tomorrow morning. Can you be there to make sure they don't try to kidnap me or anything?" Renaire asks. "I only need you to make sure I get in and out alive, nothing beyond that."

Mathieu thinks with his heart above all else, so Renaire—a friend in need—doesn't have to say anything else. "Sure. Why me, though?"

"Why not?" Renaire stands, stretching and then patting his coat down to find his cigarettes. He doesn't really feel like trying to explain the Interpol thing, mostly because Renaire himself has no fucking clue what's really going on. "And I'd be grateful if you didn't tell Emile about this."

"What? Really?" He can hear the confused frown in Mathieu's voice.

"Really," Renaire says. "I'll tell him on my own later. It's at the Arènes de Lutèce, at dawn."

"Well, I can see why Delaurier isn't going, then," Mathieu says with a laugh. "Arènes de Lutèce at dawn, I'll be there. Are you coming back home?"

"I just needed a nap," Renaire says, exasperated. It takes a lot of work to get a cigarette out of an already crumpled pack with one hand, so he props his phone on his shoulder as he fishes one out. "It was a *nap*. Why does everyone think I've abandoned you all?"

"Nobody thinks that, we're just waiting, but You-Know-Who's been pacing up and down the stairs. It's kind of funny," Mathieu says, and this is why they get along. They both enjoy when Delaurier gets snappish, although for completely different reasons.

And Renaire is absolutely not at all getting fluttery warm butterfly-in-his-stomach feelings at hearing that. At all.

"I'll be there soon," Renaire says and hangs up.

He *is* there soon, gets there within twenty minutes of hanging up. The sun's officially setting now, golden light turning to an awkward orange against the monotype blue rooftops of Paris, and light sensors are starting to flick on exterior illumination at the Café Chéron. The night bartender is missing, which is surprising, but Renaire doesn't stop to chat with the new girl. He'll do that after seeing whether or not Delaurier is actually pacing on the stairs.

He isn't. He's standing at the head of the stairs, watching Renaire walk up them. It feels vaguely like a horror movie. "Do I need to ask permission to take a nap now?" Renaire asks, amused.

"No, because I am not controlling your personal life choices," Delaurier says in that treatise-quoting way Renaire has heard far too often on long train rides. "I didn't know where you went, though. And I wanted to ask you to have dinner with me."

Renaire frowns when he sees that the room is completely full of their friends, and not one of them is speaking. They're *watching*, perfectly silent. "What the hell is going—?"

"On a date," Delaurier says.

Someone makes a strangled noise, and immediately every other person in the room shushes him. Everyone but Delaurier and Renaire, who stare at each other. A lot.

"Oh," Renaire finally says.

Delaurier takes a deep breath and says, "I know we're not exactly going in the usual order of things, so it might be strange, but a developing relationship—"

"Dear God, you'd be on-switched, wouldn't you?" Renaire realizes, so stunned he ends up saying it out loud. The thought of an entire night of Delaurier in sexual mode is both terrifying and thrilling, and Renaire doesn't know if the world could survive it, let alone Renaire himself.

Delaurier frowns. "What?"

"It's kind of late to go to dinner," Renaire says, and he can feel the smile growing on his lips. He probably looks like a brainless moron, but he doesn't actually care right now because *Delaurier is asking him on a date.* "But that'd be nice."

"Good," Delaurier says, sighing the words out as his shoulders sag in relief—Renaire hadn't even realized how tense he'd been, which is just…. Had he really thought Renaire would ever say no?

Renaire is probably going to regret this, but Delaurier looks so fucking happy because of *him* that he can't help but move forward and kiss him. Their friends are making plenty of noise at that, but Renaire is much more interested in the surprised, pleased half hum Delaurier rewards him with. He kisses back eagerly, if briefly, and when he pulls away he's smiling and holding Renaire's hand again.

"We can go another night, though," Delaurier says, and it's probably the first time he's ever said anything with deliberate sexual implications in his entire life.

"Definitely," Renaire agrees. "I have an early morning, so I should get to bed early anyway."

Delaurier frowns. "Really?"

"Jesus, you're fucking terrible at this," Renaire says and kisses him again.

THE EVENING is spent like most evenings at home in Paris. Delaurier preaches and plans, Renaire drinks and occasionally heckles from his corner table, and their friends merrily flit between their two extremes. But Renaire can't stop smiling, and Delaurier keeps smiling too, keeps glancing over even when he's in the middle of a debate or serious conversation. It's maddening in the best way imaginable, and Garrant is being a lovable asshole about it with a grin and so much exaggerated eyebrow waggling it has to hurt, and Carope keeps asking for details there's no way in hell Renaire is going to give. Renaire tries to decide if he needs to write a formal apology to Carope for losing his membership to their hopeless pining club.

Mathieu is still absolute shit at keeping a secret, since he comes over and loudly asks all sorts of questions about tomorrow morning. There's no doubt that he's overheard, but nobody comments. It's suspicious, but Renaire can't even bring himself to care, he is so stupidly happy. The zombie apocalypse could erupt around them and he'd still be grinning.

When Jules takes a seat nearby, Renaire leans forward and asks, "What the hell is an amatorculist?"

Jules looks confused for barely a breath's length, and then they're grinning wide and thrilled at Renaire. "He told you! You know! Oh, thank God, you have no idea how much we wanted to tell you," Jules says and grabs Renaire's hands in their own. "You have to take me along when you go see the gallery."

Renaire hopes he doesn't look too confused. "I heard there was a museum—"

"Oh, that too," Jules says. "But you have a show right now in a gallery here in Paris. It's very well put together. And another one in Copenhagen, but that one's not *nearly* as good, in my opinion."

"He knows about the art?" Carope asks, looking almost as thrilled as Jules. "Thank God. Now you can convince Delaurier to give up those Tripoli—"

"*No*," Renaire says immediately. "Those aren't for anything but being stuck in a dark corner."

"But they're amazing," Jules protests, obviously confused.

"Well, he's the artist," Carope says, shrugging and obviously not the least bit bothered by Renaire ripping her suggestion apart like a starving shark. She pats Renaire on the back, still grinning. "You know, we should go see them! You postponed your *date*, so you're free, right?"

"Renaire knows about the art!" Bossard calls out to the rest of the room. He'd been lingering on the edges of their conversation in his usual awkward holding pattern before he decides it's considered appropriate to get in on the conversation, because when he *does* get in on the conversation, he goes in enthusiastic and excitable and kind of terrible at volume control. The room cheers, and Renaire gets hoisted out of his chair by Bossard and Jules. Renaire flails, but when they let go, it's for the sole purpose of Carope grabbing his shoulders from behind, pushing him forward and deeper into the room.

"We are going to show the artist his gallery!" Carope commands.

Renaire doesn't want to go because *he has plans involving Delaurier and a bed*, but there's no fucking way he's telling them that. They think kissing by the stairs was risqué, and Renaire is not eager to rob them of that notion. When he glances over at Delaurier, he can tell the other man's having the same exact conflicted feelings about this.

"I haven't mentally prepared myself for the shock I will receive when seeing my work in a gallery for the first time," Renaire declares. He doesn't know which one of them snickers, but he will find out, and then they will be the first to pay. "Come on, why can't you let me have a single night to adjust to this? I already had to go hide in my apartment for a few hours to deal with this. I'm in an emotionally fragile state. You could have some sympathy, for fuck's sake!"

They've slowed down, but Renaire can tell they're not going to accept that excuse. He's not going to be able to escape with *any* excuse when Garrant and his troublemaking grin get ahold of Renaire. His only hope is outside intervention. He anxiously looks back at Delaurier, who is smiling.

"You are *not helping*," Renaire snaps at him, and Jesus Christ, Garrant is just about physically carrying him down the stairs now, the weightlifting traitor. Renaire's fingers scramble for the banister, but barely manage to touch the wood. "I hate you so much."

"You hate me *often*," Delaurier says from where he and Glasson are gleefully watching him get maneuvered into his own jacket, and God, how Renaire hates when he starts getting *clever* in half arguments like these. He's been betrayed. There are no allies in the room.

"It's going to be fine," Lile says, audibly trying to wave away any and all fears Renaire might have even while he keeps goading Garrant forward. "The owner of the gallery's had at least one of your paintings up for probably a year and a half now, and she's a huge fan. You should see the presentations she gives to visiting art critics. She's been begging to meet you."

For some reason that catches on *something* in his brain, the idea that someone wants to meet him and talk to him about this illustrious lie of a career and dissect his worthless scribbles and splashes of paint on cheap canvases decorated with the same simple case of paints lugged all over the world in a military-issue khaki duffel bag. There's no way he can lie well enough to pass himself off as whatever the poor gallery owner (let alone *art critics*) thinks he is, and suddenly it seems like the world is closing in on him, and his friends aren't actually his friends, and he can't think can't see, can't *breathe*.

He can hear Glasson shout something, and Delaurier's voice on top of it as the world seems to twirl around Renaire. His body moves, but Renaire is too busy trying to even regain awareness and *sense* to tell what's going on. All he knows is that when he finally manages to fight his way past the pathetic senseless panic, he has Garrant twisted on his knees and a hand in the man's hair yanking his head back, exposing his throat, and Lile is holding his other arm tightly, and Delaurier has his arms wrapped around Renaire's torso in a half grab half hug, keeping him away from Garrant and his wide, stunned (scared) eyes.

"It's okay, it's okay, Renaire, you're fine," Delaurier is saying over and over again, and *shit* he hasn't done this since a year ago in Vienna, and he was hoping to never do this ever again. Delaurier can tell he's closer to sane again, since his hold loosens and becomes more of a hug. "Renaire?"

"Fuck, I'm so sorry," Renaire tells Garrant, letting go of his hair and stepping aside as well as he can with two men restraining him. It doesn't take Garrant long to move. He rolls out of the way immediately, eyes still on the knife Renaire hadn't even realized he was holding, can't even remember drawing out of, what, his jacket? And his brain short-circuits again because he was about to slash Garrant's throat just because he didn't want to meet someone who likes his art.

He drops the knife as if it's on fire, and tries to breathe. Lile steps away a moment after that to check on Garrant, who looks mostly uninjured as far as Renaire can see.

"No, I'm sorry," Garrant says seriously. "It's easy to forget how big this is for you. We shouldn't have pushed."

About half of their friends have seen Renaire snap like this. Garrant is one of them. Lile is one of them too. Renaire doesn't dare look behind him and see what the rest look like.

"You're okay?" Renaire asks.

"He's fine, other than bruises," Lile reassures him, giving him a small smile. "No injuries that he wouldn't have ended up with tonight anyway."

"It was kind of impressive, really," Garrant says with a grin, and fuck, he obviously means every word of it. He'd looked terrified before, but now he's smiling and complimenting Renaire on his insane panic attack-induced violence.

Delaurier shifts away from him, gives him space, and Renaire can finally start to breathe again. He didn't actually hurt anyone, nothing beyond his own pride. He covers his face with his hands and groans because it's better than screaming. "I am so, so sorry," he says again.

"There's nothing to apologize for," Delaurier says and doesn't let him try to apologize again. He grabs Renaire's knife from where it'd dropped onto the floor and pockets it before taking Renaire's hand in his own and leading him back through the room and toward their not-quite-private staircase, without a single glance backward.

Delaurier doesn't take him up to the apartment, though. He sits on the stairs and gives Renaire an expectant look before saying, "I need to know what happened."

It's not kind or even caring. It's the fearless leader voice. There's no way of getting out of this question, and Renaire admits to himself that if he was in Delaurier's position, he'd do the same. Delaurier has seen this happen before, but they were all in situations that made a lot more sense than being playfully tugged around by close friends he literally trusts with his life. Having someone like Renaire around is generally a bad idea, and even worse when there's the potential for *this*.

He wants to pace, or look away, or just glare and stay silent, but instead he sits down next to Delaurier and pulls out a cigarette. "I'm not sure," he admits. "But something about the gallery idea scared me."

Terrified me would be more accurate, but he doesn't say that. He just lights his cigarette and doesn't look at Delaurier as he breathes in and out and watches his exhalation turn the air white-gray for short staccato moments.

"Meeting the owner scares you," Delaurier says because Renaire can't admit it. He sighs. "I guess that makes sense, for you. We'll go anonymously, then. The gallery knows us, but you don't have to out yourself if you don't want to."

"I'd rather not go at all," Renaire says.

"Too bad," Delaurier says, and it's that same old simple fist of fabric that gets Renaire immediately on his feet. He lets go once they're back in STB's unofficial headquarters, where their friends are waiting and glancing carefully between them. "We're going to the gallery, but nobody says Renaire's the artist."

"Sounds fair to me," Carope agrees, and apparently the entire group is going since they all file down the stairs chatting and joking between each other.

Not a single awkward word is said about the fact Renaire went momentarily batshit insane and tried to murder Garrant. Delaurier manages the impressive feat of being nearby but not hovering while Renaire slowly finds his feet again as they walk through the night-lit streets of Paris. Carope (whose emotional intelligence is off the charts; Renaire doesn't doubt for a moment that she and Glasson combined could negotiate peace between Israel and Palestine if they tried) makes a point of pulling Renaire back out of the natural awkwardness anyone would feel for unintentional attempted murder.

The group also manages to flirt with a group of girls on the metro who decide to come along to the gallery. And then Lile and Bossard call their girlfriend, Dominique, and she brings along some friends, and it quickly turns into a hodgepodge of a social gathering that makes Delaurier start getting rigid, and that means Renaire ends up spending most of the journey needling him for it. Delaurier can whip a group into a zealous mob with twenty minutes of rhetoric, but stick him in the middle of a party, and it's like watching one poor Doberman getting swarmed by a room full of excited cats.

The gallery is surprisingly busy, which is a word Renaire can't ever remember applying to an art gallery at 8:00 p.m. before. It's also much bigger than he expected, and there's an advertisement for *him* in the window, his R signature on top of a claustrophobic painting of Rome and—

"Why did you give them the Reykjavik paintings," Renaire groans. They're old, and terrible. Delaurier had been in and out of the city while researching for a good two weeks on that job, and Renaire had stayed put and been so high that the paintings are more of a study in what kind of shit he could do pressing his brush against a paint-soaked canvas than anything else.

They just laugh at him. He hates his friends.

When they walk in, it takes only a moment for a woman to come rushing up to them excitedly, two men trailing behind her. She heads straight for Carope, which Renaire really wishes surprised him. "Oh, Ms. Carope, it's so nice to see you again! How's our favorite mystery artist these days?"

"Very busy, as ever," Carope says effortlessly, kissing the woman who is probably the gallery owner on the cheek. "How goes hunting down the tourist art?"

"Your R's philanthropic gestures continue to frustrate, not to mention how they invite forgeries of her work," she says easily, waving a hand through the air as if it's not really important, and glances around the group, greeting most of STB before her eyes catch on Delaurier, and her entire face lights up. It's not a friendly kind of lighting up. It's the kind of lighting up people do when they see money stuffed into couch cushions. "The muse!"

"Oh God," Renaire says. Now is a good time to take advantage of his flask.

"What grand occasion brings you here?" the owner says enthusiastically, glancing around their group. Most of them have moved into the gallery itself, wandering and chatting their way into the rooms.

"Just checking up on the show," Carope says cheerily and slings an arm around Delaurier's shoulders. It's not lost on Renaire that he's now carefully blocked behind their bodies. "We're trying to convince him to relinquish some more of R's stuff so we can show it off."

Renaire needs his bigger flask. Or two of them.

"We would be thrilled to get them," she says. "Of course, I won't pressure you. I know they're probably personal."

"Very," Delaurier says, giving Carope a look that Renaire can't see but knows from experience isn't fun to be on the receiving end. Delaurier sighs and shrugs out of Carope's hold.

"Honestly, I'd be thrilled just to see them," the owner says. "The London portraits—"

"Jesus, you gave them the London paintings too," Renaire says. London (the second time) was one of the very, very awkward eye candy apologies. And they aren't exactly portraits, since Delaurier's face isn't ever shown in its entirety, but he's too frustrated with his friends and the gallery (and *himself*, fuck, why did he ever paint those?) to point that out.

Delaurier shrugs at him because he's an asshole.

"I'm sorry, who are you?" the gallery owner asks, glancing curiously at Renaire. There is definite suspicion there. Very definite suspicion.

"Put the flask down, Renaire," Delaurier says.

"I'm their drunk cynical friend," Renaire says, which is hopefully off-putting enough that she'll leave it alone.

It obviously isn't, since she gives him a long, considering look, and then holds out a hand. It takes Renaire a moment, but he shakes her hand. "I'm happy to meet you, Renaire," she says sincerely, and smiles, and fuck, she definitely knows. "I'd love to show you around and tell you a bit about the gallery and exhibit."

"That'd be great," Carope says and gives Renaire a friendly slap on the back. "Make this one of the best tours of your life, Sirine."

"I wouldn't dream of doing anything less," Sirine the gallery owner says, and with another companionable kiss to the cheek, Carope joins one of the groups meandering around the nearest room. Delaurier stays with him, thank God. Sirine winks at Renaire. "I imagine Ms. Carope wants me to concentrate on the R collection, but I know an art lover when I see one. Let's start on the left and wind our way around."

And they do.

Sirine is a wonderful guide, and after Renaire realizes she really does love talking about art, it's as if Renaire can't *stop* talking about it. Her two assistants are gone by the time they've made it through probably four paintings, and by the end of the second room, Delaurier has finally given up and left. Renaire doesn't hold it against him. His efforts were admirable. The man threw a Matisse. Art isn't his thing.

She ends up putting him so completely at ease that when they finally reach the first "R" painting, one of the Helsinki cats, and she says, "I've always felt like this piece is one of the most content and peaceful paintings of the artist's entire collection," Renaire actually answers. He gives her the whole fucking story.

"We were stuck in Helsinki because of weather, ended up stuck there for an entire second week, and there were these stray cats that I found on the way to… God, I don't even remember. But I took them back to the hotel, and they wanted to do *nothing* but cuddle," Renaire says fondly. "It was probably just the cold, but even Emile warmed up to them. I nearly tried to smuggle Chair home."

He expects to panic again, to freeze or run or attack, but he doesn't. Instead he turns to look at Sirine and wait.

When she first turns to look at him, she has a triumphant, gleeful smile on her face. It doesn't last long, though. Renaire can't even guess what he looks like right now, but she looks apprehensive.

"You know who Delaurier is," he says. After a moment, she nods, and Renaire pulls his flask back out. "Then what do you know about me?"

It takes Sirine a moment, but she says, "There's a few theories, most of which are obviously extremely wrong. But what we know for certain is that you painted him and then disappeared immediately after an attack, and now we have paintings from around the world that a known associate of STB distributes."

Renaire nods and then drinks. "And from the art?"

"Whatever you're doing, you enjoy it for the most part," Sirine says, which is true. "You feel things very deeply, and nothing so deeply as your love for your muse."

"It's obsession, not love," he says, because he wishes it was true, and tries to give her a smile. "I'd appreciate if you didn't run around exposing me."

"You can trust me," Sirine says and her smile comes back. "Would you be willing to answer some questions I have?"

"You probably won't like the answers," Renaire warns her.

She obviously disagrees, but Renaire is willing to humor her after such a refreshing time talking about nothing but art for the first time in years, no blood spatter or firearms involved even the slightest bit. She walks him around from painting to painting of his own work and tells him her own interpretation, always fascinated and eager for any input Renaire offers, and usually Renaire doesn't have the heart to tell her what they really are (which is usually just *stupid*).

Sirine walks them all the way into the official R-dedicated gallery room, and Renaire is surprised to see that his friends are all carefully loitering inside, waiting for him. They're suspiciously eager, and Renaire glances around the room to see why they're waiting for his reaction. It's bizarre to see his own work hanging on walls with expert lighting and tiny wall plaques next to them, but watching him deal with that isn't enough for this kind of expectation.

But when he sees it, he groans and hides his face behind his hands.

It's one of the many pissed-at-Emile paintings he's done over the years, but this one is truly atrocious, with Delaurier frolicking through a field of bronze bullet casings and throwing sparkles and French flags and words like *LIBERTY!* and *JUSTICE!* around while he gallivants off into the sparkly pink sunset.

His friends can't stop laughing. Sirine is a good person, but he can tell she's trying to restrain her own laughter as she pats him awkwardly on the shoulder. "I can't tell you how much money I've been offered for that one," she comments.

"I need to go drown myself," Renaire says.

It's obvious that was the highlight of the evening for his friends, since they start leaving fairly soon after that. The gallery was supposed to have already closed by the time Renaire actually begins to leave, and even then Sirine looks like she wants to keep him there longer.

"It's just that I so rarely get artists in that are more interested in the rest of your collection, and your point of view is so valuable and amazing," Sirine says, apologetic but sincerely fascinated with him, which is so wrong in so many ways. Renaire's flask is empty, which is a tragedy and also the only reason he isn't completely falling-down drunk right now, like he wants to be.

But the moment she puts a hand on his shoulder and lets it rest there for two seconds, Delaurier is there. He grabs Renaire's hand and gives Sirine a polite smile and a "Thank you for showing Renaire around," and then is not quite dragging him out of the gallery.

"What the fuck?" Renaire says. It's not quite an objection because he is happy to get away from Sirine, but he's still confused, because what the fuck?

"Not all of us got to take a five-hour nap today," Delaurier says. "You wanted to leave, I wanted to leave, so we have now left."

Renaire has a meeting with an Interpol agent at sunrise.

Renaire nods and accepts it, because yeah, that's fair enough. While they make their way back to the Chéron, the truth of Delaurier's exhaustion gets more and more obvious. He nearly falls asleep with his head against Renaire's shoulder on the metro, outright yawns on the walk back from the station. He's not tired enough to use the elevator in the building, though, or to let go of Renaire's hand. Or possibly he's too tired to remember he's even holding Renaire's hand and that the elevator exists.

When they get into Delaurier's apartment, the man just takes his coat off and kicks off his shoes and collapses onto his bed, still holding Renaire's hand. It leaves Renaire feeling a little like he's holding the leash of a sleeping dog.

"At least undress," Renaire says.

Delaurier sighs but does let go long enough to strip off his shirt and pants and then actually get into bed instead of lying on top of it. And then he gives Renaire an expectant look, so Renaire rolls his eyes and follows suit, turning off the lights and taking a moment to set an alarm because he has a meeting with an Interpol agent at sunrise, before climbing into bed with Delaurier.

The other man automatically curls around him, and Renaire wonders if Delaurier remembers they're not on a train because they're pressed so tightly together that they'd probably fit in one of the miniscule bunks.

"Are you happy?" Emile suddenly asks, lips pressed against the back of Renaire's neck.

Renaire thinks about it and is stunned to realize that the answer is actually yes. Even with whatever threat Interpol poses, Renaire feels whole and confident and happy in a way he can't ever remember feeling before. There's just enough alcohol in him that the world is a warm, smooth place, he's in a soft comfortable bed with Emile pressed against him, and for the first time, he can remember he actually feels like his life isn't completely worthless.

Obviously things are going to go horribly wrong.

But for now he sighs and relaxes into the pillow he shares with Emile and says, "I am."

HE WAS happy in Vienna.

It didn't last.

Even before the swift and stunning shift of all things between them in Moscow, there were soft moments. They were impossibly rare, to the point that Renaire could count them on one hand and still have fingers left. Still, they existed.

They were brief flits of smiles, a gentle word, a simple shred of concern and kindness that wasn't related to murder and mortal peril.

Vienna was a suddenly planned gathering of STB for New Year's Eve that Enjolras had shoved them onto a train for the second an invitation landed in his inbox. Renaire and Delaurier had been in Rome, and Glasson and Carope had been in Paris, and Sarazin, Garrant, and Jules were in Sarajevo, and Renaire has no clue where Lile and Bossard were. Regardless of their location, Carope had decided that yes, they would meet up for New Year's Eve in Vienna, and so it was that everyone would meet up in Vienna for New Year's Eve.

Renaire was excited, at first. Nowhere near as excited as Delaurier, who was practically bouncing in his seat at the idea of seeing all his friends being happy in one place at the same time, but still excited. Of all the holidays in the world, New Year's Eve was the one that actually made *sense*. No presents, no worship, no deeper meaning beyond the end of one year and the beginning of another. It was a farewell and a welcoming, memories and future hopes.

Best of all, it was just a party, no traditions required beyond shouting a few words. You laughed, you drank, you reminisced and bullshitted your goals for the next year, and then you were done. That was it.

New Year's Eve can be one hell of a time, if you do it right.

He trusted Carope to do it right.

Vienna was freezing, with the snow and ice at the stage that caused crust and crunching beneath boots. December was deep winter, when the cold was such an inevitability that people didn't even complain that much.

Well, most people.

Renaire and Delaurier agreed on very few things, but they had a deeply shared understanding that winter is fucking terrible. Ever since the first snowflake dropped in Paris, Delaurier had been picking jobs and focusing on causes that made them suspiciously active in more Mediterranean climates. Delaurier had even been making some offhanded not-quite-casual mentions of going to South America, and in return Renaire had been making very subtle statements like, "being in the southern hemisphere would be amazing because it's really fucking cold here."

Regardless, they had come to this winter wonderland of Carope's with minimal whining on Renaire's part. Delaurier's grumbling was nonexistent, which was astonishing since he can't keep his fucking mouth shut on literally *any* topic you bring up.

For example, Delaurier's insightful commentary on the entire tradition of New Year's Eve parties, which lasted the entire trip from the train station to the address Carope gave them.

"The winter solstice is actually on the twenty-first, but the Gregorian calendar doesn't end and begin on solstice for quite a few reasons, the primary one being that the Gregorian calendar was dedicated to just keeping track of Easter. Solstice was left as a less important event because of it," Delaurier had said.

They were about twenty minutes into Delaurier's calendar-based lecture. Renaire shook his head at the tragic cast-away fate of winter solstice, and said, "At least we still have the party."

"Exactly. It's just moved ten days back," Delaurier agreed, and turned to give Renaire a small smile as they approached Carope's building. It looked like it was probably a hotel. Probably. He hoped it was a hotel. "Pagan holidays were twisted to suit Christianity's needs, and none more than the winter holidays. Christmas in particular has been Christianized, and it's been warped even more by commercialism—"

Renaire was saved from the not unpleasant drone of a lecture when the door burst open and Carope slid out, beaming. "Happy New Year!" she shouted. It was so loud that people five streets away could probably hear it. The more concerning thing was the fact she had on a purple cocktail dress while they hadn't done laundry in a hell of a long time.

It took no time at all for her to fling herself toward Delaurier for an enthusiastic hug that made Delaurier laugh, surprised and happy. The hug didn't last very long, though, since Delaurier released her and said, "Let's get inside before you freeze to death."

"You can't get cold when you look that hot," Renaire said.

Carope laughed. "Delaurier looks plenty cold."

"Delaurier isn't wearing a cocktail dress," Renaire replied, and couldn't help but flick a small smile toward Delaurier while they hoisted their bags through the door.

Inside, they reached a well-kept stairwell and Carope immediately led them to the left, where there was already a door open and waiting for them.

Everyone was there. *Everyone*. It was rare in those days for all of them to gather in one place, and unheard of outside of Paris, but Renaire and Delaurier were welcomed in with excited hugs and pats on the back, and Carope got them separated enough to drag them into one of the bedrooms. It had one bed. Renaire valiantly fought off the urge to groan and hit his head against the wall.

"Before you start whining, there aren't any single beds and I'm trying to fit nine people in here so you'll just have to deal with it,"

Carope said firmly. "I've already had to fit three people in another bed, so you don't have it that bad."

"Those three people get along and don't mind sharing a bed," Renaire said.

Carope frowned. "If it really bothers you—"

"It's *fine*, we can survive, thank you for giving us the most comfortable bed," Delaurier said, not quite glaring at Renaire.

And with that comment, Renaire realized that really was what Carope was doing. The size of the bed made it pretty clear that it would be more suited for Sarazin's group than just him and Delaurier. "Oh," Renaire said, and smiled at Carope. "We've slept on trains three of the past five days and shitty beds the other two, so thanks, I appreciate it."

"You're more than welcome," Carope said, obviously amused by the change in tone, and left after giving Delaurier a twitching kind of grin.

The second she was gone, Delaurier let out a long sigh and dropped their bag at the foot of the bed. "Carope is the most well-intentioned schemer on the planet, Renaire. She wouldn't arrange this on what's supposed to be a holiday if there wasn't a reason behind it," Delaurier said. "We're the last to arrive, so she must have reserved it for us. That means there's something different. She's well intentioned, and *knows* we've been on trains and shitty beds, so she makes sure we get the most comfortable bed."

It was a very valuable lesson.

"So she's Glasson, but for friends," Renaire summarized.

"More or less," Delaurier agreed, amused.

It absently brought to question what Delaurier's domain of expertise was.

The rest of their time in Vienna was spent alternating between ill-advised drinking games, to loud embarrassing stories (apparently Delaurier went through a Mohawk phase and Renaire will not rest until he sees pictures), to quite possibly the worst game of truth or dare ever, since it was more or less a room full of criminals and watching Garrant try to rob the apartment above them by climbing up the side of the building was not a good idea.

Renaire picked dare every single time, excluding the time late into the game when Lile had grinned in a horrible way and the word *kiss* came out of his mouth and fuck no, Renaire switched to truth so fast and loud that half of them flinched and nobody dared to question his choice.

Lile, being a doctor, had immediately asked, "Do you have any diseases or medical conditions?"

Happiness evaporated.

Renaire ignored how tense the room suddenly was, and shook his head. "No, that's too broad of a question—"

"Which is why I asked it that way," Lile said, cheery and immoveable, and Renaire had absolutely no doubt that he'd planned for this. He knew Renaire would switch and wouldn't risk going back to the dare option. He is kind and friendly and evil.

Renaire let out a deep breath, and tried to think back. It wasn't exactly easy, since he'd spent a few years doing his best to pretty much not exist. "I'm pretty sure I have all my vaccinations, I remember getting pretty sick a couple times as a kid but nothing worth reporting, and I'm mostly confident that there's nothing health- or body-related that's important."

"There were an awful lot of qualifying statements in there," Lile said. Renaire had no doubt he'd noticed how there was no mention of mental health, but Lile seemed satisfied enough to let it go.

Renaire shrugged. "It's the best I can give you."

"Someone have the next dare be letting me do a checkup," Lile told the room.

"But it's almost four in the morning," Renaire said. "We should be wrapping this up, shouldn't we? Most people are already in bed. That's what we should be—"

"I'm going to stay here past sunrise if I need to," Delaurier said, sitting three people away and giving Renaire a hard look, which was... surprising.

The problem wasn't that Renaire didn't like doctors, or needles (that was a different problem entirely), it was the idea of *knowing*. He was a person who preferred to operate with as little information as possible, just glide through life without having to be dragged down by knowing he was a mess in mind *and* body.

But, it was Renaire's turn first. Not that it would do any good.

He wasn't sure whether or not he was happy that he landed on Delaurier. He certainly wasn't *surprised*, considering there were four people left playing.

"If I say dare, you're going to tell me to leave it alone," Delaurier said.

"You never know. Maybe I'd just dare you to do a handstand for sixty seconds," Renaire said, just the tiniest bit of a feeble hope peeking out. Maybe Delaurier would take the chance. He *wouldn't*, but Renaire hoped in the way you hope the firing squad in front of you wouldn't have a real bullet.

Delaurier was unimpressed. "Truth," he said.

"I fucking hate you," Renaire told him.

"No you don't," Delaurier replied.

"Why are you doing this?" Renaire asked before his brain could swim through the confused frustration and *panic*, because there was no avoiding this. He shook his head, breathing sharply. "Why are you—?"

"Because I want to make sure you're healthy and there isn't anything to worry about," Delaurier said.

Renaire couldn't even glare anymore. He couldn't breathe. There wasn't a sympathetic eye in the room, in the entire fucking *building*, nobody cared what he wanted or didn't want. "I don't want to," he managed to say, and squeezed his eyes shut, tried to calm down and failed completely. "I don't want to know, don't make me go."

"I don't fucking care, Renaire," Delaurier snapped and so did Renaire, because he sounded *angry*, and Renaire was sitting there on the floor with nothing but staring eyes who *didn't fucking care, Renaire*, and nobody cared, nobody was listening, nobody would help him and he couldn't *breathe*, he grabbed something, he didn't know what was happening, nobody would help and he was all alone and the world became a hurricane of pressure and fear and blurred blindness and there was shouting he couldn't understand because he couldn't breathe he couldn't *think*, couldn't move his hand, couldn't move at all.

He jerked to the side, but there was pressure, and fingers against his temple, and someone shouted his name, and Renaire took a deep breath, choking on it, but he could hear his blood pounding and he could hear *it's okay, stop, listen to me, it's okay* and it's Delaurier, it's *Emile*, it's okay, and Renaire gasped. He was pressed against the wall, and didn't even remember standing. He was against the wall, both Delaurier and Garrant keeping him pinned, Delaurier nearly shouting in his ear. Lile was sprawled on the floor, wheezing.

"Oh fuck," Renaire gasped, and stretched his lungs desperately for air as he stopped fighting.

"Renaire?" Delaurier asked.

"I'm sorry," Renaire said, banging the back of his head against the wall. "I'm sorry, I didn't mean to—"

"We know you didn't mean to, it's okay," Delaurier said gently, and released one of Renaire's arms, but kept a grip on Renaire's wrist, probably to check his still racing pulse. "Are you alright?"

"Is he okay?" Garrant asked from Renaire's other side.

"Is *Lile* okay?" Renaire had asked, and tried to get a good look at Lile, who was sitting up carefully. "What—"

"You tried to choke him," Delaurier said, and nodded at Garrant, who stepped away and headed toward Lile. Delaurier was taking no chances, though, still keeping him the slightest bit restrained. "He'll be hoarse but fine. I asked how *you* are feeling."

Renaire swallowed, throat feeling dry and clogged. It didn't help. "I'm not sure I should give you the honest answer to that."

It was clearly the *right* answer, though, since Delaurier let out a long exhale of relief and stepped away.

"This is something that would count as a medical condition, Renaire," Lile said, but there was no anger in it. It was all gentle humor. Renaire wanted to vomit.

But there was a part that didn't make sense. Frowning, Renaire looked over at Delaurier. "You didn't tell them?"

"Did you want me to?" Delaurier asked, incredulous.

Renaire scowled. "No, but what I want has nothing to do with it. Don't you think this might be important to warn—?"

"And what else should I tell them, Renaire?" Delaurier interrupted, glaring right back. "What other little *quirks* should I be announcing to the public?"

"Like the quirk where I want to punch your fucking—"

"Stop!" Lile shouted, on his feet again. He looked so very disappointed. "*Stop.* I'm not asking for some sort of full disclosure. I don't mean you need to tell me why you have panic attacks. I mean it would be good if you'd tell me you have a panic disorder."

"It's not a panic disorder," Renaire said.

"Yes it is," Delaurier said, because he was, is, and will always be a complete asshole.

Renaire was going to fucking punch him, just ram his fist right into the side of his head, but Delaurier looked completely serious. He wasn't just arguing. He meant it. Delaurier believed he knew better so firmly that he'd reached that unshakeable idol phase.

"Fuck this," Renaire said, and walked away, heading into their assigned bedroom and barely avoiding slamming the door. When he dropped onto the covers, the bed was rock hard, like a concrete slab, and he didn't give a shit.

It took no time at all for Delaurier to follow him in.

"I'm not doing this right now," Renaire said.

"And I'm not here to argue," Delaurier replied. He sounded direct and honest. That could be deceptive. "I'm here to ask if you're okay."

Of all times, of *all times*, it was then. Of the few impossible soft moments, it came then. Renaire was sulking like a fucking teenager, sprawled over a bed with his face planted in the duvet, and Delaurier sat next to him.

Delaurier sat down next to him and said, "I care."

Renaire could've buried himself in those two words and suffocated in absolute bliss. It was completely pathetic, but it got even worse, because Delaurier didn't just sit. He sighed, and stretched out on the bed. He was close to Renaire, but not close enough to touch.

"I really do care," Delaurier had said quietly.

It was very, very dangerous. Renaire grabbed fists full of bedding and tried to control his breathing and told himself over and over again, *that's not what this means.* He'd already had suspicions about this, but confirmation of it felt like cold water trickling down his skin on a painfully burning day.

And then he ruined everything.

Renaire freaked the fuck out and opened his mouth and said, "That's great, but I'm leaving."

Delaurier was very quiet, but eventually said, "What kind of leaving?"

"The type where I'll meet you at the train station for the trip back to Rome," Renaire said, and stood, grabbed his coat as quickly as he could with hands close to shaking.

"Because of this?" Delaurier asked.

"Because I had a fucking panic attack that had me trying to choke Lile to death," Renaire had said. "I'm not staying to see what morning brings."

"Everyone will be—"

"Don't try to be reassuring, you only make things worse when you try," Renaire said, and checked his pockets, checked he'd be okay. Mostly okay. He checked to make sure he'd at least survive. Fuck knew he wouldn't survive the *softness*.

One of the reasons the soft moments never lasted was that Renaire panicked. Renaire couldn't deal with *soft*, not while it was happening. Soft was fucking terrifying. Soft was unknown, soft was... wrong. Soft was to be thought of on rough days when Renaire could use something that wouldn't wound him if he slammed against it.

Renaire was a fool in so many, many ways.

He ran.

He spent his favorite holiday doing everything in his power to forget his yesterday and his tomorrow. New Year's Eve became an isolated day of Renaire trying to pretend his life didn't exist, and *he* didn't exist. He started the new year kissing a woman whose name he didn't know and didn't care to find out and drank himself unconscious, and when he stumbled into the train station he probably looked as shitty as he felt, and Delaurier didn't say a word, just handed over a bag and waited for their train.

Not exactly an auspicious start to 2013.

Renaire lets himself believe this time will be different. He'll swing in the new year with a smile and *Emile* and end New Year's Eve with a kind of lightness that could lift you into happiness.

Happy is rare. Renaire can only grab at the pieces that flit past him, and hope, *hope* that there will be more.

THE ALARM goes off at barely five in the morning, and this whole "sleeping with Emile" thing is much more difficult than Renaire had thought because the man makes a disgruntled noise and his hold on Renaire tightens even more than before.

"Let me turn the alarm off," he says, and it takes a good thirty seconds for Delaurier to understand the logic of turning the alarm off means the noise goes away, let alone human speech, and finally release him. It's not like Renaire actually wants to go, but he definitely needs to. Delaurier can barely raise his head off the pillow, let alone ask Renaire where he's going, so he politely leaves a note for when Delaurier is capable of rational thought.

Dawn meeting with Interpol, calm down, Mathieu knows if I'm ok is probably not something that he'll be happy to see when he wakes up, but Renaire doesn't have time to write anything gentle.

Paris is as close to silent as it ever gets at this time of day, with the gray light of near morning making everything seem both cold and soft. The metro's running, and Renaire doesn't hesitate to hop on. Even at five thirty in the morning, it's stiflingly hot on the train, but the streets themselves are crisp and dim.

The Arènes de Lutèce appears to be nothing more than a vegetation-covered hill upon approach, and Renaire can already see the sky turning a pale fuchsia. He yawns his way up the tight path and doesn't light a cigarette no matter how badly he needs to calm down. He brought his flask (refilled—one of the essential stops before leaving the apartment this morning) but that he definitely isn't touching. By the time he reaches the top of the slope and is looking down into the ancient Roman amphitheater, the sun is rising, and he's casting a long, deep shadow across the terraces.

Celine is already waiting for him, which he knows because there's a blonde woman seated at the very front row wearing a truly ridiculous bonnet, along with her fashion-forward light gray suit. Renaire wishes he didn't find it so endearing. She smiles at him and waves like he's an old friend instead of someone affiliated with the group she's trying to take down.

Renaire can't help but grin and waves back before heading down the stone steps. By the time he reaches her, she's pulled two cups of coffee out of a tray she had resting on the ground and arrayed packets of cream and sugar and cocoa next to his cup.

"At least you don't know how I take my coffee," Renaire says, and Celine cheerily shakes his hand. "Has anyone told you you're terrifyingly happy in the morning?"

"My entire department," Celine confesses. "It's wonderful to meet you. Are you armed?"

"Of course I am," Renaire says, and sits down to fix his coffee—cream and cocoa, since she's offered it. She follows his example soon after, although apparently she takes her coffee black. There's no hesitation, so Renaire doesn't think she's laced the coffee with anything. Unless it's an iocane powder situation, which is really fucking unlikely. "So what information brings me out here at this ungodly hour?"

Celine takes a sip of her coffee, which looks very strange when she's wearing a two-foot-tall bonnet. "We've concluded that you aren't fully aware of STB's threat," she says and pulls a file folder out from a plastic bag that probably also has a weapon or three in it. She also pulls out a couple of croissants. She is *good*. Renaire can't help but respect the hell out of her. "Although it was tough to conclude—I have to say, you're definitely the most confusing factor in all of STB."

"Flattery will get you everywhere," Renaire says and tries the croissant. Definitely not the best he's ever had, but not bad. Probably local. "Flattery, coffee, and croissants. You're either asking for one hell of a favor, or about to give me some *very* bad news."

"Both," Celine admits with a smile. "I'll try to be gentle with the bad news at least. The point is, we think you aren't involved in the planning portions of STB. All we've been able to see is that you're more or less a human shadow for Delaurier. We didn't even know your name before receiving Ivanova's information."

"And now you think you know everything about me," Renaire says.

Celine shakes her head. "Not everything. But we do have your military record," she says.

"I can walk out right now," Renaire warns her.

She puts her hands up, placating. "And I won't try to stop you. But that's what brought us to the conclusion that you don't know about their threat."

Renaire realizes that this *threat* she's talking about is a very *singular* kind of thing. He doesn't like the sinking feeling that is already threatening to drown him.

"The only thing we're hoping you can do is talk some sense into them," Celine says carefully. "Their threat is wildly out of character for STB's usual methods."

Delaurier had been acting very, very strange even before they went to Russia.

"It may come as a surprise to you, but—"

"Everyone knows I'm the only one who can convince Emile to reconsider," Renaire says, feeling numb. His hands are already shaking. It's barely six in the morning and his body is already betraying him.

If whatever this is has gotten to the point of a formal threat, Glasson (the only other person who can really make Delaurier reconsider) is already in agreement. And where Delaurier and Glasson go, Carope almost always goes, and when all three of them are combined, STB is unanimously decided. Excluding Renaire. Because Renaire is the one who plays devil's advocate from the corner and only cares about making holes in people's arguments instead of weaving his own, Renaire is the one who kills the man about to kill Delaurier but never for any other reason, Renaire is the one who paints and drinks instead of playing politics. Renaire is the drunken fool in the back of the room.

Delaurier plans. Renaire follows.

"It's not your fault you're in love," Celine says, quiet and painfully kind. "But what you do about it is."

Renaire sighs and drinks his fucking coffee, which doesn't have any alcohol in it. Not yet, at least. "You need to have the hardest, most irrefutable proof you have ever had in your *life* on whatever atrocity he's committed for me to actually believe it," Renaire says honestly. If there is one millimeter of wiggle room, his heart will make him take it.

Celine nods, still unerringly friendly, and pulls the file folder onto her lap. She doesn't show the contents to him, though. Instead she waits and says, "The reason they sent me isn't just because I'm friendly. It's because of my parents. So believe me when I say that I understand better than most what you're dealing with."

"Well, that's very reassuring, Celine, thank you for letting me know your father was in love with a terrorist," Renaire says with a roll of his eyes, and lights a cigarette. It doesn't help. "Okay. What's he done?"

"It's just a threat at this point," Celine says. "And we know you aren't involved, there's no doubt that you aren't involved. If you walked away right now, the only thing we'd even think of charging you with is murder as an act of defense, and I know Interpol wouldn't be interested in pursuing that if you left STB."

"Fuck, what is he doing, poisoning children's hospitals?" Renaire demands.

Celine hesitates but finally hands over the file folder with a simple, "He's threatening to bomb seven major government facilities around the world, starting here in Paris."

Renaire scoffs. "No he's not."

"I'm sorry," Celine says so seriously and heartfelt that even the bonnet doesn't dull the pain that comes with hearing those words.

He doesn't want to look, he doesn't, he *doesn't*, but Renaire looks at the folder, and shit, either Celine is an excellent forger or Renaire has to admit she isn't lying. The explosives are the same kind STB has used on the other very rare occasions they've blown something up, but so, so much bigger. *So* much bigger. There's no way the damage would stop at whatever specific area the bomb was put in—it'd take out the whole fucking building and probably the block around it. Collateral damage would be catastrophic, and the transcription of STB's threat is tone perfect for Delaurier.

"I need to hear it," Renaire states. When Celine frowns, obviously not sure what the fuck Renaire is saying, he rips the transcription out of the folder and barely restrains himself from throwing it into her face. "I need to *hear it*. I need to hear if it's really him, if he really made this threat—"

Celine shakes her head. "I don't have it, but—"

"Then it might not be Emile," Renaire says. "It could be some imposter. We've had some of those. God knows he has enough psychotic fans to do shit like this—"

"You know it's true, Renaire," Celine says gently.

"I care about one thing in the whole fucking world, do *not* take him from me," Renaire shouts, demanding, *begging*. He has to stand up, has to toss the folder to the ground and lean against the railing that separates the arena from the spectators. He can't fucking breathe; he sees trails of blood-soaked tires and feet and young faces that didn't even have time to be surprised, and he can feel Emile curled around him in bed and humming into the back of his neck, and fuck, *fuck*, he is going to be sick, he is going to vomit and pass out.

Celine is rubbing a hand up and down his back, careful, and Renaire jerks away, stumbles a few feet away before hitting the stone bench and slumping onto it, head in his hands.

The one thing Renaire could never, ever stand idly by and not give a fuck about is putting a child's life in danger. He has problems even with Chason being involved in STB, and he's never truly been a child, not really. It wasn't until Chason sassed and argued Renaire into the floor like only a world-weary optimist can that he admitted the kid was an adult stuck in a still growing body more than anything else.

Delaurier would not choose a quiet night at the office. He would choose the middle of the day, probably somewhere around eleven o'clock on a Tuesday, with as many people as possible in the area. He would make it loud and painful and so absolute that nobody could ever doubt what happened, why it happened, and who did it.

Renaire should have never gotten out of bed this morning. Or even answered the phone on the train. Or woken up in Tripoli, or killed a man in a Paris apartment, or gone on a fucking walk in the park, or, fuck, he should never have been born in the first place.

He sits up and pulls his flask out, and his watch helpfully informs him that it's 6:22 a.m. and he doesn't even hesitate. He drinks, drinks until it's empty and he can barely breathe, and fuck, it's his smaller flask, he should've pulled the bigger one out of their bag.

Renaire's phone buzzes, and it's a text from Mathieu, simply saying, *U OK?*

I'm fine, he lies back. Liquor stores don't open for another few hours.

"You can still change his mind," Celine says earnestly. She hasn't moved toward him because she's smart. "You can stop it."

Renaire sighs. "I can try," he says. "And I will try. But I seriously doubt they'll care what I have to say." If their plan is already this detailed and the threat has already been made, it's practically set in stone. He scrubs a hand down his face, trying to get some sort of clarity back in the world. He's painfully sober, the alcohol hasn't had nearly enough time to make the world a little bit easier to deal with, so this is the best he can do. He takes a deep breath and repeats, "I will try."

Celine gathers her things, leaving Renaire's coffee on the stone but putting the rest of the goodies in her bag. She doesn't even offer to let him keep the folder and its contents, but she does put a business card on top of the cup's lid. "I know I'm technically the enemy, but I really do want to help you. If you need anything, even just a place to sleep, call me. I won't even ask any questions."

"I have no idea how someone like you found her way into Interpol," Renaire says, because he *likes her*, genuinely likes her, and it's a way to try and concentrate on something other than the nausea and disgust and soul-deep pain, and fuck, what is he going to do?

She smiles at him. She's never stopped smiling at him, really. "One of my fathers is very dedicated to justice. I guess it's an inherited trait," she says. Celine hesitates, but in the end she leaves with a painfully honest, "I'm sorry for your loss, Renaire. You're a good man."

He hesitates, but he nods and says, "Thank you for telling me."

Renaire can imagine what kind of fucked-up mess everything would be if this had happened and Renaire hadn't known it was coming. He would've mindlessly followed Delaurier along to plant bombs and murder people and any doubts would've been swept away with alcohol and Emile's very existence, thinking *he would never do that*. Nobody can believe a lie quite like a fool who is in love. This is better. This way he might not end up shaking apart and then shooting himself in the head.

Celine doesn't reply. She just walks up the stone tiers and leaves, pulling her bonnet off in the process and putting it in her bag. Renaire watches her go and really wishes he hated her. It would be so much easier.

Renaire stretches himself out on the stone, staring at the monstrous shadows cast by even the smallest figure at this time of day. The bright pink quickly fades into blue, and he waits for the alcohol to soak into his blood.

CHAPTER 6

Paris: Arènes de Lutèce—Chéron—{Cote d'Ivoire}—*Hôpital*

HE LOSES himself in the streets of Paris as deeply as possible. It's easier here, the alleys are narrower and the buildings are more cramped and the slope is steeper. Renaire knows Paris, knows Paris like only a drifting waste of humanity can. He knows most of the good bars and all the bad bars and where to go for what, but that means he knows that at—*shit*, at eight in the morning, Renaire is stuck with his own company and his empty flask because he has acquaintances around here (he has acquaintances everywhere) but none who would be willing to help him drown himself as literally as possible in alcohol.

Which is another thing he can blame on Delaurier and his disgusting attempts at *you could be so much more*ing at Renaire. Fuck, he is so in love with that cruel, cold son of a bitch that he wants to scream but can't find the air to do it.

Renaire doesn't know where he is beyond that it's a park and he's sprawled on a bench, wishing he was about a million times drunker than he's been able to manage and his phone keeps ringing. The moment it sang out *I can't see me*, Renaire had turned it off and barely restrained himself from tossing it into the nearest body of water. He hasn't checked his phone since.

He has few escapes in life, even if he uses them as hard and thoroughly as possible. Drinking is out. The idea of sex right now is enough to bring back the urge to vomit, and Renaire refuses to think about why that is. He could probably find drugs, but he's been (mostly) clean for two years, and it's so, so tempting, but he knows if he goes down that path right now he'll never get back out, and he has shit to do. He can't do anything permanent. He has to escape for a while, is all. He just needs to breathe and not *think*.

Art it is, then.

Actual materials are nonexistent—he didn't exactly leave thinking *hey, maybe I'll paint something during my meeting with an*

Interpol agent. He has knives and a metal bench, which could be interesting but would dull the knives. There are trees, and that seems like a better idea. Sculpture isn't exactly his thing and neither are reliefs, but these are desperate times. There's only a few people in the park, and Renaire's pretty much as in the middle of nowhere as he can manage, and the world is just a little bit blurry, and Renaire pulls out his least favorite knife (four inch needle-point steel, really only good for precision stabbing, which, to be frank, *he doesn't do very often*) and starts carving.

He means for it to just be a pattern. It starts that way, but it all spirals out of one quickly darkening point where there used to be another branch. Lines and ovals trail away from it, but somehow the lines turn into the curve of Emile's neck when he's leaning his head against a wall or, occasionally, Renaire's shoulder, and the ovals morph into curls barely brushing his neck.

The lines are tire tracks. The ovals are feet.

Renaire feels like absolute shit for mutilating a tree. He carves a quick *R* in the remains of the missing tree branch as sarcastically as possible and turns away. There's an old woman watching him silently.

"In case the police showed up," she says when Renaire raises an eyebrow at her and points at what is easily interpreted as Delaurier in the tree. "Who's the girl?"

Renaire laughs. It's not a pretty sound. "Hypothetically, if your boyfriend was going to bomb the capitals of seven countries around the world, what would you do?"

The woman considers the question. "Which countries?"

He didn't really expect a better answer, doesn't even know why he tried. "Thank you for keeping watch," Renaire says, and walks out of the park on feet that are far steadier than he'd like.

It's ten o'clock in the morning, now. He can probably find an open liquor store, or someone that he can charm into serving him alcohol.

Instead, he finds Chason at the arch in and out of the park. This isn't as surprising as it should be—if anyone could find him, it's Chason, and if Renaire was angry and they wanted to keep casualties to a minimum, they'd send Chason. Renaire punched Delaurier once, and he's still not sure which one of them was more surprised. Chason, he can't even imagine hurting.

"Your phone's off. Delaurier is panicking," he says, obviously finding it hilarious.

"Chason," Renaire says, lighting another cigarette—he needs to buy more soon, "I am having a *very* bad day, and I really don't give a fuck what Delaurier is doing right now."

Chason's eyes light up like he's won the fucking lottery. "Do you want to put blue hair dye in his shampoo?"

He is an adult in a kid's body with the sense of humor of a five-year-old.

Renaire approves.

"Itching powder might be better," Renaire says, heading out of the park with Chason at his side. "Make him pull his own pretty hair out." Which Delaurier would do in the shower. He shakes his head, like that can somehow wipe memories from his mind. Renaire hates how impossible it is for him to forget things. "You were sent to fetch me?"

"I'm supposed to make sure you don't drink yourself to death," Chason says, which means Delaurier sent him, because Delaurier knows that is a thing that could in fact happen. "I think he wants me to bring you home, but I won't unless you feel like going. Delaurier isn't in charge of me."

"You are my favorite," Renaire says, and Chason grins at him. "I don't need a babysitter. You can get going if you want."

"Sure. Just turn your phone back on," Chason says.

Renaire narrows his eyes. "You are no longer my favorite."

Chason shrugs, and, per usual, Renaire doesn't even know the kid picked his pocket until he has Renaire's phone in his hand, turned back on. It immediately starts pinging away about missed calls and texts. Christ, he can't even look at Delaurier's *name* without it hurting.

"I don't know exactly what's going on, but whatever he did, he's sorry," Chason says. He's grown up surrounded by ruthless militant extremists who debate politics constantly, and it's turned him into a cunningly persuasive criminal. At this point he probably doesn't even realize he's trying to convince Renaire to go back.

"Give me some time and another three bottles of wine, and then I'll head back," Renaire says. Chason doesn't look impressed. Or like he believes a word Renaire says. The kid is probably the smartest of them all, really. Renaire sighs. "Fine. What is it going to take for you to leave me alone?"

"I'll leave you alone when you've gone back to the Chéron," Chason says.

"What happened to Delaurier not telling you what to do?" Renaire demands.

Chason shrugs again, unimpressed. "I take suggestions. Come on. Let's go home before he tears his hair out without our help."

"I don't like when you're more mature than me," Renaire says, but he follows Chason home.

Honestly, he's been following Chason for a while—the kid is very good at guiding someone where he wants them, particularly when they're already lost. Even following Chason, he's still not quite sure how he got here. Renaire knows most of Paris. Chason knows all of it.

Sometimes Renaire wonders if Chason's lost parents were actually Paris itself. He grew up as an orphan and never stuck around with any family, no matter who or what they were. Paris raised Chason, even if it didn't give birth to him, and now he knows every street and every person who walks on them.

It takes two transfers to get back to the Chéron, and everything comes swirling back the minute the building is in sight. Renaire freezes in the middle of the sidewalk so suddenly that Chason runs into him.

"Who is in there?" Renaire asks quietly.

Chason shrugs. "Not sure. Delaurier is definitely there, and so's Glasson. Pretty sure I saw Lile and Jules too, so Carope and Bossard might be in. Sarazin's working her day job, and who ever knows where Garrant is before noon?"

"Fair enough," Renaire says and sighs, glancing down at Chason and hoping he looks serious enough that he'll actually pay attention. "This isn't just some angry disagreement kind of fight between me and Delaurier. It's going to get very ugly, very fast." It's going to be ugly, and cold, and cruel, and potentially irreparable.

Chason nods, and because he's the smartest of them all, he says, "Give me two minutes to evacuate."

Renaire does, and within moments customers are carefully leaving the Café Chéron, Jules and Garrant emerging with them. The two stop in front of where Renaire stands and waits and watches the time on his watch tick down.

"We're going to be the impartial ruling if things really get that bad," Jules says, amused, but it fades into concern very quickly. "Oh, *Renaire*. What did he—"

"I'm going in," Renaire says because the two minutes are up. He passes Bossard on his way in too, and he looks like he means to intercept Renaire, maybe try to calm him down, but he takes one look at Renaire's face and doesn't try to do a damn thing. Chason is on the stairs, but, smartest of them all forever and ever, he gets out while he can. Or stays out of STB's unofficially private room, at least.

Delaurier is waiting for him at the top of the stairs again, looking tense and nervous, *again*. Fuck, he hates this, he hates this so much, hates how just the sight of Emile patches up some unnoticed hole in his heart. Except now the patch is acid, and he's going to be physically ill. Last time this felt like a horror movie, walking up to face something terrifying. This time it feels like he's headed to an execution where they have to flip a coin to see who kills the other.

"Are you alright?" Delaurier asks the moment Renaire is off the stairs. He stands close to Renaire, attentive and concerned, hovering just above touching his shoulders. "You should have told me about the meeting, I would have come and—"

"Stop talking," Renaire commands in a cold, authoritative voice he didn't even know he had. Delaurier is just as stunned as Renaire, stopping midsentence and carefully stepping out of Renaire's personal space. Renaire takes the opportunity to shake one of his final cigarettes (two left after this) out of the pack and light it and look around the room. The only remaining characters are Delaurier, Glasson, and Carope—the holy trinity of STB.

"What did I do?" Delaurier asks bluntly, looking more frustrated than worried now. He still thinks this is one of his *communication issues*, and Renaire wishes he was right. Slapping a hand over Delaurier's mouth sure as fuck sounds appealing.

Renaire sighs, leaning against the wall and looking at Carope and Glasson instead. Carope is frowning, confusion and worry and more than a little apprehension in her eyes. When alert, Glasson is a creature of caution and calculation, of waiting before making a precision strike on his target if it's needed, and it shows in the way he watches Renaire smoke.

"I didn't want to believe it," Renaire says simply. "But really, it's STB all over, isn't it? Just one more tier of escalation. When protests didn't work, you moved to sabotage. When that didn't work, you started assassinating people. Bombings are just the next step, and you never really do things by halves, do you?"

The bastards don't even try to deny it. Renaire doesn't look at Delaurier because he *can't* look at Delaurier. Fuck, Renaire should have stopped to refill his flask before coming here.

Carope is the one who speaks, which is surprising. "If we want to really help The Cause—"

"Don't start with that shit, we're not talking *ideals* with this, this is *blowing up innocent bystanders*," Renaire snaps, and he's up and pacing now. "Fuck, do you even understand what you'd be doing? This, right now, what you do with your psychotic well-intentioned murdering, it makes *sense*, for people like you. It's unbelievably fucked-up, but I understand. But *this*? No."

"Sometimes, sacrifices—" Glasson starts, and Renaire doesn't even realize he's moved until there's a knife shuddering in the wall next to Glasson's head. It's far enough away that they know he intentionally missed. It's also close enough to know he *intentionally* missed. For once, Renaire wholeheartedly agrees with what his body decided to do without his input.

"Don't you fucking dare try that one," Renaire says coldly. "This isn't *sacrifices*—it's *slaughter*. It's completely disregarding human life for the sake of your Cause."

And oh, they're actually taking him seriously now, possibly for the very first time. Isn't that refreshing? They're still, and *listening*, like Renaire's respectably dangerous.

"What are you even fighting for anymore?" Renaire shouts, and now he does look at Delaurier. He can't even try to figure out what is going on in his beautiful marble-cold brain right now. "You all claim to be fighting for *The Cause* and for *the people* to have all these pretty ideals of yours, but you're going to blow up the people you're supposedly fighting for? And what makes you think they even want them?"

"How much have you had to drink?" Delaurier asks.

Renaire shakes his head so violently the world spins, clenching his teeth. "You can't derail me, not this time, we *are* having this conversation, and if you don't feel up for it then *too fucking bad*."

Delaurier has already gone to that cold, still place in his head, Renaire can tell. Carope is staring at Renaire as if he's gone crazy, and

Glasson's observation has become much more precise. Renaire takes a long drag of his cigarette, and it doesn't help.

"Do *not* do this," Renaire says. It's torn between commanding and begging, and it does nothing but make Renaire sound tired and desperate, which is true. He just wants to curl up against the wall and have dreamed up this entire disgusting, fucked-up affair of STB's. Instead he stands as firmly as he can, and smokes, and breathes, and smokes.

"It's already in place," Glasson says simply, sitting carefully on the edge of a table, still watching Renaire like he's going to start shooting up the place. Which he kind of has a point about, really, what with throwing a fucking knife at Glasson's head.

"Then call it off," Renaire says, and fuck, his cigarette is already nothing but ash.

"No," Delaurier says.

It's the cool, collected tone that so many people take for distance or disinterest, but in reality means he's a finger's width away from exploding and is trying very, very hard to contain himself.

When Renaire turns to glare at him, Delaurier glares right back. "If we really want change, we have to do something big, and this is it. This is our chance to finally make a real, definite, *absolute* difference in the world."

"You are not this stupid," Renaire says because he can't say Delaurier isn't this cruel, or isn't this ruthlessly dedicated, or isn't this destructive. Stupid is the best he can do. Stupid and *heartless*, but even now, Renaire can't bring himself to throw that one in Emile's face.

Delaurier steps closer, staring at him. "This is what they told you to do," he says as if it's some sort of terrifying epiphany.

"This isn't about Interpol—" Renaire begins, but Delaurier isn't paying attention. He's moving closer, frowning and watching Renaire's face intently.

"Whatever they told you, are you sure it was true?" Delaurier asks.

Renaire shakes his head, says, "Don't do this, *don't—*"

"You *know* they're not fully informed, I don't care how much information she may have tossed at you, you're too smart to just take that at face value," Emile says.

"That's not the fucking point!" Renaire shouts at him, but Emile doesn't back off. He looks like he's on a life-or-death quest, like he's driving headfirst into a suicide mission. Renaire's heart automatically reacts, instantly wants to *help him* with whatever is making him feel like he needs this much willpower.

Except that thing is Renaire.

"With this one act, we can change the world," Delaurier says, and his hands are on Renaire's shoulders as if he can somehow transmit that fervor into Renaire through physical contact. "This is our *chance*, Renaire, don't you see?"

"You think blowing up seven major government buildings full of civilians and hundreds of innocent bystanders in collateral damage is the right thing to do?" Renaire asks, dumbfounded.

Delaurier shakes his head. "I wish there was some way to do it without hurting innocents, you *know* I do, but there's no way to—"

Renaire can't take one more word, can't even imagine what Delaurier is going to say, fuck, doesn't *want* to. He presses a hand tight against Delaurier's mouth because there is no other way to make him shut up, and he can feel Emile's soft lips dragging against his palm, and Renaire has to step away. His back hits the wall. Delaurier doesn't pursue.

He swallows and drops his hand. Delaurier is just confused now. Nothing but *confused*. It's horrific.

"Glasson," Renaire says, even if he can't look away from Delaurier. The world could be falling apart, and he couldn't look away from Delaurier. "You said you read my file."

"I did," Glasson says.

He takes a deep breath, watching Delaurier's eyes as he realizes this isn't just some sort of hypothetical moral objection on Renaire's part and asks, "What exactly does it say about Cote d'Ivoire?"

Glasson is a good man. He hesitates, because Renaire doesn't like to admit he even existed before he and Delaurier met and rarely brings anything up that happened over three months ago, even with his friends. Renaire can't run from his past, but he sure as fuck tries to ignore it. But Glasson is a good man, so he finally says, "You were dishonorably discharged for killing—"

"Executing," Renaire corrects.

"For executing two rebel soldiers, and then going missing in action for five days," Glasson says carefully. "You were dishonorably discharged instead of sent to jail, which most likely means they thought what you did was justified in a time of war, but not honorable." He clears his throat. "I'm guessing there was collateral damage in an attack the two soldiers were involved in."

"Astute," Renaire says, jaw clenched. The anger is back now, just at the memory, but he pushes it aside and moves away from Delaurier and lights another cigarette, and he only has one more. His hands are shaking again. Or still shaking might be more accurate. Either way it takes him three tries to light it. "I'm not." He takes a deep breath, squeezes his eyes shut. "I *can't* tell that story. But that was a *complete accident* that killed four kids, and they were just—"

Fuck, he can't even say it. Nobody else tries to speak, and Renaire is so grateful it hurts. When his lungs are full of smoke instead of fire, he tries again.

"I say execute because they just *waited* for it," Renaire says simply. "They were already dead inside, after that, and I was only a step behind. And if you think this plan is going to bring some sort of utopia, or *any* kind of victory, you're even more of a fool than I am for thinking this isn't how you'd all go in the end."

Carope understands it, he can tell, because Carope looks about ready to vomit, and about ten seconds after that she actually leaves the room, since she understands that the damage they're planning is a hundred times worse. Glasson is upset, and shaken, but he still watches above all else.

But Delaurier is back in that ice-cold defensive walled palace of his, because *he* had already understood this. Delaurier is willing to sacrifice his life and soul for his fucking Cause, and he would hate himself for it, but by now Renaire is pretty sure he already thinks he's irredeemable after killing those he views as corrupt and poisonous to the world for two years.

And oh, looking at that expression and letting his painfully close-to-sober mind run on its own, he starts to put pieces together. Ivanova researched STB because she heard about the threat, and when Delaurier wouldn't back down, she planned to try and stop them, and Delaurier had made his final decision on this the moment he killed the reporter in her bed.

And *fuck*, it all just spirals out from there, doesn't it? Delaurier fucks Renaire because he's read the file and he knows he isn't going to really be *Renaire* once he finds this out, so it's now or never, and

Christ, he doesn't want to think about what else might have been inside Delaurier's mind about this. Fuck, the control issues, the *you could be so much more*, the reckless headfirst dive from zero physical contact into trying to have a *permanent relationship*—

"Renaire," Delaurier says, and fuck when did he get there, when did he get this close? Renaire is sitting in one of the chairs and Emile is kneeling in front of him, tracking Renaire's shaking breath and looking something dangerously close to panicking. Renaire has one cigarette left. Emile is holding his hand tight and warm and inescapable. "Renaire, listen to me—"

"You weren't even going to tell me," Renaire says, numb. "You were just going to let me follow along until it was too late and just hope you could get the gun out of my hands—"

"No, I wasn't," Delaurier says urgently, "I wasn't. I would never make you be a part of this, Renaire. I wouldn't make you break your 'no kids' rule. I know there was a reason for that, something that you lived through, or did, or saw. I didn't *know*, but I knew there was *something*. I would have never involved you. We weren't even going to be here."

Renaire laughs, and it is a terrifying noise, and he wishes he could cut it off. "Oh, and where would we be?"

"Headed to Australia," Delaurier says.

It probably would have worked; it's a long flight, and Renaire would have been doing nothing but panicking about Delaurier for the duration. "A day-long flight wouldn't keep me from—"

"By ship. It's a mobile command center," Delaurier says. And fuck, he could've kept Renaire ignorant for anywhere from a month to two months, depending on the ship and ports, and *fuck*, why is Delaurier so smart? He had this planned perfectly. And worst of all is that Renaire would've thought it was nothing but a fucking honeymoon and Delaurier's usual amount of research and plotting and he would have been so happy that he'd believe *anything* to stay that way and Christ, he can tell it would've worked. Delaurier recognizes the instant of Renaire's realization, because his eyes shine, and he pulls Renaire forward with a hand cupping the back of his neck, fingers already familiar with the curve of his skull. "It leaves in two days, we could still—"

"You don't get to touch me," Renaire says.

It hits Delaurier harder than any slap or punch ever could. His grip immediately loosens on Renaire's neck and hand, but it only leaves him obeying the letter of the law—he hovers over Renaire as if Renaire is about to change his mind and Delaurier just has to wait him out.

"Delaurier," Glasson says simply, nothing beyond that, and Delaurier finally moves back.

Renaire takes the window of opportunity and stands without another word, headed for the stairs.

"Thank you," Glasson says, and Renaire glances back to see the frail attempt at a smile on his lips. He's seen sense. Two out of three means it isn't happening. Somehow that doesn't make Renaire feel the slightest bit better now. "If there's anything you need—"

"Get Carope a towel," Renaire says, and nods awkwardly before finally walking down the stairs, and he will not look behind him.

Delaurier calls his name, and he doesn't look back, he just speeds up and shoves his hands in his pockets and tightens his shoulders, and he isn't going to look back. Delaurier is on the stairs behind him, and he calls Renaire's name, and Renaire isn't stopping. He is getting out that door, and he is going to... *fuck*, who is he kidding? He doesn't know what he's going to do, but the only thing that matters is that he won't be here, won't be in physical pain every time he looks at Delaurier.

He wants to get on his knees and fucking *beg* for Emile to at least lie to him and say he doesn't really think it's a good idea, but somehow he has developed just enough self-worth to not become the addict clinging to his dealer's shit-covered boots.

Renaire has made it all the way to the door when Delaurier grabs his shoulder, voice desperate when he says *Renaire, please* one more time, and Renaire doesn't hesitate. He turns and grabs Delaurier by the throat and slams him hard into the Café Chéron's wide-open oak door and pulls out a knife and thinks about holding it to Emile's throat—thinks about it *very seriously*—but instead he ends up raising the knife and stabbing it into the space next to Delaurier's head so hard that the blade is driven in to the hilt, and the razor-sharp point is sticking out the other side. It's shaved off some of Emile's hair, and Renaire wants to curl his fingers around the lost golden locks, but instead he *squeezes*, and Delaurier is staring at him like he's never seen him before in his life.

"I may be so in love with you that it rips me apart *hourly*, but now I can't even *look* at you without feeling sick," Renaire says, and releases his hold on Emile's throat. "You fucked up. If you touch me again, you will bleed."

It's his favorite knife. He leaves it in the door and walks out without looking at Delaurier again.

The rest of STB is standing just outside the door, all witnesses to the threat, and every single one of them is staring at him, voiceless.

Renaire has one cigarette left. He lights it, and doesn't look behind him as he walks past his friends and into sunny, indifferent Paris with absolutely nothing left to believe in.

"THIS IS Agent Normandeau, how can I help you?" Celine says when she picks up.

Renaire wasn't sure pay phones existed anymore, but he found one, somehow, and he's kind of slumped in a phone booth, even though he wasn't sure Paris had those either. He can't really remember seeing one before now, and he's sort of not sure he's actually seeing one now, but he's kind of having trouble remembering anything at all, so, oh well.

"Hello?" Celine asks.

"Oh," Renaire says, which takes some work, the people walking past should be very impressed. "Hello."

When he doesn't say anything else, Celine hazards a, "Renaire?"

Renaire frowns at, well, nothing. "What do you want?"

"You called me," Celine says carefully, and oh, yeah, he did. "Are you okay? Where are you?"

"I found a phone booth," Renaire says because he is very proud. "I'm on the phone, inside of it. With you. *On the phone* with you, not in the booth with you. You're not in here."

"Renaire, what did you take?" she asks and sounds kind of worried. Which is weird, since… yeah.

Renaire frowns, but he'll figure this out. Maybe. Probably not, because he is bad at just about everything under the sun, which is still out, wow, weird, but he ends up shaking his head. "I can't remember." He sighs. "Why did I call you?"

"Do you have my card?" Celine asks.

Renaire shakes his head, but then he remembers she can't see him, right, so he says, "No. I shook my head no. You couldn't see it."

"Then how are you calling me?" Celine asks.

Renaire shrugs, but she can't see him shrug, so he says, "I just shrugged. And I sometimes can't forget some stuff sometimes. But I can't remember a lot of—" He stops because his brain is trying to tell him something, and he is listening to his brain and, "Ohhh, that's right. Something about Emile." He sighs, leaning against the glass. "He's really great."

"Okay, Renaire, I need you to look around, tell me if you can see any street signs," she says.

"Nope," Renaire says.

"No you won't look or no you can't see any?" Celine asks.

"This one time we went to the beach," Renaire says. "Not for swimming, for a job, pretty sure we drowned someone, but Emile was—he's sure pretty. And smart. He's really great." He frowns. "I think I stabbed him?"

"Don't worry, I'm sure you didn't stab him," Celine says, and she's very soothing, it's nice. He likes her. "Keep talking. Tell me about the beach."

Renaire sits on the floor of the phone booth, which is kind of dirty but whatever. "The beach," he echoes and tries to think. "Ohhh, the beach, that's right. Mmm, the beach."

Humming noises. "You know, when he's really happy, he makes this noise. I love the noise," Renaire says. "It's like. It's like he's breathing happy bees."

"Happy bees," Celine says, and he can tell she is trying not to laugh, which, yes, it is funny.

"You know, I really like you," Renaire says. "But not like *like* like, like, *liking* like, you know?"

"I'm just going to say yes," Celine says. "And I like you too. Will you do me a favor and check your pockets?"

Renaire tries to, but he can't. "Wow, I can't feel my hands, how am I holding the phone," he says, but then looks around and nods because he gets it, it's propped on his shoulder because it's one of those old big phones. Because it's a pay phone. In a phone booth. "Oh, I'm nodding again, by the way."

"Okay, I'm going to send someone to get you, there's going to be a police officer—"

"I don't want to get arrested," Renaire complains. "Bad things happen."

"They're not arresting you, I promise," Celine says soothingly. "They're. Okay, they're a taxi service. They're going to come get you and bring you here so I can take care of you."

"I want Emile," Renaire says, but then he feels kind of bad about it, so he says, "I mean, you're nice, I like you, but you're not him. Nobody's him except him. He's great." He thinks for a moment. "Why did I call you?"

"They're going to be there soon, Renaire," Celine says. "And I'm going to meet you either at the hospital or my house, okay? I'll be there right after you."

"Why did I call you?" Renaire says, and pats himself down with numb hands—it takes a whole lot of work. There's stuff in his pockets, some bottles and pills and stuff but—"I don't have my phone. I'm on a pay phone because I don't have my phone. Why don't I have my phone?"

"Calm down, Renaire," Celine says, words a lot faster than usual.

"Something happened," Renaire says, and when he says it, he knows it's true, but he doesn't know *what it was*, but it was something and it was awful. It was so awful and painful, and he says, "No no no no no, I don't want that, *no*," and he's starting to remember *Jesus Christ he doesn't want to remember.*

He can't feel his hands, and he complains to Celine when he tries to get at whatever pills he has, says, "Childproof tops are proof for way more than just kids."

"Put the bottle down, Renaire," Celine snaps, and *oh fuck he remembers every fucking word and shout and bloody tire tracks and Delaurier's shocked eyes and* this is our chance *and fuck he's going to be sick*, and someone pulls him to his feet, strong arms taking him out of the phone booth, and it's Delaurier, shaking him and holding him close and *don't you ever do that again you son of a bitch, don't you ever fucking make me come home to see you like that ever again.*

There are lights and radios and more lights, and he falls asleep with Emile curled around him, humming contentedly into the back of his neck.

He REMEMBERS.

He remembers Cote d'Ivoire.

Oh God, he remembers.

It was emerald landscape and packed dirt and not peaceful, but not bad. It was *angry*, it was divided, it was meeting Renaire's eyes for long enough to get the *fuck you* across.

Feelings more than actions bash through the night and into his brain, and it's eyes. Some eyes didn't flare and hate. Some eyes went wide with bright young smiles and *oh fuck* they'd shine with delight at cats drawn on their palms, light up when he was nearby and Renaire would grin right back.

They would run to him.

They ran toward him. They ran toward their friend because they were scared and young, so fucking *young*, oh God, young and scared and not listening or maybe not hearing him over the cacophony or maybe they were just fucking *stupid* or God, fuck everything to ever exist, drown the Earth and let humanity rot in the waves.

"Stop fraternizing, Renaire," they would tell him through subdued smiles.

Renaire would laugh and wave them off companionably.

They ran and didn't even make five steps, barely got out the door, *reaching for him*, and he reached back, he was reaching *back* and

and

Renaire shattered. He fell to his knees and shattered.

Tire tread smashed through the dirt, a spray of dust as it roared to a stop.

There were three men, there were boots in blood trailing into the dirt, a M16 automatic rifle they could've picked up anywhere limp in one hand and gripped tight in another—and those were the hands that went with the boots that stopped next to Mimi and hooked the filthy mud-coated bloody-soled toes of his boots against her ribs and *lifted* and no, *no*, he was kicking her over and Renaire *screamed*, fuck knows what, nothing but a broken wordless shriek.

All three of them jumped.

They hadn't noticed him.

Blood soles left her alone and turned toward Renaire, saying words that he couldn't process, but the gun aimed at him was clear enough, and he was going to die. He was going to *die*, and he didn't fucking care. The world was rolling around him, he was going to vomit, he was having a fucking heart attack, grabbing at the dirt, his hair, his chest.

The rifle pointed toward his head.

Renaire wanted to die, he *was* dying, he would be dead soon if this fucking—but. This was the man who killed them. It was him. It was his fault. *He did this*.

This man needed to die, and oh God, Renaire wouldn't be able to do it because he'd be *dead*, and he needed to, he *needed to*. He needed to stop sobbing and fucking *kill him*—

Renaire had already shattered, and there was plenty of shit he didn't want back. Getting rid of that *but you can't do that, killing people is bad*! voice of restraint and empathy was a good start.

After one decision and a long, deep exhale, he just genuinely didn't give a fuck. Bloody soles over there was busy mocking Renaire with his horrified colleagues, still far too close to the kids' bodies. Since he was busy mocking Renaire, he wasn't paying very much attention. Not enough attention, anyway. He definitely got more attentive when Renaire pulled his handgun out.

It still wasn't enough.

Killing people is easy.

He shot just once, just one bullet, nice and smooth and straight into his pretty brown eye. The left one. It left the right available for watching that gasp's length of a reaction. For this man, it was incredulity. How could Renaire get up and shoot him in the face? How could a broken weeping fool actually get off the ground and kill someone?

It was *all* so easy, it was so fucking easy.

Renaire watched the man fall with a grim emptiness that felt nothing like success, or relief, or any kind of redeeming revenge killing. It felt like nothing but a job well done.

The other two ran off, pickup bursting to life, but that was fine. Renaire holstered his pistol. He'd get them later.

People were shouting, and Renaire slumped forward, finally getting off his knees by pushing off of the dirt. The shouting got closer and closer, eventually forming into his name, and another couple of bursts of camouflage came running around a corner.

Renaire felt through his pockets, eventually coming across his lighter and an old crumpled pack of cigarettes while the two shouted at him, and then shouted at each other, and then shouted at the bodies and Renaire again.

He walked away, and they shouted some more, and Renaire kept on walking. He didn't give a fuck. Besides, he had a couple more people to hunt down, and where were *they* when it actually mattered? Where were they when it wasn't too late? Where were they when they were standing there, scared and *reaching*—

He liked the little flame that licked at the wind when he clicked his cheap lighter into action.

He liked having something else to focus on.

He liked losing the self who was losing himself. That was the addiction that hit him, left him drifting for what he'd expected to be one hell of a short lifespan. Except he kept living, and living, and *living*, close to dying but never quite managing it. The shards of Renaire had eventually molded together into some fucked-up amalgamation in the same vein as Renaire used to be, only less... alive.

No, he needed someone else to bring the *alive* part to his life. Someone who burned so bright that Renaire could actually feel the warmth.

With Emile, he can feel the heat five floors away.

RENAIRE DOESN'T want to wake up. The sheets are coarse and the lights are overly bright, and there's beeping and intercoms, and he doesn't want to wake up.

"Just open your eyes, Renaire, you're not fooling anyone," Delaurier says.

Renaire's eyes snap open wide even with the searing pain of bright lights, and holy shit, there he is. He's really there. Delaurier is sitting in a hospital chair set a polite distance away from the bed, even if he's sitting on the edge of the seat and clutching the book in his lap so tightly his knuckles are white. He has his marble face on, and when Renaire can see something other than Delaurier, he realizes it's probably because Celine is sitting on Renaire's other side. Glaring at Delaurier. Who is glaring at Celine.

"Why are you here?" Renaire asks him.

"We were legally required to contact him," Celine says.

"I don't know what I'm allowed to ask for, but I'd like to ask *her* to get out of the room," Delaurier says, arms crossed, glaring at Celine with even more passion than before.

Renaire sighs, just fucking accepts that he has to deal with Delaurier being an asshole, and turns to look at Celine. "What happened?"

Celine looks very resigned and sour when she says, "I don't have that information."

"What happened was that you were incredibly stupid and nearly killed yourself with so many different drugs that the doctors couldn't figure out what to treat you for," Delaurier says. "You—"

"Get out," Renaire says.

Delaurier looks like he's about five seconds from strangling Renaire, but he stands and doesn't even try to argue. "I'm not closing the door," he says, which is somehow a threat toward Celine, and leaves.

Celine takes over much more reasonably, saying, "You were admitted to the hospital for... well, quite a few things. And you've been in and out of consciousness for about a day." She hesitates but says, "You really do need to talk to him."

"Shouldn't you be trying to arrest him?" Renaire asks.

Celine's eyebrows rise, disbelieving. "You think I'm going to try and arrest Delaurier *in Paris*? There's such a thing as choosing one's battles."

She has one hell of a point there.

"Some other friends have been by," Celine says and points to a table with two things on it—a get well soon card in Jules's handwriting, and a massive stuffed rabbit in a 1940s nurse outfit, which is awful and therefore probably from Carope. "I'm glad you called someone."

Renaire nods because he's not sure he agrees.

"Say me too," Delaurier says from the doorway.

"Fuck off," Renaire says.

Delaurier sighs. "*Please* say me too?"

"*Why* did you call him?" Renaire asks Celine.

"We've been PACSed since Tripoli for this *exact reason*," Delaurier says, still glaring at Celine.

"How the fuck did you marry me?" Renaire demands.

"You signed a paper, I signed the same paper, someone stamped it. It's a legal partnership, so I'm primary contact for reasons like *hospitals*," Delaurier says, completely unrepentant. "They threw me out last time. They can't do that now."

"They threw you out because you were trying to strangle me," Renaire bites out.

"I should let you two talk," Celine says awkwardly, standing quietly in the corner.

Delaurier just keeps on glaring at her from the doorway. Renaire convinces himself he's not the slightest bit touched that Delaurier is restraining himself to *only* glaring at her.

"We're talking for ten minutes," Renaire finally says.

Delaurier presses his lips together for a moment before carefully saying, "I would suggest something closer to thirty minutes, if not more. We have a lot to cover."

"No, we don't," Renaire states. "Ten minutes."

Celine leaves quickly, and Renaire doesn't blame her for it. God knows Renaire wants to be out of the room.

The moment the door is closed, Delaurier says, "You were right. A victory like that wouldn't have helped anyone. We called off the plan barely ten minutes after you left."

Renaire isn't surprised, but the acid in his veins calms down a little. "And how much of that decision was you and not the fact Carope threw up and Glasson was about to follow her lead?"

"It was unanimous, if that's what you're asking," Delaurier says and shakes his head. "It's just *maddening* to see that no matter what we do, the world doesn't change. For every corrupt head we chop off, two grow in its place."

"Or you're still incapable of realizing that everyone's human and humans don't work like you want them to," Renaire says dryly and sighs, pointing at the chair. "Sit. We have communication issues."

It's remarkable how well that works. Delaurier sits, shuts his mouth, and waits.

"You are giving me yes or no answers, and elaborating only when I tell you to," Renaire states and doesn't wait for confirmation. "Do you understand why I was *and still am* completely disgusted with your willingness, if not *eagerness*, to murder innocent people?"

Delaurier doesn't look happy about it, but he says, "Yes."

Renaire nods. "*Without thinking about The Cause*, do you agree with me that your plan was a genuine atrocity?"

"Do I get to ask for specification?" Delaurier asks.

"No. Answer the question," Renaire says.

Delaurier is quiet for a long moment, and Renaire is grateful. He's actually *thinking* about this and not just spitting out fire and righteousness. Eventually he says, "Yes."

"Oh, thank God," Renaire breathes out in relief, covering his face with his hands.

"Do you think I *like* killing people?" Delaurier demands.

"I think you're so consumed by 'ends justify the means' that you scare the shit out of me sometimes," Renaire says bluntly. "Now shut up, I'm not done. Are you ever going to consider doing something like that again?"

Delaurier makes a frustrated noise, obviously struggling with being forced into yes or no answers, but finally he says, "*Consider*, yes. Actually carry out, no."

He isn't sure what to do with that answer. It's completely honest, pure Emile, and it's probably as good as Renaire is ever going to get, but the sheer lack of morality makes Renaire queasy. "I can't do this," he says quietly.

Delaurier is rigid marble. "It's your choice and I'll respect that," he says, but something suddenly seems to snap inside of him, and he's pacing, glaring at Renaire, biting out, "But *this*, I can't accept this, I never told anyone about Tripoli because I was *respecting you*, and I thought that was over, but that was obviously a huge mistake, and there is no fucking way I am letting you try this again. If this... this *obsession* with me—"

"It's not an obsession," Renaire says, and fuck, he wants a cigarette so desperately that his fingers itch for one, or for paint, or it's just one more manifestation of the ever-present ache for alcohol. Delaurier laughs at him, braces his arms on the end of the hospital bed, and watches him with cold eyes. Renaire expected nothing else, not really. "It started as an obsession. It was obsession in Tripoli, but now it's—" He takes a deep breath. "Now it's not."

Now he sees every one of Emile's many, many flaws. He sees that Delaurier is sometimes petty and often violent and always arrogant and disdainful, knows that he doesn't actually like death, but is so dedicated to The Cause that he kills remorselessly, watches as Delaurier indifferently bats away anything that he doesn't think is important. Delaurier is cruel and passionate and terrifying, and Renaire throws those facts into his face as often as possible, and it makes Emile that little bit less of a horrible person and a little bit more of a human being, and Renaire is in love with him anyway. Renaire knows Emile for himself and loves him anyway.

Delaurier believes him, which is surprising. He looks awkward and something else that's somewhere between epiphany and desperation. "I'm sorry," Emile says quietly.

Oh, isn't that beautiful. He'll fuck Renaire when he thinks it's obsession and fucking *apologizes* when he realizes it's actual love. It is the first apology he has *ever* heard from Delaurier's lips, and Jesus, Delaurier has a ridiculous concept of morality (if he has *any* concept of morality), and Renaire is so, so tired. "Just get out," Renaire says, exhausted.

"No," Emile says, immovable. "You can't do this again, Renaire."

Renaire can't bring himself to confess that it feels like he doesn't even have a *choice*, that if he gives up for even a moment, it rears up and drags him down, and he just doesn't have the strength to fight if there's not a cause, and Emile has been the only cause he's ever had. He can't even remember what was driving him before Emile—guilt, probably, the refusal to give himself any sort of way out of pain and guilt and self-loathing. But now, there's nothing. He didn't even mean to really do it. He just wanted everything to *end*.

Emile swallows and says, "It's fine if you don't ever want to see me again. That's your choice, and I understand it, and I'm not going to try and convince you or even try to stop you because God knows you're justified. But if you ever—" He stops. "If you ever need someone, I'm—*we* are here for you."

He doesn't know what to say to that, so Renaire keeps his mouth shut and meets Delaurier's eyes as steadily as possible. As he watches, the marble breaks.

"I'm just—shit," Emile says, strangely desperate, and lifts his eyes toward the ceiling, looks anywhere but at Renaire. "I'm not trying to change your mind or control you or disrespect you for making the smart choice here, but I am having a *hard fucking time* with this, Renaire. We've been together for *two years* and I only just started to try, and I swear to God I can be so much better, but, *fuck*, okay, I am *not* trying to change your completely justified and rational decision."

Emile doesn't even look at Renaire again. He just turns and walks straight out of the door and doesn't come back.

When Celine finally comes back into the room, carefully poking her head in before walking in, Renaire is very proud of the fact he is not crying, and the shaking can all be blamed on sobriety.

"I am so in love with him," Renaire says, not nearly numb enough.

Celine hugs him. She smells like honey.

CHAPTER 7

Paris: {Cologne}—Maison—Magasin—Chéron

RENAIRE HAS always been loyal. Always. He's loyal to the point of self-destructive. It's down to the bone. It's compulsive. It's inescapable. Renaire is unwavering.

But every time, every *fucking* time, he picks the wrong person.

Family? Bad idea in his case, but expected. Fellow soldiers? Limited, but trained into him just enough to count. It was supplanted by the kids. Then there was the dry period. There was the period where he didn't trust, tried not to feel, did nothing but *exist* and wish he didn't.

And then there is Delaurier.

Renaire's life is separated into *Delaurier*, and *before Delaurier*. The worst thing is he *likes it* this way. He lives like he's hooked himself to a hurricane, trapped in the eye of the storm and lazily coasting along with wherever the wind takes him.

He's loyal to Delaurier in a way that people can't understand. It's laced through his fucking skeleton, cracks of golden poison that might be the only thing holding him together.

Delaurier isn't exactly the smartest choice for such a horrific depth of devotion.

Cologne was stupid. Cologne had been yet another job, yet another cause, yet another thrilling adventure in the wonderful world of keeping Delaurier from getting his head shot off.

Delaurier prides himself on planning for everything. He usually succeeds. Renaire can admit that Delaurier's hyperdiligence is one of the reasons they're so good at this. He knew the guard dog's name and commands, for fuck's sake.

He hadn't known the bastard had a panic room.

They tore their way through the target's (Steinhauer? Steinbaum? Stein-*something*, he'll just go with 'Stein') house, headed for the office they expected Stein to be barricaded inside. Delaurier had pressed himself tight against the wood paneling of the hallway, expression harder than usual. It's usually blank determination when they're on a job, emotions buried deep. Not this time. This time Delaurier glared at the double cedar doors.

Renaire leaned against the opposite wall, eyebrows raised, waiting.

It was fast. Delaurier motioned quickly toward the lock, and Renaire did his delicate duty of unlocking the door by pulling out a gun and shooting it. There was no point bothering with secrecy and sneaking, since Stein obviously already knew they were in the house.

They'd busted through the door just in time to see Stein diving behind a secret door in the wood paneling, and Delaurier had shouted, "*Stop him!*"

So Renaire did his best. His best happened to be sprinting forward and throwing himself into the room before the autolock slammed it down.

It left him looking into the stunned eyes of Stein-something, letting out a long, low huff of air to recover from that little burst of energy there.

The panic room was nothing but concrete with a metal door. A cot waited in the corner, folded sheets sitting in the center of it. A tiny foldable table stood next to it, an equally tiny and foldable chair arranged neatly beneath. There also happened to be an emergency radio on top.

Stein didn't get to the radio. Renaire drew his gun in a snap and aimed it right at Stein's head. It was too small of a room to have a safe distance to make sure Stein didn't grab the gun, but the man had looked about ready to piss his pants, so Renaire wasn't too scared. A man who builds himself a panic room isn't going with the *fight* option when it comes to fight or flight.

"You'll never get out without the code," Stein said quickly. He was sweating so much that Renaire could see it beading in his buzz-cut hair.

Renaire couldn't help but frown, tilting his head slightly to the side. "Why would you put that in a panic room?"

Stein frowned right back. "What do you mean?"

"The point is to keep people out, not in," Renaire explained, nodding toward the little black keypad. "Plus if you want to make a quick escape or something, you're kind of fucked."

There was a moment of grim realization on Stein's face, and what little resolve he'd maintained crumbled as he said, "Oh."

"Yep," Renaire agreed, and it was an easy enough shot to take the radio out, so he took it. He also regretted it, because the sound was deafening and it was stupid of him, it was so fucking stupid. Guns are always loud. Shooting a gun in a tiny echoing room so small was idiotic to the point that Renaire fucking deserved the pain.

He heard something pounding at the door, and grimaced, holstering his gun and sliding across the minimal distance so he could pound back a couple of times. There were another few pounds and knocks that were probably Morse code or something, because that's the kind of shit Delaurier does, but fuck if Renaire knows Morse code.

"Hey, any chance you'd be willing to open the door?" Renaire asked instead.

Stein was pretty much curled in on himself, hunched over his knees as he teetered on the edge of the cot and sanity. "If I do that, you'll kill me," he said, barely audible since he was speaking directly into his hands. That, and Renaire's ears were still ringing.

"I'm not going to kill you," Renaire told him, which was absolutely the truth. Clearly the honesty came through in his voice, because Stein-something slowly raised his head, watching Renaire intently. "Really, I'm not. And Emile doesn't always kill people either. I mean, I'm just the backup, so I don't always know what he's planning."

Stein squinted, some sort of moral inquisition where Renaire was judged solely based on his posture or something. "You could convince him not to kill me?"

Renaire shrugged. "Maybe. I've never tried before." He wasn't planning to start.

And oh, how Stein-something's face had lit up, that tiny flame of hope rekindled by one of the most noncommittal answers Renaire had ever given in his entire life. "You're a reasonable man," Stein said and rose to his feet, watching Renaire carefully as he sidestepped his way to the keypad and associated door. He was even sweatier than Renaire had thought. "I'll go out second, maybe give you time to convince him."

"Sounds like a plan," Renaire said. "You're going to have to move over, though. And you have to do the convincing. I can just get you the chance to talk—"

"That's enough," Stein had said, let out a long determined breath, and typed in a really excessively long code, something like twelve digits for him to get out of his own panic room. The door slid open with a smooth hiss, and Renaire was in front, as promised.

Renaire wasn't even a little bit surprised when Delaurier's hand grabbed his shirt and yanked him forward, so hard and fast that it left Renaire not quite flailing his way into Delaurier's bright red shoulder. "Hello to you too," Renaire muttered.

"Are you okay?" Delaurier asked, loud and somewhere between frustrated and irritated and nowhere near reassuring for Stein-something.

Renaire did not at all let himself read anything into the entire situation and stepped back, nodded, and was very much no longer in physical contact with Delaurier. "I'm fine. The guy wants to talk to you, though," he said.

Delaurier had scowled at the panic room's door before turning back to Renaire. "Is that so."

"I told him I wouldn't kill him," Renaire said quietly in case Stein-something had super hearing.

"Of course you wouldn't kill him," Delaurier said, scowl fading just enough that some sort of fond confusion could sneak into his eyes. "You never do. That's not how this works."

Renaire shrugged. "Yeah, but *he* doesn't know that."

"True," Delaurier said, bemused, and looked at the open panic room door. "Okay, we can talk. Get him out."

It was easy enough to peek back into the panic room. Stein was inside, pressed against the wall, as sweaty as ever. "Okay, he'll talk. The rest is up to you," Renaire said.

Stein swallowed and nodded, and Renaire moved away to give the man some space as he emerged. Renaire's part was pretty much done, so he found himself a seat on Stein's desk and pulled out a cigarette. He got better at smoking with gloves on every single time, and there had been plenty of times by then. Experience made it nothing, plucked out like a rosebush bud or a round of ammunition.

There wasn't any rush, so he just pulled his lighter out. The flame had barely kissed the tip before Delaurier had raised his pistol and shot Stein right between the eyes.

The shot was loud, but not deafening. It was nowhere near as loud as Renaire's had been in the panic room. It wasn't unexpected either—

they came here to kill Stein, so Stein was going to die. There was no question. There was no surprise.

And yet Renaire flinched.

He hadn't flinched at gunfire for *years*. He was a fucking professional, he was *experienced*, he wasn't some wide-eyed idiot who didn't realize there'd be blood everywhere. And Renaire had a better view than Delaurier. The exit wound is always bigger. Drops of darker red reached inside the panic room.

Stein hadn't got beyond a simple, desperate *"Please—"*

Maybe it was the way Renaire had expected some kind of dialogue to pick up between them, Delaurier humoring Stein for a couple of minutes before doing the deed. Maybe it was Delaurier's put-upon sigh as Stein's body dropped to the floor, holstering his gun and stepping away.

This happened instead.

Delaurier had turned to look at Renaire, expectant. Renaire had no fucking clue why. Was he expecting a "Good job" and round of applause? Validation of some sort? Sarcastic commentary? Renaire could give it an eight out of ten, penalized for the brevity of the encounter.

Renaire simply sat on the desk, breathing smoke in and out, watching Delaurier. It was fun to watch him twitch, sometimes. This time, the silence was simply because Renaire didn't know what words to fill it with.

Eventually, they reached Delaurier's tolerance level for silence. If he's not asleep, he can manage to keep his mouth shut for an hour at the most. He gets chatty even when there's supposed to be stealth involved, turning to Renaire and saying, *We need to stay quiet.*

"You look angry," Delaurier had eventually said, neutral. It was a sign of something being wrong. Delaurier is never neutral.

"I'm not," Renaire replied honestly, glancing down at Stein's body.

It wasn't Stein's body that had him unsettled. It wasn't his death, or the fact the shot made Renaire jump. It was the fact Delaurier just fucking *did it*.

He didn't care about the death. He cared about the killing.

"You just kind of went for it there," Renaire said over his cigarette.

Delaurier had looked so *confused*, like Renaire had just told him he was moving to Panama or something. It wasn't quite a double take between Stein's still fresh body and Renaire, but it was close enough for Renaire to wonder what was going on in that fucked-up pretty little head.

"I just did what you... I got the job done?" Delaurier had said, still confused. It was careful, as if he was trying to navigate around drastic cultural differences. For someone so adept at navigating verbal minefields, he was kind of shit at this.

"Yes, you did," Renaire said, and there was no point to the argument. If it even *was* an argument. So he stood up and didn't look over at Stein's body. "Let's go."

Something had loosened in Delaurier's shoulder, and something had hardened inside of Renaire.

There was no question of what Delaurier was becoming. There was no question of what they were doing. There wasn't even the thought of questioning if Stein really deserved a bullet to the brain. He didn't care about Stein. He cared about Delaurier's steady hands. He cared about how Delaurier looked so still, so *poised*, untouchable and unrepentant.

"We might have time for one more stop before our train leaves," Delaurier had said, offering Renaire *something*. Anything. It would be just under three hours of whatever the fuck Renaire wanted.

That's why he never even *thought* about leaving. There are those three-hour handouts of indulgence and an impossible press of Delaurier's hand on his shoulder, or their fingers brushing across bottles of water. There's the rare word of praise and appreciation.

He's loyal. He follows. He watched Delaurier casually shoot a man in the head without a breath of hesitation and felt nothing but a tease of warmth between his lungs because Delaurier was willing to indulge him for three whole hours.

Now his morality had stretched to the limit and snapped to shit, sliced Renaire apart, and he's bleeding out belief. It's only a matter of time until he runs dry.

Leaving with Celine won't be the hard part. That won't come until she leaves Renaire. She'll leave, and Renaire will be alone, and Renaire will be lost and broken and desperate for something, *anything*, to hold on to.

Renaire is loyal.

Empty men don't break bad habits.

IT'S RAINING when he gets released into Celine's care, with tight frowns from the hospital staff and an awkward smile from Glasson, who had magically appeared the moment he started fighting his way through the release paperwork.

"You know we agree with you," Glasson had said, more of a question than a statement.

"You know he won't ever do it again," Glasson had said, frustrated until he really started listening to Renaire.

"You know you're one of us, right?" Glasson had asked, reaching out a hand as if he was going to hold Renaire's shoulder but stopped himself abruptly. Renaire hadn't blamed him—he did nearly stab Delaurier for doing the same thing, after all. "I know you've always felt like some sort of half member of STB, but you're as much of a member as any of us."

Renaire had patted him on the back with a weary smile and said, "That's the problem."

Glasson is a very smart man. He gave Renaire a bag of his things (most from their duffel bag) and a new phone with everyone's phone numbers in it (*"But we don't have this number,"* Glasson had said, and Renaire wondered how anyone ever thought Glasson was cold—quiet, yes, sharp and intense, often, but so gently caring at all times that they simply took it for granted) and, after a moment of hesitation, he'd hugged Renaire very carefully.

"If you need *anything*, please, let us help," Glasson had said.

And now, sitting in Celine's quiet house in the late afternoon while she's working from home in her office, being politely and not expressly on suicide watch, Renaire is seriously trying to figure out what the fuck he's supposed to be doing now.

Being an actual legitimate artist is the most obvious answer, since that's technically what he already is, but the idea of painting for a living seems like cheating, somehow. Life isn't supposed to be that simple and enjoyable. He has exactly two skill sets, and since he doesn't want to kill people for a living (he kills people trying to kill someone who kills for a living—*there's a difference*), art is really all he has left. Art and a stunning ability to make terrible life choices.

Renaire needs to buy more cigarettes.

"Can I ask you a question?" Celine calls out hesitantly from the office. She's standing in the doorway, toying awkwardly with the tail of her blonde braid. "Do you believe in fate?"

"I refuse to, purely out of spite," Renaire says, because the actual answer is sappy and humiliating and *hurts*.

Celine smiles anyway. "What about love at first sight?"

"I don't know about *love*, but sure, there can be some kind of thing triggered at first sight," Renaire says. *This* topic, he can cover. "Attraction, definitely, fascination, sure, but actual love? Probably not."

"Oh," Celine says, smile losing some of its normal soft sparkle.

Renaire frowns. "Sorry to crush your dreams. I could be wrong. That's just my experience, where the actual love took a while, but the addiction shit just kind of snapped on. Honestly, I am *not* the person to ask about this. I mean, if it's about your dads—"

"No, it's nothing like that," Celine says, warmly reassuring. "Then why did you go with Delaurier? He killed two people in front of you, and you still just... left. It's what I've never understood."

Renaire figures he has nothing left to lose, so he leans back deeper in Celine's very comfortable green armchair, and he *really* needs some cigarettes and says, "He only killed What's-His-Name, actually. I killed the security guy because he was threatening Emile." He ends up smiling. "That was the start of a very bad habit."

Celine frowns. There's something to the look that is self-reflective, like she's somehow seeing herself in his words. "Even then you were already willing to kill for him. Even if it wasn't love at first sight," she says.

"Oh, I would have done much more than kill for him," Renaire says and stands because the itch in his fingers just won't subside. "Do you need to watch me on my way to buy cigarettes?"

She smiles at him and ducks away for a moment before returning to him with an umbrella in hand. "Get some art supplies too."

"Did you know I'm worth two million dollars?" Renaire asks, looking at the umbrella. It's a heavy-duty quality umbrella, the kind that a Victorian-era man would use to beat street urchins. "I'm guessing this is your father's."

"Papa's, actually," Celine says. "The shop's just two blocks down. Do you think it'll be emotionally draining going from here to there?"

"Ha-ha, just give me the fucking umbrella," Renaire says and is out the door two minutes later with a small shopping list.

The rain is that irritating, intermittently horrible type of rainfall, where it moves from casual raindrops to a catastrophic downpour every few minutes. Renaire is stepping wide to avoid puddles and concentrating on his footing, which is why it takes his name being shouted for Renaire to actually look up and see the abysmally familiar figure standing awkwardly beneath a flimsy turquoise travel-sized umbrella.

"I am not trying to change your mind," Delaurier says immediately after they make eye contact. He looks like he stood under a waterfall.

Renaire gapes at him. "How the fuck are you that wet?"

"I didn't have an umbrella," Delaurier says. "A woman offered hers, though."

And Delaurier probably just said thank you and took it and completely ignored the expectant look she gave him. Delaurier knows he's attractive, but it is genuinely baffling how actual *attraction* seems to fly right over his head.

Delaurier doesn't say anything else. He just stands there, staring at Renaire.

Renaire can't help but take pity on him, even if he is a horrifically misguided human being with zero moral fiber. He sighs and says, "I'm going to the shop."

"Can I come?" Delaurier asks. It's very assertive of him, for something to do with their relationship. That's probably why he then backpedals, says, "If that's okay. I should buy some things, but I can wait, or we could both buy things at the same time in the same place."

It's very strange to be both hopelessly in love with a complete loser and also disgusted with a ruthless terrorist all at the same time. It's strange that the two can even be the *same person*. Renaire's mind settles on affectionate irritation, and he says, "And what are you going to buy?"

"A towel," Delaurier says.

Renaire can't help but smile. "Fair enough," he says, and when he starts walking, Delaurier naturally falls into step with him. "By the way, what exactly are you doing out here?"

"I'm not trying to change your mind," Delaurier says again.

Renaire rolls his eyes. "Yes you are."

"Fuck, I really am, I'm trying not to, but I absolutely am trying to change your mind," Emile says. Their umbrellas keep Renaire from seeing his expression or anything beyond the more rigid stride he gets when he's restraining himself from exploding. "I'll leave if you want, I swear."

"I know you will," Renaire says. "Honestly, I'm kind of impressed with how you're taking this." How well Emile is taking this is the only way Renaire can keep himself from running back, really. If he genuinely tried to change Renaire's mind, Renaire would crumble in an instant. He needs to not do that.

When they get to the shop, Renaire opens the door, and Delaurier is the first one through, and Renaire doesn't even notice it until he's closed the door behind him. It's surprisingly big for a local neighborhood store, with an eclectic blend of goods. Renaire's real target is behind the counter and its very bored attendant, so it'll be his last stop.

"How are you?" Emile asks him intently. He doesn't even pretend to look for a towel.

Renaire, on the other hand, is determined to be at least a little bit useful to Celine. When he realizes Emile is just going to hover, he sighs and hands over the shopping list. "I'm as good as you would expect," he says simply.

Awkward silence descends once again. Emile is obviously trying, but Renaire will admit it's not easy to have a conversation under the circumstances, even for someone more socially adept.

"Am I allowed to try and change your mind?" Emile asks carefully when they're five items in on the nine-item list.

"Do you understand why I can't really deal with you and STB right now?" Renaire asks.

Emile nods. "I do."

"And do you regret it?"

"Yes," Delaurier says firmly. "There are actions that are so reprehensible that any positive results that came from them would be completely negated and always tarnished, solely because of how they were achieved."

"That's one hell of a twist to make to your ideals in a couple of days," Renaire says, not entirely sure if he believes it. Delaurier sounds sincere, but he's a charming bastard when he wants to be, and Renaire isn't always the best at avoiding being charmed by him.

"When your partner not only objects to something for the very first time but also has an objection so extreme it leaves *knives embedded in walls and doors*, you pay attention," Emile says dryly, which, yeah, he can see the logic behind this.

"So you understand that you need to have morals, but haven't quite developed them just yet," Renaire says dryly. It's a step in the right direction, to be sure. The fact that he's realized it's necessary for his precious Cause means it's a lesson that will remain permanent.

"I'm trying," Emile says quietly and fetches item number seven. He gives Renaire something close to a hopeful smile. It's small and sweet and beautiful. "I could use some help."

"Stop that," Renaire snaps because he suddenly wants to do absolutely nothing but push Emile onto the floor and ravage him then and there, and that is *not okay*. He chooses his own actions, and that action needs to not be the one he takes and *fuck*, Emile is gorgeous and *wants him* and is practically pining, it's awful—how the fuck is he supposed to fight this?

Emile immediately backs away and reverts to his cold marble expression and clears his throat. After a moment he says, "I don't know what I did wrong."

Renaire takes a deep breath and shakes his head hard enough that he should have flung the urge to kiss Emile breathless out of his head—hell, out of the shop, shattering the windows in the process—but it doesn't help. "You didn't do anything wrong," Renaire says, and fuck, he needs a cigarette (or a drink, which is why he needs a cigarette; he knows it's a substitution and not a very healthy one, but it's all he's got, and his entire life seems to be about the lesser of two evils anyway).

They have existed around each other for two years, but it's still surprising when Emile pulls out a pack and wordlessly offers Renaire a cigarette. Emile is a strange sort of social smoker. He has to be both comfortable and talkative to even consider touching a cigarette. It doesn't happen very often.

Renaire never really thought about it, but it seems painfully obvious now that Emile only carries a pack around for him.

He takes it, and Emile makes sure their fingers don't touch.

"Okay," Renaire says, hands shaking again as he lights it and tries to calm down because, *fuck*, he is so in love, and he needs to not be. Deep breath, deep inhalation and exhale and seriously consider telling the bored clerk to fuck off when she glares at him for smoking indoors, and Christ, does Emile look good when damp in this lighting. "Okay, you get five words."

Emile frowns. "Five words of what?"

Renaire tosses a sketchbook into the pile of purchases along with three packs of cigarettes and twitches his way through the entire slow disdainful transaction before casually blowing a lungful of smoke at the woman behind the counter. He walks out with a plastic bag in one hand, the umbrella in the other, and Emile trailing behind him. He is being unnaturally patient about this, and the rain is pummeling hard enough against the umbrella that he can't even hear Emile.

It's probably a good thing.

He picks his way back to Celine's house easily enough, and every time he glances back, Emile is following. It isn't a long walk, but it gives Renaire enough time to realize he's about to put Emile and Celine in the same room again. That didn't seem like it went very well last time, so when he reaches the front door, he fights two years of instinct and manages to get through the door first. It unsettles Emile enough that he's three steps behind, which gives Renaire time to actually step inside and close his umbrella.

Celine steps out of the office to smile at him and his bag, saying, "You survived!"

The smile evaporates when Delaurier steps through behind him. She watches him like the Interpol agent Renaire keeps forgetting she is.

"Renaire," Celine says, obviously starting to pick her way through a polite way to say *get that son of a bitch out of my house*, but Renaire holds up a hand to stop her.

It doesn't stop Emile, though, since he bites out, "If he wanted me gone, I'd be gone."

"Jesus Christ, can you just calm the fuck down," Renaire snaps at him. Really, Emile had been doing such a good job of being decent that Renaire forgot he categorizes people as *STB* and *Not STB*, and Celine is relegated to the "I don't give a fuck beyond your theoretical oppression" column. He sighs and turns to Celine. "We met outside. The rain is too loud to actually hear anything. He'll be gone in five minutes."

"I'm not leaving the room," Celine says, and it's somewhere between reassurance and a threat.

"What do you think I'm going to do to him?" Emile demands.

"Seriously, calm down or I'm kicking you out," Renaire says. He has no idea why Emile is so violently opposed to Celine. It could have something to do with how meeting her ruined the strange bits of happiness they'd managed to scrounge together in Russia, but it seems more personal than that. Renaire's betting there was probably a hospital bedside argument. Regardless, it makes the tension in the room almost unbearable.

Delaurier takes a deep breath, obviously fighting to manage a civil conversation, and says, "I respect his boundaries and wishes, and I'm not going to push for *anything*, just ask him."

"It's true, he's annoyingly passive about this shit," Renaire admits.

"I'm patient, not passive," Emile says.

"And I'm still not leaving the room," Celine says, frowning. "You may have forgotten, but I'm still on suicide watch, and whatever you're doing, it's going to be more than a little emotional for Renaire."

"Oh," Emile says, probably because he forgot big formal suicide watches exist when someone almost kills themselves, deliberately or not.

Renaire sighs and thinks about screaming about how he's not some delicate daisy about to be trampled under Emile's cruel, cruel feet, but neither of them would believe him, so he just points a finger at Celine and says, "No commentary. This is my choice to make."

Celine immediately nods in agreement. She puts herself in a chair in the corner, rather decorously turning it so she's looking at the wall parallel to where Emile and Renaire are currently standing, her back to them.

"I don't like this," Emile mutters.

"Deal with it," Renaire says and closes his eyes. "You want to try and change my mind."

"I won't," Emile says immediately. "You're completely justified and rational, and I have no—"

"You get five words," Renaire says.

Emile gives him an assessing, not quite calculating look. "Are you sure about this? I have no right to even ask, and you know exactly what I am."

He's persuasive, terrifying, passionate, charming, and capable of inciting riots or crippling politicians with five minutes of rhetoric. Giving someone like Emile Delaurier five words in this situation is like giving a warlord a nuclear warhead with no strings attached. What he chooses to do remains to be seen, and Renaire can't even begin to guess.

"Five words," Renaire repeats, shifting his weight awkwardly. "And then you leave. I have your number if I want to get in touch."

Emile nods and purses his lips, looking over at where Celine is watching the wall, before looking at Renaire for a long time. He watches Renaire's lips and then his gaze traces Renaire's throat before finally looking into his eyes, steady and devoted. Even with Emile's hands tucked tight in the pockets of his brown coat, Renaire still feels like Emile is touching him.

"You're what keeps me human," Emile finally says, quiet and honest, and leaves.

Celine is completely silent as Renaire stares at the door and then moves to the window. He watches the turquoise umbrella fading into the rain.

"Good choice," Renaire says and opens his new pack of cigarettes.

HE DOESN'T even really mean to do it. Renaire is desperate to get his mind off *things* for at least a few minutes, sketching some fantasy megalopolis in his admittedly rain-crinkled sketchbook with a ballpoint pen he stole off Celine's desk. He just glances over at the paperwork she has spread on the coffee table and says, "That is a really terrible plan."

Celine looks up from her laptop, confused. "I'm sorry?"

Renaire long ago perfected the art of smoking while drawing and also holding a sketchbook. He can add a bottle to it if he gets really ambitious. It has impressed thousands, but apparently Celine is not one of those thousands. He points at the estimated times on a sheet, about targets of some sort in what looks like China—it's been a while since they were in China. "The only way you could manage that time frame is if you start trying to do some *Mission: Impossible* bullshit," he says.

Celine's lips twitch into a smile. "You've managed it," she points out.

"Yes, while doing *Mission: Impossible* bullshit for something a lot more important than stealing some—what is this, corporate data? Please," Renaire says, rolling his eyes. "Don't waste your time with these fools, Celine. They're going down in a blaze of stupidity, thanks to underestimating Chinese security guards. That company does *not* fuck around."

She laughs, tilting her head to the side and giving him a fond look, which is.... Really, Renaire has no idea what to think of Celine sometimes. He's only really known her for two days, but somehow he feels like they've been best friends for years despite not even knowing whether or not he can trust her beyond this room. "What happened to never being involved in the planning?" she asks, amused.

"There's a difference between planning something and enacting it," Renaire says and turns back to his sketching because he doesn't want to get into that. "A Chinese security guard managed to shoot Delaurier. It was just a graze, but it still taught us all a very valuable lesson about fucking with China."

"I really don't understand you," Celine says after a moment. "You're so smart—"

"Do *not* start that," Renaire warns.

"I'm sorry," Celine says, immediately backing off.

"It's fine," Renaire says and finds himself looking at the information Celine has spread all over the coffee table. "So who are they?"

Celine sighs. "They're a militant offshoot of PETA." When Renaire laughs, she shakes her head. "I know. Not everyone has the lofty goals of STB. *Or* as much precision."

Renaire nods, wonders if Celine has met Glasson, and twists to look more closely at the blueprints and Interpol's gathered intelligence on the attack. He catches terrorists for Celine without ever putting the sketchpad down.

RENAIRE MAKES it about five hours after that. It's five hours longer than he ever thought he'd last.

Celine doesn't even look surprised when he finally gives up, stops scratching the pen across his water-warped sketchbook, and says, "I have to go."

"I feel like I should tell you you're stronger than this," she says.

"But I'm really, really not," Renaire agrees.

"I meant that you wouldn't listen, not that you aren't capable," Celine says, just enough admonishment in her voice that Renaire knows it's sincere. She puts her papers into an organized stack and stands up. "Let me get my coat."

Renaire frowns at her. "It's past midnight."

"And you're giving me a bedtime?" Celine asks, already dressed for the still present rain, purse in place and holding an umbrella that is almost identical to the one she loaned Renaire, excluding the fact its white with off-white polka dots.

Renaire continues to enjoy her fashion choices, which is very strange. He can't remember ever actually paying attention to shit like this. She's just naturally fascinating.

"They're not going to be happy to see you," Renaire warns her, already pulling out his new phone—Glasson didn't go cheap. It's quite a nice phone, and Renaire *almost* knows how to work it. He does text Carope, since he isn't going to chance walking into the Chéron with an unannounced Interpol agent.

BRIEFLY coming home & bringing Celine do NOT fuck with her i know where u sleep—R

"You might be surprised," Celine says, amused.

CELINE!!!!!!!!!! <3 <3 <3 Carope texts back at that exact moment.

Fuck, he really misses his friends.

"We're just going to say hello," Renaire says firmly as if he can actually make it true if he says it the right way.

Celine nods, obviously as aware of the horrible lie as Renaire is, and says, "I'll be here for support the whole time."

She lives on the outskirts of true Paris, and it takes two transfers to get to the Chéron's closest station, but they manage to fill it with idle chatter that keeps him from vibrating to death. The trip is too long and too short, and when Celine carefully puts a hand on his shoulder, Renaire has to take a deep, calming breath because her hand isn't the one he wants, and he is going to have to survive this. And he will.

The Café Chéron greets him with a soft affection, where what would normally be shouts and slaps to his back are now friendly greetings and soft pats to the shoulder. They act like he's survived some horrible life-changing experience with each and every customer by his side, and now they need to greet him with more *meaning* because of it. Celine gets polite apprehension, which is better than he expected. No glaring is a victory that very few new faces achieve.

Even at one in the morning, the Chéron is active. There's a different bartender tonight, which is strange, but the new woman gives Renaire a wink. Renaire smiles back, but Celine subtly shifts his path away from the bar—not explicitly toward the stairs, but definitely away from the bar. And that direction just happens to be toward the stairs.

"You don't have to go, you know," Celine says simply, and really, just that is plenty of incentive.

Delaurier is not waiting for him at the top of the staircase, thank God. Renaire walks up with Celine tight on his heels, and they're all there, every single one. They start to greet Renaire, all rising with smiles (except Delaurier, who is not in the room, and he has no idea where Delaurier is, but it's all fine—there is obviously a reason for him to not be here; there is no reason to panic), but it's cut off sharply when Celine finally steps into the room.

"Who is that?" Celine asks immediately, grabbing onto Renaire's sleeve and staring at something in the room like it's about to eat her.

"Who?" Renaire does his best to follow her line of sight and frowns, not sure he'll get the target right. But overall, he can guess. "Do you mean Mathieu?" It's good to see he's doing okay, since he hasn't heard from the guy since Renaire used him as an emergency contact. Then again, Renaire's been kind of busy. Checking up on amiable little Mathieu wasn't his number one priority.

"Mathieu," Celine repeats, breathless, entranced, completely focused on nothing else.

Renaire nods. "He was there with me when—"

"I *know*, I saw him," she says, eyes wide and shining, lips tilting into a causeless smile, and oh fuck, Renaire knows this. Sort of.

"Are you telling me you saw him in the park and can't get him out of your head and now you're completely infatuated without saying a word to him?" Renaire asks, incredulous, because *no*, no way this is happening to poor Celine.

"Yes," Celine says. Her grip tightens.

"Well fuck," Renaire says, and wonders if saying *sorry for your loss* would be appropriate here. Probably not. Still, he looks down at Celine, making sure she's actually looking at *him* and not Mathieu for this conversation. She deserves a warning, even if she doesn't know she needs it. "You can still walk away. We can turn around and—"

"It's her!" Mathieu practically screams, literally *jumping* out of his seat next to Carope at the sight of Celine, who is completely awestruck, hands clasped together in front of her chest like she's some sort of medieval damsel being wooed by lute. Mathieu isn't done with the jumping, though—he sprints past the people who had started to stand, dodging tables. He stops barely a body's width away from Celine, staring and smiling and anxious and awkward. He is adorable, the poor bastard. "It's *you*. I kept looking—"

"I never thought I'd find you again!" Celine says, taking Mathieu's hands in her own and beaming. "You were there and then you vanished!"

"Because I went looking for *you*," Mathieu says.

Celine keeps on smiling. "I'm so happy to see you again. I want to take you to dinner. Can I take you to dinner?"

"Of course you can take me, I'd follow you anywhere," Mathieu gushes, probably genuinely seeing stars and sparkles around Celine's head.

"What have I done," Renaire says, stunned. When he looks away from the shiny new couple, Carope is completely frozen in her chair, expressionless in a way that's more about composure than shock. Renaire starts hurrying over, since the rest of STB doesn't seem to notice because they're all justifiably staring, excluding Delaurier.

Renaire freezes.

Delaurier must have emerged through the back door at some point during the show, and his eyes are fixed on nothing but Renaire. When their eyes lock, Renaire has to fight to breathe.

After a moment Delaurier looks meaningfully around at the (understandably) hypnotized group, nods back the way he came, and gives Renaire a questioning look. It doesn't take much movement even at this distance—they've negotiated entire battle strategies without words. For the same reason, all Renaire has to do is give a miniscule nod of agreement, and Delaurier is back through the door. Renaire carefully weaves his way through Celine and Mathieu's audience to join him.

He's standing in the stairwell with impeccable posture, so Renaire immediately slouches onto the stairs, sitting in as sprawled of a position as he can manage. There's the tiniest bit of pacing before he stands firm and rigid and slightly awkward next to Renaire.

"You came," Emile says, and Renaire can tell he's trying not to smile, even if he has no idea why he's hiding it. "It's nice to see you."

Renaire preemptively pulls out a cigarette. He knows he'll need it. "How long were you standing out in the rain earlier?"

"A while," Emile says.

"Long enough for a woman to give you her umbrella out of sympathy," Renaire says. "And you were still wet when I finally caught you stalking me."

Emile's mouth drops open, and it's an interesting thing to see him go from righteous indignation to horrifying realization in less than a second. "I *was* stalking you. I didn't even realize I was doing it."

Renaire just nods and lights his cigarette, not really bothered by the stalking. Emile is bothered enough for the both of them. "My point here is that I want to know what you *did* think you were doing standing out there for a minimum of half an hour, and at least an hour if you include transit time."

"I don't really know," Emile admits. "I had tactics, but no definite plan of attack."

"Knocking on the door would have been a sensible first strike," Renaire says. "It's a good opening gambit. Very traditional, but tradition isn't always a bad thing." He points at the stairs next to him and straightens slightly. "Sit."

Emile sits down carefully, separated by a cautious distance but resting on the same step, at least, and takes a deep breath before jumping straight to the point. "I can't promise I'll never think it's a good idea, or that I'll never wonder what would have happened if we had carried it out, or that I won't horrify you again. But I do promise I'll never actually carry it out, and I will always listen to you," he says. "You're the closest thing to a conscience we have."

"Which is really fucking tragic," Renaire says and nods, what little decision that remained having been decided. "Hold out your hand."

Emile frowns. "What?"

Renaire reaches into his jacket pocket because he is in fact capable of being slightly tricky and says it again. "Hold out your hand."

Emile finally follows orders, hand stretched out awkwardly, and Renaire pulls out his (small) sketchbook and pen. He puts them on the step above them and presses nothing but his hand against the one Emile offered. Renaire carefully laces his own clever fingers together with Emile's own rigid digits, and fuck, his heart is racing like he's running for his life just from this.

Emile's eyes are wide and stunned, and his grip alternates between painfully tight to featherlight as if he doesn't know what he's meant to be doing or how long this is going to last. When Renaire doesn't pull his hand away, simply letting them rest together as he tries to sketch *something—fuck, let's go with rabbits*, Emile says, "I'm not as good of a person as I should be."

"I know," Renaire says.

"This is going to happen again," Emile says. His thumb cautiously traces the side of Renaire's hand, light and soft and beautiful. "I don't have the limits people are supposed to have. One day I'm going to go too far and you won't be fast enough to catch me before it's too late."

"And one day I'll drink myself to death or end up accidentally murdering someone during a panic attack or just fall to pieces," Renaire says and looks Emile in the eye, straight and simple and honest. "One day I won't be fast enough. But I'm sure as fuck going to try and make that day a long, long time from now."

Emile squeezes his hand so tight that Renaire worries he can feel the snap of bone, squeezes until he worries their hands might end up irrevocably fused together. Renaire doesn't really mind.

"You know, instead of trying to get rid of the evil in the world, maybe you could try to add good instead," Renaire suggests.

Emile looks at him as if he's insane.

Renaire shrugs. "Just a thought," he says and goes back to drawing. His rabbits look more like fuzzy fanged monsters. He is weirdly okay with that.

They fall into the strange standard routines of trains and cars and hours spent alone with zero outside entertainment, but there's a warm tension beneath it all. Emile tries to tell him about The Cause and some of his plans, Renaire casually shoots holes in them, and they end up half arguing about absolutely nothing.

Eventually, Emile starts trying to talk with his hands. He ends up yanking Renaire into his side, and looks mortified about it. Renaire can't help laughing. He laughs and leans into Emile's side, softly brushing his thumb across the top of Emile's hand. He's completely sober and yet his entire body feels warm and buzzed, like that beautiful moment of intoxication where the world is vivid and breathtaking, and he is so giddy he can't see straight.

"Renaire," Emile says, and it's all he really needs to say. He's rigid and hot, and his eyes are shut as if his entire body is barely fighting the urge to move. "Either—"

"Fuck morals," Renaire says and kisses him. It's harder than he intended, because Emile twists to meet him halfway, hand already embedding itself in Renaire's hair as their lips move, and God, it's only been two (three?) days, and Renaire missed this so desperately that he already is having trouble breathing. What was a warm, giddy buzz suddenly *explodes*, and fuck, the only thing he wants is to climb onto Emile and start begging into his skin.

Emile can tell because he can always tell. He's always three steps ahead, and he pulls away to press a kiss to his cheek, hand shifting to slide softly along Renaire's neck. "You don't have to," he says seriously and kisses the corner of Renaire's mouth. It's not quite teasing, more of a promise than anything else.

"I swear to God I would let you fuck me right here in the stairwell," Renaire says and means it.

Emile's grip on his hand tightens roughly for a moment, long enough for Renaire to realize he can imagine it just as vividly as Renaire—barely undressed, panting frantically, and trying to stay quiet (and failing) as Emile thrusts inside him again and again, trying to stay steady while losing their minds and hysterically thinking *this is such a bad idea* and not giving a shit—but Emile Delaurier is about control.

"I know you would," Emile says and kisses him softly, chastely. "But I want you in my bed, on my pillows. Please."

Renaire feels something very strange for a moment, but it cuts off sharply. He squeezes Emile's hand and says, "That sounds dangerously romantic."

"Nothing dangerous about it," Emile says and gently pulls him to his feet with a wry smile. "And it's not *nearly* as dangerous as a stairwell."

That makes Renaire laugh, and he follows Emile up the stairs, still wondering how he can feel so warm and *giddy* from nothing at all. It's enough of a climb that they have to stop on the stairwell when there's an immediate urge to touch, where Renaire finds himself pressing into Emile's body and kissing him like they have all the time in the world, kissing him for the sake of being together, like he can't stay separated for more than a few moments.

It's strangely quiet but comfortably so. He can't remember ever feeling like this before, both of them unrushed and warm and something else he can't even try to name, something accepting and affectionate and desperately sweet passing between them with every kiss and touch. He's vaguely reminded of honey, somehow, something slow and golden and dangerous to acquire.

Emile's front door is unlocked when they finally reach it, and when they're in the apartment, Emile turns and locks it not once but *three* times—standard doorknob lock that all of STB has a key for, second lock that the Holy Trinity of STB has a key for, and the simple security of a chain in the door. Renaire isn't quite sure what to make of it. "Expecting company?" he asks, hoping it sounds casual.

"Dreading it," Emile says, frowning at the wood, and then seems to realize Renaire isn't actually casual about this because, let's face it, *that's really fucking weird* and kind of creepy. He trusts Emile, but still. "I just don't want to be interrupted or for anyone to walk in for anything beyond the apocalypse for a few hours, but we can—"

"It's fine," Renaire says. Weird, but fine. It makes sense for Emile, though, if he feels even the slightest bit insecure about this thing between them. Renaire has only seen him truly out of control probably twice, and each instance was a nightmare of someone else's design—control is safety, and something feels *loose* right now, organic and unplanned. If he wants his door locked like this, it's the least Renaire can give him.

Emile glances at the locks and then looks back at Renaire, saying, "If you want it unlocked I'll—"

Renaire cuts him off with a kiss, hot and slow, pressing Emile back against the door with gentle force. "It's fine," he says again, this time firmly, and it's so strange to be the reassuring one. He must do a decent job, though, since Emile leaves the locks alone and concentrates on getting them into his bedroom.

It's a decent-sized room by Paris standards and has the same tall, airy windows and neat lines of furniture as the rest of the apartment. The only word to really describe the place is *serviceable*, since everything in it is functional and fitting with the décor, and that's about it. Renaire knows for a fact that the unimpressive queen-sized bed almost constantly decked in beige and white is comfortable, and really, what else does anyone need?

The hour is long past midnight, leaving the room dark save for the city's ever-present light pollution and lit windows that seem like distant rectangular stars when Renaire glances out the uncovered glass. It's enough light to see, but not enough to do it well, and the rain distorts it just enough to make the dim light flutter around the room.

The moment they're through the door, Emile freezes, and it leaves Renaire feeling like he's clinging to a statue. He frowns, because this isn't normal behavior, at all. And not just compared to what semblance of normal behavior they're slowly cultivating when it comes to sex—it'd be abnormal even if they were in the middle of a firefight or downstairs with the rest of STB or even sitting on a train bored out of their minds. He is still, and he is contained, and he is *controlled*, but this is an entire new level.

"I should tell you," Emile says, words halfway to an apology.

"No you shouldn't," Renaire says because fuck, no, *no*, not right now, he thought they were... fuck, he doesn't know what he thought they were, but it was *something*. It was warm and safe and as close to truly content as he's ever managed, and now Renaire can't breathe again. He grabs onto Emile's shoulder, bends forward just enough to rest his forehead on Emile's collarbone, and shuts his eyes. "Don't tell me, don't, *please* don't."

Emile sighs, but he's less rigid—probably lack of eye contact—and he pulls Renaire close. "I'm not trying to break up with you, Renaire, that is the *complete opposite* of what I want, where the fuck are you getting that from?" he says, more than a little irritable. "How long is it going to take for you to believe that?"

"Probably a year," Renaire admits. "A few months at the very least."

"I'm not that patient," Emile says, like Renaire can suddenly change his fucked-up brain because Emile doesn't like waiting. He shifts them toward his bed, tugging almost politely at the hem of Renaire's shirt. Renaire pulls it off immediately, and when he looks at Emile, he can see the humoring-you smile. "And *you* are not that ridiculous."

"Oh, I'm pretty ridiculous," Renaire says, and he still feels unsettled and awkward, the pleasant *whatever* they'd had before now replaced by a jittery anxiety he doesn't like at all. Emile must notice (because he always notices) but doesn't say anything, just pulls his own shirt off and kisses him again.

It's slow and feels strangely filthy, with the way Emile is dragging his lips and tongue into it, and Renaire has no idea what's happening anymore. What once was sweet and warm is quickly turning into an ache to somehow prove this is still real.

This isn't on-off switch Emile. It's some blend of the two that's created rational passion, and what little confidence Renaire had about this *thing* is vanishing in the face of it.

Emile pulls away, and after a moment spent watching Renaire wait for him, he says, "You left me."

Renaire is pretty sure his heart stops. And then when it does start beating again, he's trapped in adrenaline and fight or flight or beg forgiveness or scream at him for being something very close to monstrous sometimes.

Emile spares him the decision, though, quickly stepping away and dragging a hand down his face. "Fuck, that was creepy, that sounded so bad," Emile says, and starts pacing. "Okay. Empirical method."

"What?" Renaire says, more than a little confused because this is…. Well. Kind of fucked-up. They've somehow gone from making out and the first steps of clothing removal to Emile pacing and talking about *the empirical method*. Renaire can barely remember what that even is, something about hypotheses or experiments or something—overall, not a topic one usually starts ranting about in a bedroom.

"I can lead you there. I can do this," Emile says, the words obviously meant for himself, and Renaire moves to turn on the lights, but Emile holds out a hand and says, "No! No, this is better."

"You were only slightly creepy before, now you're kind of acting like a serial killer," Renaire says and wonders what the fuck it says about him that he thinks it's kind of adorable. He obeys, though, and sits on Emile's bed and watches him pace in the half light.

"I told you I'm terrible at this," Emile says and takes a deep breath. "First, things we already know. One, I am attracted to you. Two, I consider you a friend. Three, I am invested in this relationship and want it to be a steady long-term romantic partnership."

"Oh God, more communicating," Renaire groans and falls back onto the mattress, everything but his dangling legs sprawled on the sheets.

"This is important, Renaire!" Emile says.

"Fine," Renaire says. "I'm listening, I promise. Yes, I know these things already."

He doesn't take promises lightly, and Emile knows it, so there's no further objection. Emile stops pacing and stands almost directly over Renaire, looking down at him intently. "You know I can, will, and have already killed and risked my own life for you, and I will keep doing it."

Renaire frowns and moves to sit up in the hopes of getting a better view of Emile's face (in times like these, it's all in the eyes), but Emile presses a hand to Renaire's bare chest and keeps him down. He's leaning over Renaire now, dedicated and beautiful and so very serious while he waits for acknowledgement. Renaire gives it to him, saying, "That goes both ways."

"It does," Emile agrees, and it's like watching him spiral his way down a drain. The hand on Renaire's chest is hot and sliding cautiously up his body, headed faceways. "And you know that no matter how I complain or how often we fight or how close we get to killing each other sometimes, I'm a mess when you aren't with me."

"No you aren't," Renaire says, confused, and he would say more, but Emile's hand has slid its way up the line of his throat, and a thumb is suddenly pressed into his mouth. He ends up biting it, almost purely by instinct, but Emile doesn't budge. If anything, Emile is nearer now, and leans down to press a close-mouthed kiss against Renaire's jaw.

"I don't feel wholly myself unless you're near me," Emile says into his skin, and Renaire's mind starts to catch up on two fronts—Emile is standing between his legs, bowed over him, and pressing kisses along his bare neck and jaw while Renaire almost unintentionally finds himself licking the thumb pressed between his lips, and he's being.... Well. He's being *very affectionate*, and Renaire's heart is racing, and oh, there's that buzz again. "And I want to keep you safe and give you everything you ever want. I bought you an incredibly expensive painting just because I thought you'd like it, and I wanted to make you happy."

Renaire very carefully bites at the thumb keeping him silent, and Emile removes it, replacing it with his mouth and tongue, and *oh*, the kiss is so sweet it burns through him. He can only see the light in Emile's eyes, but even in the dim wavering illumination of a rainy Paris night, it's fierce and bright and terrifyingly eloquent.

"Follow me, Renaire," Emile says when he pulls away, and Renaire releases the hold he'd had on the sheets in favor of wrapping his arms around Emile's bare torso. "All this time I thought you obeyed me, but you don't. You never have. You don't obey me—you *follow* me. And you *know* where I'm leading you, even if you can't believe it."

He shakes his head, but that doesn't last long. Emile keeps his head still with the lightest of holds, just two fingers keeping his jaw aligned with Emile's own. Renaire should have known there was no way to escape this. "I don't know what—"

"Yes you do," Emile says, and Renaire is glad he has his arms around Emile because the man straightens, and twists, and fuck, sometimes he forgets how bizarrely strong Emile is. He follows, as ever, shift for shift, until Emile is finally satisfied with their positioning on the bed—Renaire clings to Emile because he is having trouble telling what way is up or down while Emile twists them around. Renaire is pressed prone into the pillows with Emile braced above him and warm between his legs, and he finds himself actually thinking about what Emile is saying and *oh.*

"No," Renaire breathes out, gaping at him, and holding him so tightly it has to hurt and will probably leave fingerprints on Emile's back.

"*Yes,*" Emile says, and there's a savage glee in his eyes as he slides a hand across Renaire's cheek, coaxing him forward.

"No fucking way," Renaire says, because *no fucking way* did he just reach the right conclusion. Emile is so close to him that he could try and count his eyelashes, but Renaire can't stop gaping, can't even imagine kissing him because... *what.*

"I knew you could follow me there," Emile says, and he sounds so fucking smug, halfway between proud and arrogant as he makes that humming noise of his, and his teeth begin toying with Renaire's earlobe. It's the happy content oh-so-pleased noise, and holy shit, it's true, isn't it? This is an actual reciprocal thing between them.

Renaire has no idea what to do, but Emile knows that already, probably knew it would happen the minute they stepped into the stairwell earlier and has been ready to lead Renaire wherever he wants him.

"You can come back any time now," Emile says, amused and still so smug it's obnoxious.

It's probably that thread of irritation that finally snaps all the restraints in his brain. He doesn't have to worry if he's welcome. He doesn't need to tread carefully in case Emile pushes him away—if anyone separates them, it'll be Renaire. He pushes himself up from the pillows until he's flush with Emile, and keeps pushing, pushes until Emile falls back and is staring up at him from the mattress.

"I know what I want," Renaire says, because he knows the question is coming, and for once he really does, he has a *goal* here, and like hell is he letting the opportunity of having an actual stationary, reasonable-sized bed pass them by. He has to quickly put a hand over Emile's mouth because the man is incapable of staying silent, *ever*; he criticizes Renaire for it while preaching at empty rooms. "I want you to fuck me."

Emile looks like he's waiting for something, so Renaire carefully removes his hand. "Is that all?" Emile asks. When Renaire just stares at him, he wraps a hand in Renaire's hair and continues, "I thought there'd be adjectives. Hard or slow or—"

Renaire presses two fingers hard over Emile's lips. "Just fuck me like *you*. That's all I want. No adjectives necessary. Just be the passionate, possessive, arrogant as fuck asshole I know you to be."

"That was almost sweet," Emile says when Renaire moves his fingers away, a hand sliding down Renaire's skin and into his waistband. "Take your pants off."

"The romance is dead," Renaire says but rocks back onto his knees as he unzips his fly. He expects to have to work around Emile's hand as he efficiently divests himself, but Emile isn't even touching him. He's *literally* kicking his pants off by the time he realizes that maybe this would have been a good time for showmanship.

Emile is still stretched out on the mattress, eyeing the clothing Renaire tossed against the wall with a frown. "Very seductive."

Renaire is very glad their light source leaves the room in flickers of dim light. It means Emile (probably) won't mock him for the blush quickly spreading across his cheeks. He's already fucked-up. He knows it isn't going to change anything, other than how much ammunition Emile has, but he still has to fight the urge to shrink and apologize. He shuts his eyes and takes a deep breath and reminds himself he can leave, but Emile will never *actually* want him gone, not long-term at least.

When he opens his eyes, Emile is directly in front of him, pressing a hand against Renaire's cheek. "I'll be more specific," Emile says dryly.

"Oh fuck you," Renaire snaps.

"That *was* my original plan for tonight," Emile says, like it's an offhanded comment, and Renaire is so stunned at that information (and image, oh dear God) that he simply follows where Emile guides him. He's kneeling in the middle of the mattress, hovering two inches away from officially sitting in Emile's still-clothed lap as he trails kisses down Renaire's neck, their hands joined again. Renaire tightens his grip, and Emile presses back just as hard. "Is it really that surprising?"

He wants to say *of course it is*, but it really shouldn't be. "That explains the locks," Renaire says, and his voice is rough from far more than the lazy press of Emile's lips on his chest.

"Partly, yes," Emile says and lifts his head to look Renaire in the eye. The dim light makes his eyes shine almost unnaturally. "There are three reasons I locked the door, but if you want it unlocked, I'll go do it right now."

Renaire glares at him and finally lets himself grind down into Emile's lap as he says, "No, you will *not*."

It catches Renaire by surprise, Emile's dropping Renaire's hands to instinctively grab Renaire's bare hips. Renaire gasps. "I'm not going anywhere, I swear, not unless you want me to," Emile says, forehead pressed to Renaire's collarbone, and lets out a deep breath. "Christ, I had plans but…. Okay. Turn to face the wall and put your hands against the headboard, comfortably. Kneeling."

Renaire obeys almost immediately, rocking off Emile's lap and hooking his palms against the top of the headboard expectantly. "That was good and specific," he says, and he'll admit this isn't exactly how he'd hoped to do it, but Renaire is *not* complaining, breath already sharper just at the *thought* that Emile is going to fuck him. But Emile isn't replying. Hell, he can't even hear him, but he doesn't know if he's allowed to turn his head—Emile was specific but apparently, it's *still* not specific enough. Time stretches on, but he knows Emile won't leave him, and won't kick him out, and—

A hand presses softly against his hip and lips press against his lower spine, another hand wrapping around his waist and pulling him close, holding him. "I've got you," Emile says softly, and his breath is warm and soothing against his skin, and Renaire finally exhales. His hand moves away from his hip, but the grip on his waist pulls him down onto Emile's lap. "I'm still here. I just had to get something."

"I know you're still here," Renaire says harshly, and he doesn't even know why. "I'm not stupid—"

"Turn around," Emile says like he thinks Renaire is some sort of human swivel chair, but he obeys, a leg on either side of Emile's own hips.

Renaire takes a deep breath and begins to say, "You don't have to treat me like—"

"You're amazing," Emile says firmly, and... *what*, that cuts Renaire off immediately, leaves him frowning at Emile's fierce expression for one baffled second, and then *oh shit*, fuck, Emile has a lube-slicked finger just pressed against his ass. It's not moving.... It's cold and still and *waiting*. "You are brilliant and beautiful and wild and talented. Stop insulting my partner."

"I didn't," Renaire says, wide-eyed and torn between awareness of Emile's single questioning finger and the light in his eyes.

"You were thinking it," Emile says, and his finger moves the slightest bit, making small spirals, toying with him. Renaire clenches a hand in the sheets and does *not* shiver when he presses a little harder, other hand sweeping up his side to cup the back of his head. "Do you trust me?"

He shouldn't. "I do," Renaire says, nodding and leaning into Emile, and Christ, he's moving his finger just that little bit faster. "Fuck, you are such a tease."

"You'll like it," Emile says, not a shred of doubt in his voice, and he pulls Renaire's mouth to his, kissing him almost gently while his fingernails graze their way across his scalp, and that single fucking finger suddenly jerks inside of him, sharp and tight, and he gasps against Emile's smirking lips. Emile's finger withdraws, only to thrust back in, and Renaire has to squeeze his eyes shut and whimper as he bites back a moan. "Told you."

"Hate you so much," Renaire says.

Emile makes his pleased humming noise and says, "We're at home. You can be loud."

Renaire laughs breathlessly. "And give you—*fuck*." It's *one finger*, he should not be feeling this broken apart from one fucking finger, even if it's Emile's finger. "I will *not* give you the satisfaction."

"That sounds like a challenge," Emile says, and shit, this is going to be bad, isn't it? Why couldn't Renaire just shut his stupid fucking mouth. "I'm going to throw you down face-first onto the bed, and you are going to put a pillow beneath your hips, and you are going to tell me if you don't like something, and you will end up a gibbering, shouting, purring *catastrophe* before I even fuck you, do you understand?"

"Oh shit," Renaire says.

"Good," Emile says, and Christ, he is strong, Renaire is on his stomach and frantically grabbing a pillow moments after Emile's promise-threat. He can feel Emile's hand sliding hard down the curve of his spine, lower and lower until Emile is cupping his ass. His finger abandons Renaire, and it feels strange already, like he's not whole but somehow is still getting ripped apart.

That sure as fuck doesn't last long because where there used to be an inquisitive finger, there's now Emile's very determined tongue, mercilessly licking him open, and Renaire can't hold back the moan at the feel of every nerve rippling through him. It travels up his spine, and Jesus, if this keeps up he is going to tear the sheets with the grip he has on the fabric as Emile smugly shakes him apart—achieving the gibberish goal takes him approximately zero point five seconds. Renaire can't help the miniscule thrusts against the pillow beneath his hips, doesn't even know what he's saying beyond *oh please don't stop. Oh fuck please, Emile, please.*

After no time at all, his head is twisted to the side, and Emile is there, kissing him almost carefully, fingers toying with Renaire's hair. "Are you usually this sensitive or—"

"I don't even know. What do I have to do for you to get your tongue back in my ass?" Renaire says, hand grabbing onto Emile's arm because he has to hold on to *something.*

Emile kisses him again, deep and slow and so fucking *smug* that Renaire wants to strangle him, except he also wants to kiss him forever. He pulls back, eventually, and Renaire barely manages to stop himself from chasing Emile's lips with his own. "I bet I could get you off just from that," he says and shifts away from Renaire again, always keeping a hand pressed to his back, almost petting him. "But I have a goal here."

"You do?" Renaire asks, voice high, back to thinking *oh no*.

"Oh yes," Emile says, voice low and smooth, and he thrusts that same finger in. There's nothing gentle about it, coated in cold lube and jabbing in as deep as he can go, and Renaire *yelps*; it is the least sexy noise ever. Emile pulls his finger out completely, and Renaire pants into the sheets.

"Fuck, how are you this sensitive?" Delaurier says.

Renaire clears his throat, finding words again. "This is usually a third-date kind of thing for me," he says.

"But you don't—oh," Emile says. His grip on Renaire's hip tightens until it will leave bruises in the morning, and it shouldn't make Renaire shudder, but it does—it absolutely does—and Emile starts doing that fucking humming of his again, and that only makes it worse. "Renaire, are you telling me nobody's fucked you for two years?"

His voice is dark and smooth, and he croons it out into the small of his back, and Renaire can't tell if he sounds more like he's about to fuck Renaire so hard he breaks the bed or he's about to call off the sex to snuggle Renaire to death. It is quite probably the sexiest thing he's ever heard.

"Not exactly," Renaire manages to say. "Fuck, when was Antwerp? I can't remember."

"Fifteen months," Emile hums into his skin and carefully nips at his skin. "I should've known you don't like getting taken down by strangers."

Renaire twists to glare at him. "Nobody's *taking me down*, what the fuck does that even mean?"

Emile is completely unimpressed by the glare. He meets Renaire's eyes, and *fuck*, his finger thrusts in again, cold and slick and gliding in like it's meant to be there, and Renaire's body just opens up for him, and fuck, Renaire has fucked people with an eighth of this amount of lube.

"That's better," Emile says and starts to explore, twisting and thrusting and watching Renaire so intently that Renaire fucking blushes as he bites his lower lip because he will *not* give Emile the satisfaction. He moves faster and deeper, and Renaire can't stop his small thrusts back onto the finger and forward onto the pillow, can't keep his choked back moans from escaping as a low keening noise.

Emile starts to smile, slow and wicked. He pulls out completely again, looking away for a moment and saying, "Any last words?"

"I hate you so much you arrogant, beautiful, amoral asshole, you are vicious and cruel and you are *killing me*, fuck you, you merciless tease, what do you *want* from me?" Renaire demands.

"That'll do," Emile says and thrusts two fingers inside of him (slick and smooth and cold, and *fuck*, how much lube does he *have* back there?). They hit his prostate like a train wreck, and Renaire is seeing sparks and feeling lightning and it is *glorious*. He grabs at the bedding and groans loud and harsh into the mattress and spreads his thighs as wide as he can.

Emile does it again, and again, and Renaire's shouting into the sheets as Emile fucking narrates, says, "Fuck, I need to put a mirror in front of you and just fuck you against the glass in the first place, and Jesus, how will you look when it's my cock and not my fingers, will you want to ride me? Or should I fucking *claim* you, like you want me to? You're so desperate for it you can't even get the right words out to ask."

"*Yes*, oh please," Renaire says, and Emile's fingers are *gone*, Renaire whines at the absence and turns and manages to grab Emile's hand in his own, grip tight and hard as he finally gets Emile to look at his face instead of whatever he's toying with. "I *need* you to fuck me, please, Emile—"

"I will, I swear," Emile says, and there's *even more lube*, this time with no fingers, just spread around his rim, and it's fucking dripping, and Renaire *will* strangle him. He will throw Emile down and wrap his hands around his neck and ride him like his life depends on it if Emile doesn't fuck him soon. But no fingers and more lube might mean it'll finally be *Emile*, and his breathing sharpens, and he feels coiled and tight. "I've got you. Soon."

"*Now*," Renaire counters.

"*Soon*," Emile repeats and thrusts three fingers into him, slick and warming and just gliding right in, and it's maddeningly good. Emile is good at anything and everything, he is great, he's the best thing to ever exist on Earth and possibly the entire galaxy, and he is hitting that sweet spot with every single thrust.

The pillow beneath his hips is going to be so wet and soiled from dripping lube and Renaire's painfully hard cock that Renaire will have to buy him a new one, and then Renaire would own a pillow on Emile's bed. Renaire is *on* Emile's bed, Emile wants him here, wants him so bad he'll wait in the rain just to *see him*, and he is what keeps Emile human—Emile wants him, and even better Emile *needs* him.

Emile is pulling him up, pulls him until he's splayed out against Emile's chest with his legs spread and his cock pressing hard against his own stomach as Emile's fingers keep thrusting inside of him. Emile's other arm is wrapped tight around his chest, and he's whispering into his ear and hair and kissing his neck as he says, "I've got you, Renaire, fuck, if you could see yourself."

"Please," Renaire begs and twists to at least breathe against Emile's lips, and he fights the desperate urge to try and jerk himself off, to even touch himself, he wants to, but Emile probably wouldn't like that. He will beg for absolutely anything. "*Emile*, please—"

"I think if I don't fuck you right now, I'm going to die," Emile says, and Renaire moans like he's being tortured, barely capable of kissing back when Emile leans forward and latches their mouths together, just for a moment. "But." He takes a deep shuddering breath and presses his forehead against Renaire's shoulder. "Fuck it, that'll be next time."

"What will?" Renaire manages to ask, hands wrapped around his knees because he wants to touch himself, wants it so, so bad, but he won't.

"I wanted four fingers," Emile says, and Renaire can feel the head of his cock pressed against him, and it is fucking fantastic. He wants to rock back and feel him slide inside, but instead he stays rigid... he stays still and good and *waits*. "You'd take it so easy, even after *fifteen months*."

"Come on," Renaire says, his own hands sliding up and down his thighs because he has to do something with them, has to restrain the itch to touch and grab and stroke and reach back and drag Emile where he wants him. "Come on, Emile—"

"Were you waiting for me to fuck you, before?" Emile asks, thrusting just the head of his cock inside of Renaire. There is absolutely no resistance, Renaire's body is so slick and prepped and gaping for him that Emile could have thrust in with one merciless slam of his hips, but *no*, he barely lets himself thrust in even that far. Fucking control freak of a tease. "Or is it just trust?"

"Both," Renaire says, not even meaning to, but now that it's out, why not just say it? He tries to breathe. "I don't want anyone but you. I don't trust anyone like I trust you. I just needed *someone* to touch me."

Emile pulls out, all the way, not even the almost imperceptible thrusts of before, and Renaire is going to snap at him or beg, but Emile seizes one of his hands, and curls their fingers together, holding tight and somehow sweet, kissing the curve of Renaire's neck. "Ask, and I will give you anything," Emile says and presses their joined hands right above Renaire's heart. It's beating harder than Renaire can ever remember, for so many, many reasons.

"I just want you," Renaire says.

"You already have me," Emile says, calm and absolutely certain, Jesus *Christ*. "You have me, and I have you, for as long as you'll let me." Renaire moans like he's dying, he can't think or breathe or stop panting, and the only place Emile is touching him is his hand and his chest.

He leans back until he can look at Emile, pressed tight against his chest with his head resting on his collarbone, and he doesn't know what to do. Emile looks deadly serious, *enraptured*, and Renaire has never felt this desired. He ends up smiling, slow and giddy and so caught up in the idea of Emile *wanting him* like this and really seriously meaning this shit that he doesn't even realize he's purring out, "Fuck me like you own me."

Emile moans. Something rips apart in Emile's eyes, and Renaire barely has time to take a deep breath before Emile thrusts inside him, hard and slick and groaning into Renaire's skin, ramming into Renaire's prostate, and fuck, this is going to be embarrassingly fast. Emile is merciless, rocking in and out of him in a harsh rhythm that ends up pushing Renaire forward, bowed at the waist as Emile wraps his arm around Renaire and thrusts harder and harder.

Renaire can't catch his breath, can do nothing but squeeze his eyes shut and hold on to Emile's hand just as tightly as Emile is and sweat and feel about two seconds away from hyperventilating.

"I've got you," Emile breathes out against the nape of his neck. "Touch yourself."

Renaire whines, shakes his head. "But you—"

"You're going to jerk yourself off and I'm going to feel it from inside of you when you come, and then I'm going to lick the come off your fingers after I've taken you apart," Emile says, and *oh*. "Now *do it*, I've got you, Renaire, come on, I want you to."

He obeys, and fuck, it feels so good. Renaire strokes himself fast and tight, tighter than he likes it, but *God*, the way Emile is moving inside of him, if he doesn't hold himself back a little he is going to be gone within three strokes. What little breath he had before is lost to him, and he couldn't stop even if he wanted to.

Emile keeps whispering praise into his skin, keeps telling him *that's good, you're so good, I've got you, come on, Renaire, come for me*, and he'll never hear the end of it. It's brutally fast and viciously good, and he comes with a ragged shout, clenching around Emile and feeling so dizzy that he'd fall if it weren't for the way Emile is holding him.

"Oh, Emile, wow," he says, making a low, rumbling noise without even realizing it, and after a moment he gathers his breath and feels so fucking *sated* it's amazing. He rises up to meet Emile's thrusts and makes a noise somewhere between a chuckle and a purr. "You have the best plans."

"Jesus *Christ*, you're so fucking beautiful," Emile pants into his shoulder, full of lust and excitement and desperation. "Come on, tell me—"

"You're a horrible person, and I am hopelessly in love with you," Renaire blurts out, and Emile lets out a high whine, thrusts more erratic. "I am going to cuddle the shit out of you."

Renaire didn't even know Emile could make this noise, a single giddy, desperate laugh full of sunshine and frantic sex on picnic blankets, and he comes with a groan, holding Renaire tight. He takes a moment to catch his breath before pulling out of Renaire, and he doesn't know what he expected, but it wasn't for Emile to roll off the bed with somewhat shaky legs and pull Renaire forward to follow. He carefully grips Renaire by the wrist, eyeing his sticky, drying hand with intent, and how the fuck is this his life now? Who the fuck would even *believe* him if he tried to explain Emile?

"I can't stay awake for a bath," Emile says when they're in the bathroom, and at least this statement makes sense. He leads them into the shower and is making his humming noise, sounding inches away from actually singing when he turns on the water. Renaire doesn't know what he's looking for, but after a few seconds of Renaire standing there staring at him as the shower pours down, he starts nonchalantly licking the come off Renaire's hand.

"You are very confusing," Renaire states, watching.

Emile watches him back before softly turning Renaire's hand to give him a better view. "It's not confusing," he says simply, and smiles like the insufferable dick he is. "This happened because of me. I made you come."

And he loves that fact, Renaire thinks.

It doesn't take long for Emile to finish—he's *very* dedicated—and then he scrubs them both down and washes Renaire's hair, batting away any and all of Renaire's attempts to do *anything*. He gets to touch and kiss, but any actual showering efforts earn a gentle swat on his hand. He's tired anyway, so he lets Emile pamper him, soap and shampoo feeling almost like a massage, it's so unexpectedly soothing.

Unlike the last time Emile decided to do this, there's no clothing involved after they step out, and Emile dries him off. They fall back into Emile's exceptionally mussed bed, clean and smelling lovely, even if the bed doesn't, and curl tightly around each other.

The message light on his phone is blinking. Renaire doesn't care one bit, and falls asleep in Emile's arms.

CHAPTER 8

Paris: Chéron—*Palais du Luxembourg*

A PHONE is ringing.

It's not any of Renaire's ringtones, and it's not the annoying beeping Emile has his phone set to, so Renaire tries to ignore it. But it's persistent and *incredibly* annoying and making Emile actually wake up, even when it's—he glances at the clock—only seven in the morning. It takes Renaire a while to finally accept that yes, he has to move, because yes, that's his new phone. If this keeps up, he'll throw this one into the Seine too.

Which is strange, since from what he remembers, nobody actually has his number. Carope has it since Renaire texted her, and Celine has it for emergency purposes, but that's the end of the very, very short list.

Emile is mumbling discontentedly into his collarbone and has his arms wrapped around Renaire's waist, and it's a painful ordeal to move because *he really doesn't want to move*, and Emile seems to agree with him, but he manages to extract himself and grumble his way to the phone.

His voice is rough and awkward when he answers. "What?"

"We need to talk," Celine says, quiet and serious, and all Renaire can think is *oh God, not again.* But it can't be like last time. STB has officially called off their insane plan. There should be absolutely no reason for that tone, unless it's something like his tiny apartment is burning down. Which wouldn't actually be that much of a tragedy, although he'd miss his toaster and Chason would be short one hideaway.

Renaire takes a deep breath. "Just tell me," he says.

Celine hesitates, and fuck, that is not a good sign. He doesn't like this, at all, he wants to just curl up with Emile and stay in bed until two in the afternoon with nice morning sex and then eating lunch naked in the kitchen and then afternoon sex. Is that so much to ask? No, it is *not.*

But Celine is hesitating, and Renaire has accepted that he has to know whatever it is.

"Tell me," Renaire repeats as calmly as he can manage. It's much calmer than he expected.

"I should preface this with the fact we're certain it's not Delaurier," Celine says.

Renaire wants to say that he knew that already, but he doesn't trust himself when it comes to judging Emile. Not anymore. He sees all his flaws and is still in love with him, and really, no logical person would ever be able to do that. But in the end, he says, "I know that already."

"Of course," Celine says, and she does sound relieved. Emile is actually waking up, fighting his way through his natural inclination to pretend sunrise is just a myth. "I'm assuming he's nearby?"

"How could you guess," Renaire says, deadpan.

"We couldn't get into contact with him, and nobody seems to be willing to try and contact him—both of you, I suppose—in person," Celine says, and Renaire isn't sure if she's actually giving him an answer or just explaining because it's in her nature. "But I'm guessing he has an alibi."

Emile makes a muffled whining noise into the pillow that Renaire thinks might possibly be his name. Or just complaining. Renaire often wonders if he mentally regresses to a toddler between the hours of five and eight in the morning. "Yes, he does," Renaire says and is very proud that there's only a little bit of smugness in the words. Okay, more than a little bit. The point here is that he isn't screaming it at her, and he deserves an award for that.

"Good," Celine says. She's nervous, and it makes her sound a little bit fluttery. "Now, are you sitting down? Is Delaurier awake?"

"Just say it, Celine," Renaire bites out.

Emile actually manages to sit up then, even if he ends up flopping himself onto Renaire's shoulders and mumbling nonsense into the back of his neck.

"We received another threat about STB's bombing plan," Celine says. "It's a recording of Delaurier, most likely made at least a week ago."

Renaire is infinitely grateful for the fact Emile is still mostly asleep because this way Renaire can get up and walk out of the apartment and never stop walking, or he can just pretend this never happened, or he can shake Emile awake and demand groggy, honest answers.

"Maybe it was mailed weeks ago, and only just got there," Renaire suggests, even if it's weak.

"It wasn't," Celine says simply, and Renaire can hear some shifting, probably papers. She's a hard copy kind of person. "But we know it wasn't anyone in STB, or at least from the core."

Renaire frowns. "The core? Who's that?"

"That's *you*, Renaire. The original STB. It sounds less intimidating than inner circle," Celine says. "I'm guessing you aren't familiar with how many STB-related branches there really are, so I'll just say that there are many of them, at least one per nation. Most of STB's branches are political groups that focus on protesting and trying to right wrongs in ways that aren't murder. They leave that to you."

"Very kind of them," Renaire says. He knew there were groups, and he knows Emile goes off and preaches while Renaire does whatever the fuck he wants, but... *wow*. Maybe Wikipedia wasn't so wrong. "And you think one of those groups stole the bombing stuff?"

"Whuzzat?" Emile says, fighting closer toward conscious. "What'd she tell you?"

"I've been speaking with Glasson, and the information he's shared makes me think someone didn't get the message that the plan's off. That, or they just didn't care," Celine says. "Considering it's a coordinated attack on seven different cities over thirty-three days, it's very likely *someone* is out of the loop. We don't know what country or city, and STB won't tell us what the targets are, so it's *very* frustrating. We could use your help."

"And Glasson didn't stop this?" Renaire asks, genuinely confused because Glasson doesn't want it to happen, and Glasson could probably control the entirety of France if he felt like it. If it's beyond Glasson's abilities, this is an extremely serious threat.

"I've been told he's trying, but doesn't know who the rogue supporter is. He did a good job of hiding information in case of interrogation, even from himself. The point was to make this unstoppable, and undoing his own work isn't going to be easy," Celine says.

"If anyone can do it, it's Glasson," Renaire says.

"Oh, I'm well aware of that," she says, words tinted with Interpol agent frustration. There's a cautious pause. "But if this does happen—"

"I'll stop it or die trying," Renaire says.

And that definitely wakes Emile up because he jerks forward and snatches the phone out of Renaire's hands and is scowling at the wall, and Renaire can't breathe because Emile is holding him so tightly. "What the fuck are you saying to him?" Emile demands.

Renaire watches closely as his face falls from outraged scowl, to silently attentive, to the dangerously intense expression he gets before something life threatening and unpleasant happens.

"I'll take care of it," Emile says and hangs up on Celine. He's still holding on to Renaire like he's moments away from flying off, but it's not strangling him anymore. He's quiet, tense, and somehow somber, and Renaire presses his hands on top of Emile's own.

Someone is going through with STB's horror of a plan, and this time Renaire doesn't know who is doing it. He doesn't know why they're affiliated, doesn't know why (or if) they're going against orders. Emile is warm behind him, chin resting lightly on his shoulder. Renaire desperately wants to just fall back into bed. They've had four hours of sleep, at the most, and Renaire can feel himself already dragging along. Neither of them is in good shape for a crisis. They're tired, trapped between razor-sharp stress and a relief so deep it leaves you incapable of getting off the floor, and they have yet to figure out the new balance between them since this *thing* started.

"*We* will take care of it," Renaire finally says because there's nothing else to say.

Emile presses his lips against Renaire's neck, soft and calm, and pulls away.

They get dressed. Emile goes downstairs. Renaire lights a cigarette and stares out of his massive windows for a long time, and then he goes upstairs to pull together their armaments, piece by deadly piece.

WHEN RENAIRE hears the target, he nearly vomits. He feels sick down to his soul, and if Emile was anyone else, *anyone*, Renaire would be seriously considering killing him. Or would have done it already. As it is, he sits in one of the chairs and leans down, bends in half to put his head between his knees and desperately try to remind himself that this isn't happening, they're going to stop it. Emile will never even consider doing something like this.

Consider, yes. Actually carry out, no, Emile had said because he doesn't *feel* it's wrong, but now he knows it is, intellectually. They'll be fine. They'll stop this, and he will keep convincing Emile that he needs to develop a conscience, and the only people who die will be the mostly precise strikes they already do.

Emile is hovering cautiously by his shoulder, obviously torn between trying to reach out and comfort Renaire and stay far away to give Renaire space.

It's an endless dilemma, figuring out what to do and how to act when you're in love with a monster.

"And everyone was going to go along with this plan," Renaire says when he's able to speak. It sounds dead and cold, and he raises his head to scrub his hands over his face, trying to wipe away actually feeling things. He used to be good at that. Not so much these days.

Fuck, he wants a drink so bad, but they have a job, an *incredibly* important job. He needs to be vaguely sober, so he settles for a cigarette. The ritual behind it—pull out pack, pull out single cigarette, put pack back, pull out lighter, watch it light, inhale, exhale, inhale, exhale—is calming. Not calming enough, but it gets him under control just enough to survive.

He still can't look at Emile, but he doesn't want to push him away either, so Renaire shuts his eyes. "Well, it would certainly bring about a need for change," he says, but there's little humor in it.

"We're not going to let it happen," Carope says firmly from the table they've tossed their plans across. Their very thorough, well thought out, exceptionally difficult to stop or sabotage plans. She's lost a lot of her usual sparkle. "At the very least, we can evacuate the building and area."

"And then Plan F goes into effect," Glasson says, and Renaire can't even imagine what it'd be like even if they only lost the building. And probably the grounds along with it. It makes the artist part of him curl up and sob. "No, the original approach is still the best one we have."

"Which is what?" Renaire asks, finally opening his eyes because this is *productive*, this is STB at its best.

Every single person in the room is suddenly looking at him. Well, everyone but Emile, who is still torn between awkwardness and attentiveness, now with an added burst of that stubbornness he gets when he thinks Renaire's about to launch a particularly damaging attack during an argument. When Renaire stops being amused, Emile clears his throat and says, "We can talk about this outside—"

"No, we can't," Renaire says. And STB is back to business, all of them looking very very busy and not the least bit like they're listening. Renaire points to the closest chair and says, "Sit. Explain."

Emile obeys and purses his lips and then lets out a breath before saying, "We have a way in. If we use it and steal a couple of badges, you and I might be able to just walk right in, unimpeded. From the research we've done, it sounds like we could even get assistance from the security in the building if we talk fast enough."

Renaire is impressed. "Then why aren't we using that right now?"

"Because it's your brother-in-law," Emile says.

"My what?" Renaire asks.

Emile sighs and moves over to the table to grab a file, and oh, that's right, his sister is married and his parents are dead. Renaire never really did go the whole way through Ivanova's file—he got to his hospital records and gave up after the fourth page of *nothing wrong except poor life choices*. When Emile comes back, he's holding a picture of Renaire's sister looking like an adult and marrying a handsome enough man who has a painfully wide smile on his face. It's a newspaper clipping, with a headline that reads "Senator Mannon Marries Childhood Sweetheart Michelle Renaire."

The childhood part must have been *very* childhood because Renaire's never even heard of a Dax Mannon. He would remember a *Dax Mannon*.

Probably.

He can see how this plan starts, and Renaire can feel the grimace long before it surfaces on his face. He keeps staring at the picture and the associated article, and Delaurier keeps staring at Renaire, and fuck, he does not want to do this.

"We can find another way in, but this is the easiest," Glasson finally says when the staring's gone on long enough. "A missing brother who sees the picture for the first time realizes his older sister is alive and married and rushes to the first person who could tell him where she is—"

"I understand, thank you," Renaire says, and rubs a hand down his face. Again. Fuck, he isn't even done with his first cigarette. "So I can get us into the Palais du Luxembourg, but I have to play the part of a long-lost baby brother."

"You *are* a long-lost baby brother," Emile says.

Fucking logic. "Fine, but how does that get *you* in?"

"Long-lost baby brother-in-law," Carope says with far too much pleasure.

"So basically everyone but me knew I'm married," Renaire says.

"Yep," Carope says.

He doesn't even bother being surprised. He could find out he's the mother of five children and not be surprised at this point. "This gets us physically present in the building," Renaire says. "And relies on them ignoring the fact Delaurier is Delaurier."

"We think they'll be distracted enough by your drama to ignore that, so make it *very* dramatic. It also helps that our uninformed bomber will probably see Delaurier's presence as support rather than a threat. It's shaky, but it's the best we have right now if we don't want to make things worse," Glasson says.

It makes sense—if this plan was as well thought out as Renaire suspects (*knows*—Glasson and Emile were planning with the entirety of STB, so it's damn near foolproof), the only chance they have is of being incredibly unobtrusive. One bizarre blip of a long lost relation making an unarmed ruckus is probably the best they could ever manage. Renaire just happens to be the lucky bastard who has to reunite with his family to save hundreds of lives and a national treasure.

Renaire nods and takes a moment to think about how this could be so much worse, and how much better it would be if STB was something very simple. Like a sheep farm. They could all just herd fluffy, placid sheep all day.

"Let's go, then," Renaire says and stands up, patting himself down quickly and handing Emile his usual preferred weaponry. Nothing fancy this time. Renaire only has his knives; most of his pockets are full of art or smoking or drinking. He's attired for Paris, and Paris isn't supposed to be armed conflict. Paris is supposed to be sleep and friends and excessive *everything*, not bombs and reunions.

"We probably won't make it inside armed," Emile warns. Unlike Renaire, he tucks a pistol away along with the usual versatile gear he can fit in the red coat.

"Consider it my single act of optimism for the day," Renaire replies and finishes off his cigarette.

They leave with nothing more than a good-bye and some hurried organization and commands on Emile's part before walking in tense, anxious silence to the metro.

It's bitterly cold out. Renaire is completely underdressed for the weather even with his coat on, and it's barely eight in the morning when they actually get near the front gate. It's too early, and he's too cold and tired and he doesn't want to do this.

"How long has it been since you saw your sister?" Emile asks while they stare at the gate from across the street.

"About twelve years," Renaire says. And fuck it, he doesn't care how much he hates Delaurier's amoral cruelty right now, he loves him desperately, and he *needs that*, needs *him*. Anxiety and panic are clawing his mind to shreds, so he grabs Emile's hand. Emile is right there with him, squeezes tightly the moment their fingers are joined together, and Renaire knows the only way Emile will let go is if Renaire tells him to. That or someone saws his hand off, and even then it might not work.

They're together. They'll stay together. Emile will take care of him and Renaire will take care of Emile, and if they're together, he can absolutely face the fact he has blood relations.

Emile doesn't talk about it, but Renaire knows that where familial relationship is concerned, they're on the completely opposite ends of the spectrum. Renaire left of his own choice and did his best to forget they even exist. Emile was tossed out and disowned but still occasionally stalks his parents, in that affectionate stalking way of his.

"We can escape after this," Emile says simply, and when Renaire looks at him, Emile is completely serious. "We can get you lost again, I mean. You don't have to be found if you don't want to."

"Or we can get blown up along with hundreds of other people," Renaire says.

"Or that," Emile agrees.

Absently, Renaire realizes this is where he first saw Emile.

He concentrates on that. He thinks about the way it'd been breezy and warm, how Renaire had just needed *out* and away from What's-His-Name and been drawing in the *Jardin du Luxembourg* feeling dead. The wind had picked up and tossed drawings into the air, and Renaire had deftly snatched them back before they got too far, but he *saw him*, saw Emile Delaurier smiling in his direction, probably at someone behind him, smiling beneath a sun-soaked tree sending dappled light down through the leaves, and he'd glowed in Renaire's mind.

He was, and still is, the most beautiful thing Renaire has ever seen.

And now they're holding hands, and Emile wants that. Emile wants *Renaire*, wants them to be together and wants it to stay that way for a long time. He concentrates on that, and they walk across the street.

Renaire has the article crumpled in his pocket and his hands were already shaking slightly from his truly depressing level of sobriety at the moment, and the anxiety has them shaking even more. He lets himself look as terrified as he is—they're going to die, they're going to destroy the upper house of the French judicial system and a major public park and the entire surrounding area of the city, and he's about to face the fact he has an actual past. He doesn't want any of those things.

By now, they know how to get in and out of places they aren't supposed to be. For example, it's early morning and people are flooding their way in to work. They flood right along with a larger group, just two more faces in a mass of tired humanity on a Tuesday morning whose stolen entry badges slide past tired and busy security at the entrance. They're good at looking like they belong, even if they're holding hands, and Emile has his bright red coat on while Renaire is wearing a shirt so casual it's about five threads from being classified as pajamas.

Emile had already told him what he'd known even without hearing the words—the explosives are already in place. Apparently, it's been there for days, if not weeks, planted and ignored by all the right underlings. Sometimes, STB's (Emile's) ability to get people to go along with plans is terrifying.

They follow the flow of bodies past the entry gate until the group starts to thin out, leaving them with no idea where to go or who to ask. After a quick, shared look of Emile telling him *you're leading right now*, and Renaire eloquently informing him how much he hates him and the present situation they are in, Renaire takes a deep breath, crinkles the newspaper clipping even farther in his pocket, and pulls it out like it's a badge and he's a detective at the first person he sees. "I'm looking for this man," he says, making it as urgent sounding and commanding as possible, which more or less means he's imitating Emile. "Senator Dax Mannon, where is he?"

The woman gapes at him, but when Renaire asks again, she finally points to their left and says, "Senator Mannon should be in the conference hall—"

Emile is already dragging him along, and Renaire thanks her while they rush through the beautiful halls. Emile knows the blueprints, so Renaire tries to concentrate on how shockingly well this is all going so far. They're in, they're armed, they aren't arrested or dead yet, and they could theoretically have just rushed around the building and tried to dodge (or alert) the guard.

"There's a major vote at 10:00 a.m. If it's exactly according to plan, detonation's at 10:28 a.m.," Emile says, because *of course it is.* "I don't know where it is, but—"

"Why don't you know where it is?"

"In case of capture," Emile says, like it's ridiculous he has to explain this. "There were seven major targets, Renaire. This wasn't going to be something we could hide from. The second it started, every single person even vaguely related to STB would be chased down for interrogation to try and stop the other attacks. There's no risk of someone giving away information if they don't have it in the first place."

They step into the conference hall, and Renaire gapes. It's breathtakingly beautiful, coated in gold and marble and sculpture and paintings, all elegant and symbolic and perfect. He's barely looked at the place before he glares at Emile and ends up shouting, "Why the *fuck* did you pick here?"

There are people milling around, talking and doing what Renaire assumes are very important instances of newspaper reading. They all look up and frown at the two underdressed men holding hands in the doorway looking sleep-deprived and stunned. Renaire is too busy staring at the room to play long-lost brother, but Emile squeezes his hand hard enough that he doesn't have the luxury of staring at the artwork. Job to do, right.

Renaire steps forward awkwardly, holding the newspaper clipping up like it's a cross among vampires and lets himself babble out, "Please. I just need to find Dax Mannon. I think he's married to my sister, and I haven't seen her in twelve years. I didn't even know she was alive until I saw this, and I haven't slept more than a few hours for the past—I don't even know how many days. We've been traveling almost nonstop to get here."

All of which is mostly true.

Bizarrely, nobody calls for security.

"That's me," a voice at the end of the hall says, and a man walks toward them. He looks at Renaire like he just smashed a shovel over his head. "I'm Dax Mannon, and I can't possibly believe this."

"I saw this picture," Renaire says and hands it to Dax. After spending so much time getting deliberately crinkled and worried at in his pocket, the paper looks like Renaire has been messing with it for a minimum of four days. "I—we were in, fuck, I don't even remember where we were, but I saw it, and it's Michelle, and you'd know where she is if you're married."

"How on earth do you expect me to believe this?" Dax asks, but he's faltering. He's looking from the article (which makes zero mention of their family beyond that their parents are dead) to Renaire's frantic, panicking eyes to the death grip he has on Emile's hand. Somehow, he hasn't actually really *looked* at Emile. From the lack of security streaming in and trying to murder them, nobody has. Renaire didn't even know ignoring Emile was humanly possible. "Prove you're related."

"There's always blood tests, but mostly I'm really confused by the article since I've never seen you before in my life, and it says *childhood sweetheart*, so unless you were sweethearts before kindergarten, it's a lie," Renaire says.

Dax clears his throat and looks hard into Renaire's face. There's only vague family resemblance between him and Michelle, but it must be enough since Dax nods and says, "Follow me."

They do. He takes them into another breathtakingly beautiful room off the side of the massive ornate hallway. There are comparatively simplistic tables and chairs set up, and Dax leads them to one that is, preposterously enough, almost directly next to Napoleon's throne.

"This is a very strange day," Renaire says, and Emile squeezes his hand reassuringly while they sit with their backs to the wall, Dax vulnerable and calculating on the other side of the table. It's still over an hour before the vote and most of the senators aren't there yet, and Renaire can only assume Dax is because it's his very first year in office. He has yet to become the sort of jaded statesman that STB observes very, very carefully.

"You're right about the childhood sweethearts being a lie. That was Michelle's idea," Dax says, which isn't even a little bit surprising.

She always liked playing rich. "And I can see her in your face, just enough for me to believe it. But do you really expect me to believe you're only here to hear about your sister?"

"That, and save lives," Renaire says and realizes that shit, he actually kind of means it. Michelle was eight years older than him and never around for the worst of it, too busy trying to get her career as a soprano going. He remembers her fondly. Seeing her might actually be kind of nice.

Dax frowns at them. "Save lives?"

"There's an attack planned on the senate today," Emile says, and Dax's mouth drops open. "We're here to stop it, but there has to be absolutely no alert to the bombers—"

"*Bombers?*" Dax hisses out, starting to panic like any sane person would, and shit, if he gets loud this is going to end so badly.

Renaire reaches across the table to grab Dax's shaking hand and give him a beseeching look. He quietly says, "We can stop the attack, but we need your help, and you don't say a *word* to *anyone*, or it might go off ahead of time. You give us a tour while we 'wait for Michelle,' and we use it to sweep the building."

Dax nods, and Renaire makes himself do something that vaguely resembles a look of relief, he thinks. It's modeled after the people they *don't* shoot in the head. "And you really are her brother," Dax says. Renaire nods. "You know she's been looking for you nonstop for fifteen years."

"Twelve years," Renaire corrects, and no, he definitely didn't know that. At all. "But I really didn't know she was alive, or married, until just a few days ago. And I do actually want her to meet Emile."

"You do?" Emile asks, completely surprised.

Dax pales, finally really looking at Emile. Finally recognizing him. *Finally.* Renaire's not so sure about Dax. "You're here to *stop* an attack," he says.

"Above all else, STB believes in justice," Emile says. "And *this* isn't justice. It's an act of frustration and impatience, which causes a death toll that's inexcusable. We will stop it, or die trying."

Dax nods and pulls his phone out of his suit jacket. "And you two are…?"

"Partners in all ways," Emile answers simply, and after a moment of hesitation, he releases Renaire's hand to offer it to Dax. "It's nice to finally meet the in-laws."

"Wonderful. My brother-in-law is a terrorist," Dax says, resigned, but shakes Emile's hand. Briefly. He then starts toying with his phone, probably sending a message. "It's nice to meet you too. Is my wife's brother also a terrorist?"

"He's an incredibly talented world-renowned artist," Emile says, an unexplainable snap to the words. It must make sense to Dax, since he looks up and his eyes flick between them, and he nods something like an apology to them before putting his phone to his ear. "We're in a bit of a hurry here, so if—"

"It's ringing," Dax says, and offers the phone to Renaire.

They can all hear the click of the call being answered. They can all hear a woman saying, "Hello? Dax? What's going on?"

Emile is holding his hand again, this time on top of the table. Panic is screaming out of every pore of Renaire's body and he is terrified, he's panicking, and Emile is holding his hand and watching him patiently, trusting him. "You don't have to," Emile says.

Renaire snatches the phone out of Dax's hand and squeezes Emile's hand so hard he can feel bones shifting as he says, "Michelle?"

"Oh, God. What happened, is he okay?" Michelle says, and Renaire tenses all over. He can't speak. He can't even breathe. He's eight and watching Michelle shout at their parents. He's thirteen and trying to do the shouting in her stead. He's sixteen and looking at her picture—bold and wild on the stage—before tiptoeing out the door. "Who is this?"

"Hi, sissy," Renaire finally says, and clears his throat. "I just broke into the senate to save the world and meet your senator husband. He seems nice. I'm kind of busy right now, but we should catch up. When I'm not busy."

"Oh my God, *Valentine*? Val, is that you?" Michelle says, and Renaire has to hang up, he can't breathe, he hangs up and immediately tosses the phone to his left purely out of habit, and Emile catches it, as ever. He usually uses Emile's phone. Renaire's phone is almost exclusively used so Emile can find him. Therefore, if he's talking to someone, and Emile is present, he gives the phone to Emile.

It starts ringing again the moment Emile catches it, and Emile hands it back to Dax, since he can actually think. Dax answers it, and

Renaire can barely pay attention to what's happening other than that Dax is saying, "Yes, he's fine, he just needs a break, I think ... I know it was five seconds, dear, you ... well of course he is. They'll be here for a while ... no, I don't know how they're saving the world, can you ... look, Michelle, just ... Michelle ... Michelle, dear ... *Michelle*!"

Emile plucks the phone from Dax's exasperated fingers and says, "This is your brother-in-law, it's nice to meet you, speaking to you has been severely emotionally draining for Renaire. He'll be capable of speaking to you again in an estimated two hours." He then immediately hands the phone back, gets a fistful of Renaire's shirt, and Renaire knows this, at least. They stand. "Let's walk."

Dax obeys because everyone obeys Emile. He's still on the phone with Michelle, but he escorts them out of the room and back into the hall, where senators are shamelessly watching them.

"We're going downstairs," Emile says, and again Dax obeys. There's security lurking around them, but while they're escorted by a senator who is backing up their story with every word he says to his wife, they stay back. Renaire just has to be the emotionally unstable, long-lost baby brother. He manages that pretty fucking well.

"I need you on this, Renaire," Emile says.

He tries to shake himself out of it, but it doesn't really work, not until Emile pats his lower back right where he knows Renaire keeps his biggest knife. And... right. Right. Fuck, there are much more important things going on, and he needs to concentrate on *those*. "You said it's around ten thirty?"

Emile lets out a relieved breath. "We have about two hours," he says, purely professional, and he lets go of Renaire's hand as they fall into Job Mode. "I'm betting it's either in the actual senate chamber or somewhere around it. If they're our usual supporting demographic, they could be anyone, and gotten anywhere."

Dax frowns at them. "How?"

"Cleaning crews, security, all the hard-working people that your kind ignores and treats like invisible servants you're entitled to," Emile answers easily.

Dax gapes at him. "I do no such thing!"

"How many people have we passed on these stairs?" Emile asks. When Dax can't answer, Emile says, "You didn't notice because you don't care about them. They're angry, and mistreated, not to mention underpaid, and *you* are all they have to speak for them in the government."

"Is now really the time to preach?" Renaire asks.

"I'm walking with a senator in the Palais du Luxembourg," Emile says.

Renaire sighs and pulls out a cigarette. "Fair enough."

"There's no smoking in the building," Dax says. He's off the phone with Michelle, probably because she's on her way here. Which Renaire immediately makes himself ignore. Or tries to, at least.

"That makes a lot of sense, considering the priceless architecture, art, history, and library in the building, not to mention the comfort of the government officials in here," Renaire says, and lights the cigarette efficiently. "But since we all might be dead in two hours, and even if we *aren't*, I'm going to have to deal with a sister I haven't seen in over a decade, I really don't give a fuck." One person smoking to try and calm down a little bit instead of the entire building and associated area blowing up? Not exactly a difficult choice.

They sweep the ground floor as efficiently and nonchalantly as possible, with Emile on and off the phone with the rest of STB while Renaire dodges his brother-in-law's questions about what he's been doing for the past twelve years and how their childhood was, and all those questions that normal people can answer, and Renaire really can't. After figuring out he'll get nothing about their old family situation, he moves on to other things. Things like *how'd you two meet* and *how long have you been married* and *what do you do for a living* and even *what do you do for fun.*

Dax answers his own questions easily enough, though. Renaire isn't sure how he feels about that either.

"We're looking for a construct that's over two meters high or wide," Emile says, obviously frustrated. Renaire is too. Shit like that isn't exactly easy to hide, and it's also fucking terrifying to imagine how big of a blast it would cause. "Carope is trying to get details on our rogue supporter, but it sounds like they're as rogue as you can get. Chason is tearing the city apart for more information."

If they can't get information, nobody can.

When they've reached the end of the lowest floor and found absolutely nothing, they head to the next floor. They don't have *time* for this. Renaire finally pulls his own phone out, dialing the single phone number he has that Emile doesn't.

"What's happening on your end?" Celine asks immediately.

"Oh, I'm meeting my brother-in-law and looking for an explosive device that there's probably no way to disguise," Renaire says. "How about you?"

"There have been other developments, but you should just concentrate on that for now, I think," Celine says. She sounds haggard, and there's a worrisome lack of humor in her tired voice. "Please, if we can help in *any* way, let me know."

Renaire looks over at Emile, who is scowling for no reason Renaire can think of. "Anything you can think of for Interpol to do?"

"Have them go forwards through maintenance records since two months ago," Emile says. "We're going backwards from two days ago."

Renaire frowns. "That'd mean telling them where we are."

"We have sixty minutes left. Our priorities have changed," Emile says.

"Shouldn't we at least *try* to evacuate the building?" Dax asks.

Emile shakes his head. "That'd bring out Plan F, and we do *not* want that to happen. People enter and exit as naturally as possible."

"We need you to go through maintenance records of the Palais du Luxembourg since two months ago, paying particular attention to anything that's coffin-sized or bigger," Renaire says.

"Oh Jesus," Celine says.

"And do it *subtly*. You can't get anywhere near the building, you can't even look like you're considering it. If you find anything, call me immediately," Renaire says and hangs up. He sighs and frowns at Emile. "Why do you have to be so fucking competent?"

"We should ask some of the maintenance staff to help," Dax says.

"Did you miss the part where they're the most likely to be responsible for this?" Renaire asks.

Dax shakes his head. "The other problem is the vote starts at ten. If you're keeping suspicions low—"

"You have to go in," Emile says. They're already back into the breathtakingly ornate rooms and didn't even bother with the library. If there's something enormous and new in the library, the librarians would have known immediately. And if there is one thing they are certain of, it's that librarians aren't planning to blow up the Palais du

Luxembourg. "What's the absolute latest your entry could be considered normal?"

Dax looks down at his watch grimly. "In about twenty minutes."

"Where's the curator?" Renaire asks suddenly. If librarians would immediately know a change in inventory, so would a curator.

"Usually, the curator isn't around when the senate is in session," Dax says.

Emile's phone rings, but Renaire concentrates on this because oh, he has an *idea*. "Then where is he?"

Dax shrugs, but it's enough for Renaire. Emile is on the phone with Carope, so Renaire calls Glasson and says, "Call the curator and ask him if there have been any changes to the collection."

"You think it could be a forged sculpture?" Glasson asks, but he can already hear him giving orders, typing away. "The collection isn't exactly in flux, but I'll check into it. It's a good idea."

"We have no known affiliates here, but an affiliated moving company came in about three weeks ago," Emile says. "They're still trying to figure out what was moved, since they were hired for removal instead of delivery."

"And something that big is gone with nobody noticing?" Renaire asks. Maybe a column was removed and a new explosive device was put in its place.

"I'm already going to be late," Dax says, voice getting higher. He's starting to panic. Why it's starting *now*, when they might actually be getting somewhere, Renaire has no idea, but Renaire puts a hand on his shoulder. Dax takes a deep breath. "You either keep searching on foot and run the risk of being arrested, or you come to the public gallery area of the hemicycle."

Emile can't afford to get arrested, or even detained. Renaire technically has no record for the past two years, and a little before that as well, but Emile can't afford it. "You wait in the observation area, text me any information you get," Renaire says.

But Emile shakes his head, immediately saying, "We stay together."

"This is our best bet to stop it, and you know it," Renaire says.

"And what if you get detained or arrested and I'm stuck in the gallery, waiting for you?" Emile asks. He looks confused after he says it, but then he's shaking his head again. "No. We can slip out if we need to."

Renaire really, sincerely wants to argue, or just tell him to fuck off and stay out searching, but he knows Emile has a point. They've been searching the building for over an hour now, and it's gotten them nowhere. Now that they have *some* idea and information, the smart thing to do would be wait until they know how to act.

"Come on, then," Dax says, and they follow him to the senate's massive, breathtaking room, although Dax escorts them to the public observation level. It's as close to a packed house that the senate ever gets during regular session, with only a few scattered seats empty. Emile gets them situated next to each other, and they spend the next few minutes texting and e-mailing furiously, trying to consolidate their information.

But when Renaire looks up, and looks into the room, he *knows*.

"Fuck," Renaire says, and people shush him, but Renaire has grabbed onto the railing with a white-knuckled grip. Emile is staring at him, apprehensive. "Fuck, Emile. Okay. Okay, which one do you hate most?"

Emile frowns. "What?"

More shushing.

And when Renaire points to the interior of the room, directly at the seven very large sculptures of famous Frenchmen looking out on the senators, Emile says, "Shit."

After some more furious texting, it's confirmed—one of the sculptures was removed for maintenance and preservation efforts. Nobody can name which one it is. Or why someone decided it needed to be removed. One of the statues is a very big, very terrifying bomb.

"So," Renaire says. "Which one would you want to murder hundreds of people and change the world with?"

Emile says, "I'll figure it out."

"And while you figure it out, I'm going to get down there and try to make sure nobody even gets close to it," Renaire says. "How much time do we have?"

"They're about to start, so about half an hour," Emile says.

Renaire takes a deep breath, and nods to himself before standing. Emile doesn't let him get away unscathed, though. He deftly snatches one of Renaire's hands, and Renaire expects hand-holding. Instead, he watches Emile breathe against his palm, and then kiss him lightly in the center. He doesn't say anything. He doesn't even look at Renaire. He kisses Renaire's hand again and then releases it, turning away as if it never happened, staring down the long-dead men.

The trip out is easy enough, when Renaire once again makes a point of looking like he knows where he's going. By now, he's actually being greeted by some of the people in the building, and Renaire has to wave curious people off. It is very, very strange. And impossible. And he has probably a little over twenty minutes left to stop the bomb going off.

He manages to sneak down into the astoundingly ornate conference hall, using one of the curious senators as an escort past the guards. It's a dangerously easy way of getting around, and Renaire ends up chatting himself all the way to one of the entrances into the senate chamber. They're in full session, actively debating, and still the senators want to stop and chat about the soap opera that is Renaire's life at the moment. And they want to do it *outside* of the room.

Renaire knows that the moment he steps into that room, security will be on him. It doesn't matter how welcome he might be. Their luck *will* run out, if you can call a runaway abandoned bombing plan lucky. But there is a clock on the wall, and he has no time. He has to get out there and pray that Emile has figured this shit out. There is going to be a timed device, and a triggered device, and Renaire's job is the timed device—but thankfully he knows it *is* the red wire, definitely cut the red wire on the timed device since Sarazin made it. The triggered one he doesn't know, but he could guess it's also red, but he is concentrating on the timed device. And the red wire. He can cut the red wire.

He takes a deep breath, smiles an apology to the nice senator who wants him to know how pleasant Michelle is, and bolts into the room. There's shouts, and then there's a *lot* of shouting, and Renaire concentrates on getting up to the president's plateau. Security is trying to stop him, and Renaire *really* doesn't want to kill them, but there's enough chaos that he manages to jump up the stairs, and he can hear Emile over the din, because he can always hear Emile, and he's shouting, *Malesherbes*.

Renaire doesn't hesitate. He pulls one of his knives out, and it's absolutely no easy feat getting to the statue. It's a good ten feet off the floor, but he has plenty of adrenaline and determination to scramble his way up the wall as frantically and quickly as possible, using the beautiful wooden panels on the wall as nothing but extremely dangerous footholds before he lunges up and finally reaches what is so blatantly *not* marble or even plaster that Renaire despairs for the entirety of France, being led by these fools.

On Malesherbes's back, there are two devices. Thankfully, only one of them has a clock on it, so he immediately concentrates on it, loosening it from the statue and looking at the device and the wires and the small nonticking digital clock.

There's a cacophony on the other side of the statue, and he can hear Emile over it. Nobody is trying to shoot Renaire, so he assumes Emile has it taken care of. And fuck, fuck, *of course* Renaire doesn't have pliers. Emile has the pliers because he *always* has the pliers, and shit, why didn't Renaire think of this? He is going to end up electrocuting himself. But the timer gives him approximately 00:01:39, and he doesn't have time to figure this out. He doesn't have gloves, or anything to use as an insulator. He has his knives and cigarettes and alcohol and art, and that's about it.

When he glances around the statue, he can see that Emile has actually climbed his way down from the public tribune and is walking toward Renaire, talking to a man on the plateau. The *only* man on the plateau. The only other man in the entire room, aside from Emile and security lurking in the edges of the room. The man is wearing a suit, and Renaire realizes that he's not a senator. Or an oppressed worker. He's the senate stenographer, and he has what is definitely a detonator in his hand. Emile is being fiery and convincing and charming and a fucking force of violently persuasive nature, and Renaire is in love with him and has absolutely no time to enjoy the show.

Renaire meets Emile's eyes very quickly. He's positioned behind the stenographer here, so he holds out his knife and points at the man, but Emile shakes his head in the negative. He flawlessly turns the move into part of his speech, and Renaire doesn't let himself pay attention to his preaching. Renaire glances back at the timer (00:00:32) and shit, he doesn't have time for this. He takes a single second to smile and wink at Emile, and he ducks back behind the sculpture and prays he doesn't die because his knives have metallic handles. He takes a deep breath, thinks about how he's saving hundreds of lives and most importantly he's saving Emile, and Renaire first saw him in a place that will explode if he doesn't do this.

He slices through the red wire.

Sharp darkness jolts into his mind.

CHAPTER 9

{Brazil(?)}; Paris.

THERE IS an impossible beach in Brazil. The sand is a golden white and the ocean is a rapid shift from deep blue to aquamarine to a light emerald Renaire had never been able to replicate quite right. The beach had been surrounded by towering cliffs, covered in lush green hedges and bushes and the occasional stubborn tree, with enough of a breeze to tousle hair but not blow things away. The sky was clear and the air was sharp, and it was completely impossible, but Delaurier somehow led them there anyway.

They left the hotel long before dawn, which was the first sign something unusual was happening. South America was the land of driving instead of taking trains, and it was an exhaustive alternative. Delaurier's controlling tendencies had left them both irritable and resulted in a system—they drove for three hours, and then they took a break. More often than not, the break was simply switching drivers or stretching. Sometimes, it wasn't.

When Delaurier pulled over in the middle of nowhere after two hours of driving, Renaire was prepared to switch over and take the wheel. Delaurier is not a morning person, so it made sense that he'd want to switch early. But when they were out of the car, Delaurier had instead opened the trunk and pulled out their bag and quickly tugged Renaire's battered reliable art kit out. And then another bag, and an easel and *canvas*, which was impossible—Renaire's not stupid enough to try and take that sort of shit on a road trip.

"What is this?" Renaire had asked.

Delaurier had simply said, "You'll see."

They walked through rigid vegetation that bent willingly, only to snap back once it was past. Renaire had carried the kit and canvas, with Delaurier stubbornly holding onto the easel and mystery bag for the entire hike. It was rough, and downhill, and Renaire had followed blindly because that was what he always did. He trusted Delaurier, and there would be light at the end of the tunnel, there would be a prize at the end of the trial. Renaire believed in only one thing, and that was Delaurier.

His faith was rewarded. They stepped out of the underbrush and onto sand, and into heaven.

Delaurier obviously had no idea what he was doing with the easel, let alone what he was doing with it on sand, and by the time Renaire had argued him away from the fucking easel because *Jesus Christ, Emile, you are terrible at this*, the sun had been rising, and for the first time since they'd met, Renaire had forgotten Delaurier was even there.

He painted, and Delaurier had sat in the sand with a book from the mystery bag. The mystery bag also had a very basic and honestly not-that-good picnic breakfast in it, but Renaire could have been eating gruel and still marveled at it. They wasted only God knows how long there until the tide was coming in, and Delaurier had declared they were leaving.

They left the easel behind, standing quietly on the beach as the tide rolled in, and they drove off through light-drenched highways of Brazil.

Renaire can see it now, a creaky bone-white skeleton of an easel somehow still proudly erect on the beach. He could reach out and touch it. He can almost feel the sunlight, feel the sand beneath his toes. His battered, reliable paints are waiting, and it's warm and peaceful, and all he has to do is reach.

He doesn't.

Renaire's knives are just as reliable, and the flat of the blades are pressing into his back.

Renaire's life has been absolute shit, and it is full of pain and emptiness and trying to pick the lesser of two evils and being trampled down over and over again and so very often he just wants to be at peace and wants it to *end*; nobody wants him, and he's not worth anything, and he only ever gets in the way, a pathetic shadow lounging drunkenly in the corner—and Renaire realizes that *it's not true*. None of it is true. His hands hurt, his chest hurts, and all he has to do is reach out and touch, doesn't even have to actually touch, he just needs to *reach*.

He doesn't.

He *won't*.

Renaire grits his teeth and tries to curl his grasping fingers into a fist, but he can't because Emile is holding his hand tightly, refusing to let go. He squeezes Renaire's hand, and it's even warmer than the impossible beach.

Renaire breathes.

He breathes and squeezes back.

"—OH THANK God, move, *move*, come on, Renaire, open your fucking eyes," Emile says. There are other voices, voices and sounds echoing around, but Renaire really does not give a fuck about those because Emile is panicking.

"Ow," Renaire rasps out, and it hurts. Everything hurts. He aches like he just... well, got electrocuted. Which is what happened. He manages to open his eyes a sliver and that hurts too, but Emile is looking down at him, and fuck, he is so pretty, how is he so pretty? How is he even real? "Safe?"

"Yes, you saved France, please stop doing this to me," Emile says, moving his free hand to cup Renaire's cheek. "We're going to take you to the hospital and run you through every test known to mankind, and you are going to tell me right now if anything specific hurts."

"I'm fine," Renaire says, even if he feels like his veins are stuffed with cotton balls and his ribs ache twice as much as the rest of him. He groans and looks around—they're still in the senate, almost directly beneath the bomb-statue. "How long was I out?"

"How long were you *dead*, you mean?" Emile asks, his voice rising with every syllable. "Is that what you're asking me?"

Another man kneels awkwardly on Renaire's other side, and he's got emergency medical services written all over him. He clears his throat and says, "You were in cardiac arrest for around ninety seconds and unconscious for an additional three minutes. We're prepared to take you to the hospital whenever you feel ready."

He wants to snap at Emile for panicking over *ninety seconds*, but after imagining what Renaire would do in his place, he focuses on calming him down. "I'm okay," Renaire tries to reassure Emile.

"No you fucking aren't, Renaire, oh my God," Emile says, and he's shouting now. "This is the third time I have had to see you like this, and I *die every fucking time*, and it just gets worse and *worse* and you *actually died*, you were *dead*, you—"

"Sir," the other man says, firm and awkward.

"*What?*" Emile shouts at him.

"You're on camera," the man says.

Emile freezes. And dear God, he actually *blushes*. It's not the light blush that occasionally happens when he's sleep deprived (which he is) and his defenses are lowered (which they really, really are). It's a full-body flush that is somehow painful and adorable at the same time. It makes Renaire laugh, and that makes Renaire really, really hurt, and *that* makes Emile forget to be embarrassed, turning to look at the medic. "Let's get him to the hospital."

"But I was *just there*," Renaire complains.

"Renaire, I swear to God," Emile says.

"Your ribs are bruised, if not broken. It's going to hurt when we move you," the man warns.

Renaire rolls his eyes and sits up, and yeah, it hurts like a bitch and everything, and Emile looks like he is going to strangle him at any second, but it also calms Emile down. If Renaire is aggravating him, Renaire is alive. He can loosely follow Emile-logic, so he waves off the other man's hands and tells Emile, "Help me up."

Emile does so readily, even if he is muttering insults under his breath. Renaire can't really make them out, mostly because there are people *clapping*, what the fuck. Emile seems unsurprised, but Renaire grabs onto Emile in a tight hold as he looks out at the packed senate, swarming with statesmen and police and medics, and they're all clapping. It's the most surreal moment of Renaire's already very strange life.

"What the fuck," Renaire manages to say past the pain in his ribs.

"I told you, you saved France," Emile says, obviously not the least bit impressed with the senate. That makes sense, since Emile had been planning to kill all of them. The surrealism gets ratcheted up another notch. "I'm putting you on the gurney the moment we get you down these stairs."

"I don't want to be on the fucking gurney," Renaire says, even if he knows it's the smart thing to do. The stairs are already hard enough to manage, and Emile keeps having to glare and smack people's hands away when they try to help. "Are *you* okay?"

"I'm fine," Emile says, and it's softer, reassuring. "I'm fine and you'll be fine and everything will be okay now, I promise. We're going to take you to the hospital and get you looked over, and then you'll be perfectly fine, and I am going to take you home and keep you safe and happy."

They finally reach the bottom of the very small staircase and the gurney is ready and waiting for him, which is just.... He grimaces. "Do I have to?"

"I'd strongly advise it," the medic from before says. He's been not quite hovering, but definitely attentive.

"Just get on the gurney, Renaire," Emile says, and Renaire sighs, but obeys. It's an awkward fall down to where they have it at practically floor level, but Emile helps, and when they pop the thing up to a more reasonable height, Emile is still there. He hasn't let go of Renaire's hand even once. When they start rolling, there's more clapping, and Renaire does his best to ignore it. Emile, meanwhile, looks confident and annoyed just walking next to him and holding his hand like they do this every day and he's deigned to tolerate their spectators.

When they get out of the actual senate, the ornate hallways are swarming with law enforcement and confused workers and firemen and every other kind of emergency services people. Renaire can only assume they're not arrested because Renaire is headed for the hospital and Emile would probably shoot anyone who even tried to touch them right now. It's hard to not feel completely safe with Emile in this kind of mood, which probably says something horrible about Renaire.

The minute they're out of the building itself and into the courtyard, the press swarms over them, and their police escort is suddenly a lot less intimidating since they're there just to make the press back off. Emile gives them a disdainful glance every now and then, but he's in threat observation mode. It won't stop them from plastering Emile's face all over their front pages and then the bedroom walls of every teenager who sees it. He was already on quite a few walls before this because of STB, but now it'll be *everyone*.

"I'm sorry, sir, but you're going to have to let go of his hand when we get him in the ambulance," their designated medic says.

"No, I won't," Emile says, and smoothly hops onto the gurney to sit with Renaire. Cameras flash. He takes up very little space, and Renaire is just fine with the pain that comes from moving over to give him some more if he wants it. The medics are probably used to dealing with twice their combined weight, and the shift barely slows them down.

"Thank God I don't work in the hospital," their medic mutters.

"I like you," Renaire decides.

"Wait. You four, move aside," Emile says, and Renaire frowns until he sees they're directly in front of the ambulance's doors. The people at the foot of the gurney look confused, but when Emile tells you to do something, it's done. They move. What they're waiting for, Renaire has no idea, but Emile isn't done. He says, "Renaire, sit up."

"I'd *really*—" Their medic starts.

"Don't make me change my mind," Renaire interrupts, and (with Emile's help) he manages to obey. It's exhausting; he admits they had a point about the gurney. He does manage to smile at Emile, though. "What now?"

"I'm sorry I'm such a possessive asshole," Emile says—Emile *apologizes*, holy shit—and Renaire is still busy gaping at the apology when Emile leans in and kisses him, soft and *loving*, and Renaire wouldn't even feel it if someone amputated his leg. Emile kisses him thoroughly, and his spare hand is cradling Renaire's cheek, and Renaire is *flying*.

Or maybe they're just being lifted into the ambulance.

The doors slam shut behind them, and Emile's lips pull away to press a light, sweet kiss to his cheek. "I just wanted to make sure everyone knows," Emile says.

It doesn't take long for Renaire to figure it out. Emile *wants* the press to have pictures of the kiss. He really does want *everyone* to know. Renaire is simultaneously blushing and pleased beyond words and terrified at what the repercussions of today might be. Emile is very obviously not worried about it, though. That or he's doing an excellent job of faking confidence. Sometimes it's hard to tell the difference.

Renaire finally sinks back down again, and Emile sets about texting people with one hand while the other loosens its grip on Renaire's hand to instead run fingers through Renaire's hair. That's probably what puts him to sleep.

RENAIRE WAKES up in a hospital bed. Celine is seated to his left, and Delaurier is glaring at her from his seat to Renaire's right, and Renaire tenses at the horrible feeling of déjà vu, or maybe he never even woke up. Fuck, he could have just imagined it all, it'd make sense, wouldn't it? That he was so fucking broken that—

"Calm down, everything's fine, aside from *her* being here again," Emile says.

"Oh my God, Emile, stop it," Renaire says, shooting him an angry frown. "What has Celine ever done to you?"

"I'll step out for a while," Celine says awkwardly and stands, headed for the doorway.

"No, don't," Emile says, actually jerking to his feet and reaching for her, but Celine opens the door and there's a woman waiting on the other side of it, standing in front of the door like a bullet in a chamber just waiting to go off, and Renaire can't breathe, although he can hear Emile saying, "Shut the door, Celine, he's not—"

"Please, let me see him," Renaire's sister says quickly, but Celine slips out the door so quickly that it's all Renaire can hear out of her mouth.

"Fuck, are you okay?" Emile asks, hands cradling Renaire's head, watching him intently. "I told her she could wait outside, but she's been—"

"No, it's fine," Renaire says, and it's actually not, it's *obviously* not, but he can deal with it. He carefully removes Emile's hands and gives him a shaky smile. "I really should say hello, right?"

"You shouldn't do anything you don't want to," Emile says bluntly. "Nobody should, ever. You don't owe her anything, and this wasn't even your idea. We used her. We used *you*. You have no obligation to have some grand family reunion you don't want."

Renaire actually thinks about it. "Is Dax out there too?"

"Senator Mannon is a little busy," Emile says dryly, which, yeah. Renaire should have expected that.

He sighs. "Can I talk to her when I haven't had such a busy day?"

"That's reasonable," he says, and Emile actually stands up and walks over to the door and slides outside, and Jesus, Renaire didn't think he would actually go talk to Michelle or anything, he thought it would just be waiting and hoping she got the message. Fuck, what if she gets mad at Emile or starts shouting or something?

It takes no time at all, though. Renaire hasn't even started hyperventilating by the time Emile slides back in just as quickly.

"She'll talk to you another day," Emile says simply.

Renaire keeps an eye on the door, trying to figure out what the fuck he wants to do when that other day eventually shows up. The answer is that he has no clue, and he wonders if she'd even recognize him if they walked past each other on the street. Hell, he probably wouldn't recognize her even if they were sitting two seats away from each other on a bus. He distracts himself. He starts thinking about the present, and tempts his way to thinking about the recent past. And after a moment, Renaire pauses. "You drugged me," Renaire realizes.

"I did," Emile agrees, not even a little bit guilty.

"That's kind of fucked-up," Renaire says. "As in *really* fucked-up."

"No it wasn't. You fell asleep naturally; I just kept you asleep for safety reasons. It's been about four hours, and your tests are done. You broke your ribs, and you're bruised all over from the fall, but other than that, you're fine."

Renaire nods, slowly. "Then why am I still in the hospital?"

Now he does look a little guilty. It doesn't bode well. "There have been a few changes, recently," he says and pulls his laptop (someone must have visited) out from the table it had been resting on.

"Oh fuck, we're under arrest, aren't we?" Renaire says.

Emile hesitates, glancing up from whatever he's doing on the laptop. "We're being detained, and they're disguising it as you being under medical observation. They're figuring out what to do with us."

"At least there's a question," Renaire says dryly.

"You have no idea," Emile says and turns the laptop around so that Renaire can see the screen.

Leader of STB Saves French Senate, the headline reads. The first headline, at least. The article includes pictures of Renaire's much more impressive-looking sprint for the bomb than he'd felt it was, and the senators evacuating and tripping over each other in an effort to get away while Emile jumps onto the senate floor and starts talking down the stenographer, and then a picture of Renaire falling, and then there's a flurry of Emile looking panicked, and running past the stunned stenographer, and shouting at the stenographer from next to Renaire's (dead) body, and then the stenographer had just fucking dropped the trigger to go sit on the other side of Renaire just because *Emile told him to*. And then police and medics swarm in, and it all concentrates on Renaire being dead and Emile freaking out and Renaire has to put that down, has to click away, he doesn't want to see that.

He looks at the headlines on a standard Google search—all of them declare Emile (and Renaire) heroes and saviors, and there's *thousands* of images already on the Internet. There's countless interviews with Dax looking shaken and firm and telling the press about how *heroic* and *dedicated to the people* they were. Over and over again there's praise and awe and people declaring that they deserve medals.

In some places it mentions what STB *actually* does, but it's all portrayed in a dangerously positive light, listing "alleged" crimes, and then the oh-so-righteous reasons behind them. They're heroes, willing to go above and beyond, willing to do the dirty deeds humanity needs because the people are too afraid to do it themselves. Emile's not-quite-propaganda pictures are *everywhere*, and so is Emile's intentionally photographed ambulance kiss. *So sweet and in love!!!* comments say, massive amounts of people typing in all caps about their relationship.

Absolutely nowhere does it say that it was STB's plan in the first place.

"All of France loves us, and most of the world is following. It's an uncomfortable situation for the government," Emile says needlessly. Renaire's pretty sure he says it because he is so fucking happy that he's about to scream; probably the only thing keeping him from a victory dance is the fact Renaire kind of died to get them here. The rest of STB probably *is* doing a victory dance. Carope is doing a five-act interpretive dance of victory.

Renaire ends up on more of the him-and-Emile pages, and he has to hand the laptop back to Emile and *ignore it*. He doesn't even know what the *it* is, he just needs to not deal with it.

Emile might think this is the greatest event in human history, to have the people finally on his side, but Renaire isn't so sure. "Moving around before was difficult enough," Renaire says carefully. "With this—"

"No, you don't see it," Emile says, and his eyes are shining, that Cause-dedicated fire burning him up. "I might not even have to do it anymore."

Renaire frowns. "What?"

"If the support stays a constant thing, if they *keep listening* to us—Renaire, why do we go on jobs in the first place? Why do we do this? We do it to make a *difference*. It's all a means to an end, to bring about change that seemed impossible to ever reach because nobody ever *listened*. For years and years, before you and I met, before STB was what it is now, we just kept trying, and it never worked, and when the people wouldn't rise up to overthrow the corrupt, I resolved to take the oppressors down personally," Emile says, and Renaire has a horrible sinking sensation.

It's going to be temporary. Renaire *knows* it's going to be temporary. Emile looks so fucking happy and *relieved*, and Renaire realizes the bright shine in his eyes isn't just from believing in The Cause.

Emile hates killing people. He hates it, even if he doesn't regret it. He does it because he believes he's doing the right thing, and because he thinks *someone* has to do it. The non-Cause killings were always to finance their other work. He's shut down as much of himself as he can, sworn his soul to The Cause, a vague yet unbelievably important entity that Renaire long ago figured out is a catchall term for STB's varied interests, since the individual focus of someone didn't retract from them having a cause in common— justice, freedom, equality, the core of every person's cause, and therefore The Cause. Emile has been ruthless in its pursuit, and given up on that tiny hope of someone else caring as much as he does, and now, he thinks it's happened. He thinks the people won't need him to do it anymore, that they'll take care of themselves for once, and Emile can lock up his guns and weapons and do nothing but preach all day and get the same results, the same *action*.

Emile thinks it's over.

"We're going to save the world," Emile says.

Renaire is of the opinion that there's nothing to really save. Life always hurts, there's no such thing as a happy ending, and mankind's true nature isn't the golden shining thing Emile thinks it is. Everything Emile didn't shut down, all his belief in a better world and a deep innate kindness existing inside every person—those are the things Renaire gave up on long ago. Emile has seen the worst of humanity, and he *still* believes. He's always held himself above the cesspool they've navigated for the past two years, shining and untouchable while he ruthlessly ripped through people.

And now he's so relieved and happy he's close to crying.

"I never thought, I never even *dreamed* that this could happen, Renaire," Emile says. "The rest of STB, *all* of STB, every single fucking group around the world, is out making a difference right now, spreading the word. And people are listening because we're heroes."

"We're not heroes," Renaire says, because someone has to.

"I know that," Emile says, so easily that Renaire knows he actually does. "We know that, but *they* don't, and everything has been so quiet while they 'assess the situation' and it's amazing, Renaire, and it's all thanks to you."

Renaire is going to scream, Jesus *fucking* Christ, because they stopped *Emile's plan*, and he just.... Renaire has to close his eyes and take very deep breaths, and Emile wraps him in a tight hug that hurts so much Renaire has to bite his inner cheek to keep from shouting, but he doesn't move because Emile is shaking. Renaire hugs him back, even if it's not as tight, and fuck, Emile is *crying*.

"It's over, and—I'll try to be normal, and you don't have to—we can—" Emile says, and the words are very confusing, practically gibberish cut off between tears, but it's all probably even more confusing for Emile. Renaire coaxes him onto the hospital bed and ignores the pain while he tries to figure out what the fuck he should do or what this even is because he never imagined Emile hated it this much; he's seen Emile look so *satisfied* when people are dead that it shot ice into Renaire's veins.

He settles for just holding Emile and whispering soothing nonsense into his hair and staring at the wall with wide eyes as he tries to figure out what the fuck happens now, because he has no fucking clue. Shit, after *this* he wants to hide every weapon either of them owns and make sure Emile never gets near so much as a butter knife. There's no clock that Renaire can see. He doesn't know how long it lasts, and he doesn't *want* to know. He just wants Emile to be okay again. But it eventually ends, with Emile pressed against him, silent and still but not asleep.

"I don't mind killing people," Emile finally says. "It's just... exhausting. No matter how fast or how far I go, nothing ever changed beyond a slightly less corrupt person taking the place of their predecessor. I can't do it alone. Nobody can."

"Let's just wait to see how this all ends, alright?" Renaire says. "For all we know, we're going to jail for the rest of our lives."

"I'll make sure we share a cell," Emile says.

"It'd save them a lot of trouble. You'd probably keep starting riots until they figured it out," Renaire agrees. "Might be kind of bad for our sex lives, though."

"We'd make it work," Emile says. "At least we'll make do until we break out and go to ground somewhere for the rest of our lives. Any suggestions?"

Renaire presses his lips to Emile's cheek and says, "There's this beach."

SEX IN hospital rooms being used as temporary unsuspicious holding cells while the government decides what to do with them is not a thing either of them want to do, so they end up talking. And arguing. And napping. And arguing some more. Emile tries to read aloud some of the commentary about how brave and noble Renaire is, and Renaire has to fight the urge to strangle him.

Renaire has no cigarettes or alcohol, or anything to draw with, so he gets stuck with a fucking paint program on the laptop, and it is *miserable* because Emile is in such a good mood that he wants to compliment every fucking squiggle. He'd say it feels like he's finger painting, but that would be an insult to finger painting. Finger painting can be very respectable, and according to Emile, people have paid hilarious amounts of money for Renaire's finger paintings, so Renaire just curses at the laptop and absently listens to conversation after conversation Emile is having with only God knows who.

They don't go stir-crazy because by now Renaire and Emile are mostly incapable of going stir-crazy while around each other. The private hospital room is three times as large as their usual train compartments are. It's more the fact that this is possibly the happiest Renaire has *ever* seen Emile, while this is the most worried Renaire has ever been in his entire fucking life, and they're clashing just a little because of it. And by "a little," he means that he banished Emile into the very large bathroom after a while, and Emile went *willingly*, and that was even worse.

They get hospital food two times, so Renaire assumes it's night when Celine comes back. They're sprawled on top of the bed, legs idly tangled together while Emile has an arm around Renaire's shoulders, and they're leaning against each other while not even remotely concerned with what the other is doing—Renaire is fucking around with a slightly better art program and swearing off all digital art, Emile is doing something or other with his phone, for all Renaire knows he's playing Angry Birds, and Renaire has an audio news program streaming for Emile, even if it's currently playing some jingle about carpet cleaning. It's not exactly the image of two murderous terrorists planning to bomb important government buildings.

Another man, older and intimidating-looking, with eyes that have the same look in them as Emile's when he's getting ready to do something dangerous, walks in with her. He doesn't bother introducing himself, though. He looks at them, and then looks at Celine. Finally, he says, "We have conditions."

"Conditions for what?" Emile asks smoothly, not even looking up from his phone.

"Your release," the man says, practically grimacing around the words, and Renaire finally mutes the laptop, even if Emile shoots him a quick, irritated frown. "With the gratitude of the people of France for your actions today, the government is willing to pardon you both, *conditionally*."

"What about the rest of STB?" Emile asks.

"They're part of the conditions," Celine says cheerily. "The core members of STB, and STB in general, have to stop any and all illegal activities in France immediately."

"All activities *in France*," Emile repeats, half-sarcastic, half-disgusted. "Of course."

"Let's hear what they have to say before you get us sent to jail, alright?" Renaire says with a sigh.

"Fine," Emile agrees but still doesn't look up.

They've done negotiations this way before too. Renaire's a lot better at being the irritant, but Emile does it *pretty fucking well* too. Still, it works—the man dismisses Emile and starts talking to Renaire, and since this time it's more about being dangerously intelligent than good with knives, it's perfect.

"If STB stops all illegal activities in France, *permanently*, and you two never harm another person in *any* country, the government of France is willing to pardon you, out of gratitude," the man says.

"What if I get in a bar fight?" Renaire asks.

"Those do happen," Emile points out.

"If it's an act of self-defense, the nation's clemency wouldn't be immediately revoked," the man says. "An act of defense of another person would be viewed on a case-by-case basis."

"Renaire has post-traumatic stress disorder, which results in panic attacks that turn physically violent," Emile says, and he's actually looking up from his phone, any and all arrogance or flippancy gone from his tone. It's actual Emile, business-Emile. "What if he kills someone?"

Renaire protests, "I'm not going to—"

"Yes you will. It won't be intentional, and it won't be your fault, but eventually, you will," Emile states and doesn't break eye contact with the man.

"Case-by-case basis," the man says, unmovable.

"Do we get this in writing?" Emile asks. When neither the man nor Celine offers anything, Emile sighs. "Of course not, that'd be physical evidence, wouldn't it?"

"It's a good deal," Celine says.

It's an *amazing* deal, but Emile is the one who would actually be giving something up. Renaire can't imagine a world where Chason wouldn't do at least a little bit of pickpocketing, but he also can't imagine a world where Chason would actually get caught. So it goes with every other member of STB. Crime is a duty, not a calling or a passion.

"There's one other point to it," Celine adds. "If your assistance is requested by any law enforcement or military—"

"No," Emile says immediately.

"Just law enforcement, then," Celine says. When Emile gives her an assessing look, she smiles and says, "Only consultation. No active duty required."

"I really don't like this one," Renaire says. Honestly, prison isn't all that troubling of a thought anymore, now that he and Emile already have their escape plan plotted out. Per usual, it's mostly *Emile leads, Renaire follows*. "Can we object for ethical reasons?"

"No," the man says.

"But we *can* specify the crimes and task forces allowed to call on you," Celine says. When he and Emile don't immediately jump on the idea, Celine lets out a huff and says, "You do realize you'd be getting off completely free for *forty counts of murder*?"

"It's way more than forty," Renaire says.

"Stop talking," Emile says. "And *you* don't realize that we aren't scared of you. The entire reason we're being offered this deal is that the only parts of France that would support us being arrested at the moment are the ones supposedly *giving* us freedom. You couldn't keep us locked up if we walked into the cells and closed the doors ourselves." He smiles. "You need us to say yes. And to *this* part, we say no."

The man is close to turning blue with anger. Celine looks like she might hate Emile just as much as Emile hates her, but is much better at hiding it.

"The cessation of criminal activities, we'll concede," Emile says. "And that's all."

A concession which, Renaire realizes, Emile was already planning to do. He thinks he can save the world without killing anyone now. If it's all based on public opinion, he'd have to have STB as clean and admirable as possible. Violence as an act of defense, which is on a "case-by-case" basis, would be the core of their controversial activities.

Emile isn't conceding a damn thing.

It's very hard to keep a straight face.

"It's the *least* you can do," the man snaps, and glances over at Celine for a moment before sighing. "For now, you are free to go. Good luck with the reporters." He takes his own orders and leaves with a clench of his jaw and a pat to Celine's shoulder, striding out the door like it's personally offended him.

Celine looks stricken, torn between her job and her friendship, but says, "I was looking forward to working with you."

"You still could," Renaire says simply, and smiles. "You just have to *ask*, now."

He can see the moment she understands. It's not that they wouldn't be willing to help—it's that they don't want to be ordered to do so. If it's a worthy cause, if it's a genuine crime and not the government trying to assert itself, Renaire wouldn't mind helping. Emile wouldn't either. But it is very important to be able to say no.

Celine gives him a small smile, and it almost extends to Emile. Almost. "I'll talk to you later, then," she says.

"Wait," Emile says, and she pauses to watch him. Emile watches her back; Renaire vaguely wonders if this is what a net feels like during a game of tennis. "You didn't tell them."

Renaire hadn't even thought about that. Celine knew about STB's plan, after Renaire had finally asked for her help. She knew where it was, she knew when it was, and she knew that it was originally STB's plan. And for some reason, she didn't tell a soul that the entire incident was just them stopping their own terrorist plot. Interpol already knew there was a bombing planned, but Renaire had told her that it was called off. From Interpol's point of view, this was probably a vaguely related member of STB (true) commandeering their plan, like a copycat serial killer.

"I didn't," Celine agrees with a smile, and leaves.

Renaire watches her go and wordlessly reaches for Emile's hand. It's there in an instant, holding tight.

"What the fuck do we do now?" Renaire asks.

"We go home," Emile says.

Renaire rolls his eyes. "Helpful."

"It's better than nothing," Emile points out, and it's a good point. Small steps can get them there until they find their new road. "Now get up, you need a drink."

Renaire gapes at him.

Emile wordlessly holds one of Renaire's very shaky hands in front of his eyes.

"Oh," he says, and he doesn't pout. Not quite. "And here I thought you loved me."

"I do," Emile says and presses a very simple, quick, completely inappropriate for the statement kiss on Renaire's stunned cheek before he rolls off the bed, tossing Renaire's coat at him from the nearby chair. When it just smacks into Renaire's stunned face, he makes an irritated noise. "I swear to fucking God, Renaire, if you are *still* surprised by this I am going to—"

"No, I'm just…," Renaire says, trying to find the right words. He'd hoped, and he thinks he already knew, but it's still, fuck, he doesn't even know. He ends up laughing. "It's just that if someone told me two weeks ago, hell, *one* week ago, I never would have believed them."

"I'm planning to have a lot more time to fully convince you, hoping to have years to do it, but now is not that time," Emile says simply and steals the laptop from him, packing it up. The conversation seems like it's of secondary importance to him, like he's trying to brush it off, but Renaire knows better, and he ends up smiling because it's so fucking *Emile* to think he can avoid having to deal with potential consequences by saying it in a high-pressure situation with an opening like that. His smile makes Emile wary, saying, "What?"

"We should get married again," Renaire says simply.

Emile stares at him, but he slowly starts to smile, shy and gleaming. He's actually surprised for some reason. "Really?"

"I want rings," Renaire says.

"They're in the room with the guns," Emile says, and he's *grinning*, blushing even though he has no excuse for it, smiling like he's high noon on the summer solstice. "I was—let's go home. Right, can you walk? We'll get a taxi, but—seriously? Are you...?"

Renaire doesn't even know what question he's asking. Luckily, the answer to all of them is yes.

THE TRIPOLI Triptych goes up in Sirine's gallery for about a week, and then it's removed so it can get stuck two rooms away from where the museum put the stupid first blood-spattered painting of Emile. The order of the three paintings is supposed to be rotated every week, by artist's orders. Renaire's favorite configuration is when Emile goes from tired to confused to happy, so that's how they are during the party.

He still hates looking at them. It's not as painful now, and it's not as shaming now, or bitter or disgusting or just about every negative thing someone can feel. The freakish critics are claiming they're his *best work yet* and Renaire is so fucking tempted to grab one of the paintings and smash it over their heads.

Getting outed as R is part of the plan because apparently they are going to change the world through fame and fortune and a whole lot of preaching.

Renaire preferred killing people, he really, really did.

"Your sister is requesting entry," Emile tells him quietly.

Renaire has been ducking Michelle for three and a half weeks, blaming recovery time for his ribs and his, well, *everything*. Thankfully, all the serious damage was from falling ten feet while unconscious instead of from electrocution. Except he was actually dead. Either way, it's gravity that's to blame for him avoiding his sister, not Renaire.

"I can tell her to leave," Emile says, and it sounds nice. He's taken that option repeatedly, and liked it every time.

Still, he will take literally *any* excuse to get away from the fucking paintings, so he takes another drink of his champagne and walks toward the door. Emile doesn't seem surprised, just following him along, taking Renaire's right hand in his left.

Renaire wears his ring on his right hand for this exact reason; they both love having that little hint of metal trapped between their fingers. Emile was going to do it, since it was his idea, but there is *no fucking way* that Renaire is going with that. He knows Emile has no problem telling people no, but he's stupidly pretty, and Renaire needs *something* to discourage people; Emile had seemed astounded and incredibly confused by the idea, but he agreed. Eventually. The point is they like wearing the rings. They're bad for when he needs to punch people, and they mess with Renaire's aim a little bit, but *again*, apparently that's not the plan anymore.

He can still see Emile's hands twitch for a pistol when he gets into a debate with a particular type of person, the type that not too long ago would have been shot in the head instead of debated into a pulp on live TV. But this is why Renaire always goes with him, and not just out of habit. He gets glared at while he smokes and drinks and sketches and watches Emile rip people apart and preach people into believing, and doesn't care because he has Emile's back, and Emile knows it. Occasionally people are stupid enough to invite Renaire to debate, too, like they're trying to pick on him. He isn't as dedicated to *deductive reasoning* and *obvious conclusions* and generally being followed by the audience as Emile is, and usually just slices them off at the feet with a few words. People don't try that too often anymore.

As it is there's cameras and people eager to meet them, and Renaire doesn't know how long he'll be able to deal with this. But Emile is happy. Sometimes he looks lost, and sometimes Renaire will be watching him and realize that Emile is still more than capable of killing everyone in the room if he thinks it's for a good cause and would just keep moving on with his life. It's like watching a lion prowling through rooms full of not-wary-enough meerkats.

"You can do this," Emile says, simple and sincere. "And if not, we leave."

"I'd say you don't have to hold my hand, but you do," Renaire says. They both need to. It's probably unhealthy. Renaire does not give a fuck.

He knows her the second he glances out the main entrance, looking lovely and slumped and her eyes widening at the sight of him. She smiles at him, and Dax is at her side, looking happy for her as she pushes her way toward them.

Renaire didn't have a painful parting with his sister or a good parting. There was no parting to begin with, really. Michelle ran away from home and became a renowned soprano. Renaire ran away from home and became an alcoholic teenager stupid enough to join the military just because it was a thing to do. She looks every inch a lady, and Renaire can't even say anything. Michelle doesn't seem to expect anything else—she sweeps him into a tight hug the moment she's within range, and she's crying into his chest.

Renaire had expected panic, or to freeze up, or *something*, but instead he hugs his big sister right back, and it's fine. It's not easy, but it's fine. It's years and years of catching up to do, it's complete strangers who don't even bother to finish each other's sentences because they already know what words come next.

"I went back for you, but you were already gone," Michelle says.

Renaire wonders what it would've been like if she'd been faster or Renaire had been slower, but life is what it is. He's started to understand that, now, so he tells her, says, "But it all turned out alright in the end, didn't it?"

Michelle looks confused and worried and asks, "Did it really?" She asks it as if she wants a genuine answer, and Renaire starts thinking about it.

STB is turning into a viciously influential and cutthroat political entity that's trampling its way through France and seeping into the rest of Europe as well, with the world precariously intrigued by Emile and his friends. Celine is happy and already engaged to Mathieu (which Renaire knows absolutely nothing about, and he doesn't *want* to know, except she's hinting at making him her man of honor), which Carope is actually thrilled about for both of them, and Renaire helps her with Interpol stuff sometimes, if she asks. Which is weird. She and Emile have some sort of wary, disdainful truce, but mild verbal jabs are as far as it ever goes. And Emile is so fucking happy—he smiles, he *hums*, he sometimes honest to God serves Renaire breakfast in bed, which is completely ridiculous for many, many reasons, and Renaire is so completely certain that this is all a dream, or, much more likely, he's dead and this is the afterlife, or *something*.

Then again, it isn't all good—Emile is still an amoral powder keg Renaire is waiting to watch explode and take hundreds down with it, and STB's meetings still have distinctly violent *fuck the government* leanings that have been anything but hypothetical for far too long for it to stop at just talk, and Renaire is *still* a complete fucking mess, it doesn't matter that he can say no or stand up for himself or actually look in the mirror without having to restrain the urge to break the glass. One day Renaire is going to have a panic attack and kill someone, and that someone might be Emile. One day, one inevitable day no matter how long from now, Emile is going to die, and Renaire knows he won't be able to live without him, *knows* it.

He's the alcoholic, chain-smoking wreck of a husband to a man determined to take over the world and make it how he thinks it should be and ready to kill if people tell him he can't. But the best part of that is that he is married to Emile. Renaire and Emile are married and together and it's so good, it's so, so good. Every time Renaire knows it's going to fall apart, it just ends up tighter and deeper and *better*, and his sister is staring at him now, shit, he has to say something.

Renaire clears his throat and starts patting himself down for a cigarette, but there's no real need because Emile is already handing him one and lighting it for him and looking distinctly *unimpressed* while he does it. Renaire breathes in, and breathes out, and watches Michelle's face fall slowly. He ends up smiling as he shrugs and says, "Well, it's alright."

LUCHIA DERTIEN is a recovered agoraphobic who climbed a 14,400 foot mountain to prove it. She does not enjoy mountain climbing. Luchia received a B.A. in English from the University of Denver and started writing when she was three years old, dictating a modern classic called Castle Castle, which is a close examination of the societal impact of overpopulation and also fighting dragons. She is an advocate for mental health treatment and the encouragement of young writers. She currently lives in Denver, Colorado.

Luchia Dertien is a pen name in the way someone's call sign is a pen name. Luchia is her Ice Man, her Maverick, her Goose. Like Goose, she probably won't talk to you. She does not enjoy volleyball. She was also not born when *Top Gun* was released in 1986. This does not keep it from being timeless and relevant to every generation of fighter pilots. Luchia is not a fighter pilot.

When not making references to movies she's never actually seen in entirety, Luchia Dertien spends time wishing she had a pet dog. This wish, this ceaseless day-lit dream, has haunted her since birth. Alas, it is not to be, since Luchia is also dangerously allergic to all forms of pet dander. A cat sent her to the emergency room when she was in fourth grade because it slept in her sleeping bag at science camp. The situation was very awkward. Particularly for the cat.

Twitter: @luchiadertien

Lurking in the digital underworld, he lures, seduces, and charms.

RICK R. REED

http://www.dsppublications.com

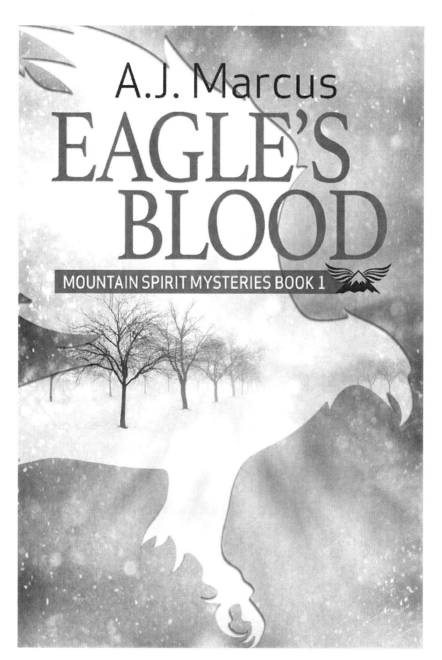

A.J. Marcus

EAGLE'S BLOOD

MOUNTAIN SPIRIT MYSTERIES BOOK 1

http://www.dsppublications.com

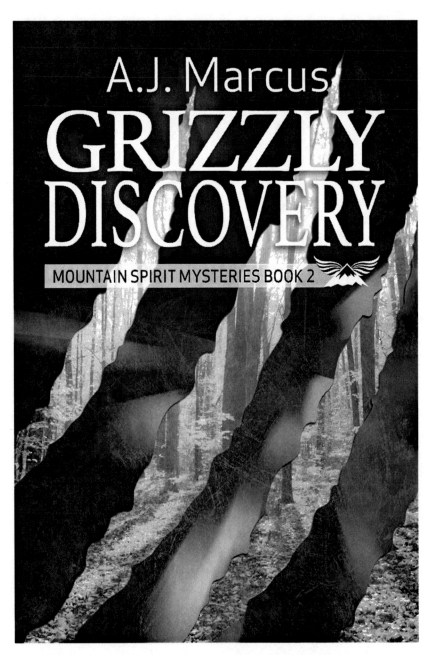

A.J. Marcus

GRIZZLY DISCOVERY

MOUNTAIN SPIRIT MYSTERIES BOOK 2

http://www.dsppublications.com

A Flesh novel
ETHAN STONE

In the
Flesh

http://www.dsppublications.com